The
Cat Sitter's
Cradle

ALSO BY BLAIZE CLEMENT

The Cat Sitter's Pajamas
Cat Sitter Among the Pigeons
Raining Cat Sitters and Dogs
Cat Sitter on a Hot Tin Roof
Even Cat Sitters Get the Blues
Duplicity Dogged the Dachshund
Curiosity Killed the Cat Sitter

The Cat Sitter's Cradle

BLAIZE AND JOHN CLEMENT

MINOTAUR BOOKS

A Thomas Dunne Book

New York

A THOMAS DUNNE BOOK FOR MINOTAUR BOOKS.
An imprint of St. Martin's Publishing Group.

THE CAT SITTER'S CRADLE. Copyright © 2013 by Blaize and John Clement. All rights reserved. Printed in the United States of America. For information, address St. Martin's Press, 175 Fifth Avenue, New York, N.Y. 10010.

www.thomasdunnebooks.com
www.minotaurbooks.com

Library of Congress Cataloging-in-Publication Data

Clement, Blaize.
    The cat sitter's cradle : a Dixie Hemingway mystery / Blaize & John Clement. — First edition.
        pages   cm
    "A Thomas Dunne book."
    ISBN 978-1-250-00932-6 (hardcover)
    ISBN 978-1-250-03028-3 (e-book)
    1. Hemingway, Dixie (Fictitious character)—Fiction.   2. Women detectives—Florida—Fiction.   3. Ex-police officers—Fiction.   4. Missing persons—Fiction.   5. Murder—Investigation—Fiction.   I. Clement, John.   II. Title.
    PS3603.L463C38   2013
    813'.6—dc23

                                                                                    2013009818

Minotaur books may be purchased for educational, business, or promotional use. For information on bulk purchases, please contact Macmillan Corporate and Premium Sales Department at 1-800-221-7945 extension 5442 or write specialmarkets@macmillan.com.

First Edition: July 2013

10 9 8 7 6 5 4 3 2 1

For Blaize

Acknowledgments

Deepest thanks go to Marcia Markland, my mother's longtime editor and friend, without whom this particular Dixie Hemingway mystery (and quite possibly all of its predecessors) would not exist. Marcia was the catalyst for true joy in my mother's life—for that, and for her invaluable role in the shaping of this book, I am eternally grateful.

I am also deeply indebted to Hellyn Sher for improving my life in every way; to Dana Beck for inspiring me to dig deeper; to Mike Harder for playing the bad cop; to Detective Sergeant Chris Iorio of the Sarasota County Sheriff's Department for his patience and insight; to the team of Linda Sher, Stanley Sher, and Jeremy Sher for their advice on immigration law; to Dr. Anna Owren Fayne for her priceless advice on veterinary medicine; to India Cooper for her extraordinary copyediting; to associate editor Kat Brzozowski for providing wise answers to my dumb questions; to Al Zuckerman, my agent at Writer's House; to Elizabeth Cuthrell and Steven Tuttleman for their love and support; to Suzanne Beecher for being an angel on Earth; to my family for loving each other in good times and bad; to my brother Don, the only idol I've ever known; to Dave, who opened the window that time; and finally, to my mother's readers, who make it possible for Dixie to enjoy yet another glorious sunset.

The best thing about the future is that
it only comes one day at a time.

—*Abraham Lincoln*

The
Cat Sitter's
Cradle

1

It was about 6:00 A.M. when Rufus and I saw Joyce Metzger on the walking path that runs around the perimeter of Glebe Park at the north end of Siesta Key. Rufus is a scruffy-faced schnauzer who firmly believes that he's in total charge of whatever street he happens to be walking on, so he let out a little *wuf!* to announce our presence. Joyce had Henry the VIII on a leash, and they were both studying with intense curiosity something that was lying on the path. Joyce had squatted down low to see better, and Henry the VIII, being a tiny miniature dachshund, was already down low. When Rufus barked again they both looked up, and their faces brightened in recognition.

I'm Dixie Hemingway, no relation to you-know-who. I'm a cat sitter on Siesta Key, a semitropical barrier island in the Gulf of Mexico, just off Sarasota, Florida. It's tiny. The whole place is less than four square miles, and probably at least one of those square miles is taken up by ponds and lagoons. Most of my clients are cats, with just a few dogs. Occasionally there's a hamster or a bird or something with scales, although I prefer to let other pet sitters take the snakes. Don't get me wrong, I admire snakes. In the Garden of Eden, the serpent was the only honest one. But anybody who knows me knows I can't stand dropping live, squirming mice into a snake's open mouth.

Until about five years ago, I risked my life every day as a deputy sheriff, but after what you might call a bump in the road of life, I went a little nuts. Well, a lot nuts. The sheriff's department and I came to a mutual agreement: I was too messed up to wear a sheriff's badge or carry a gun, and it was probably a good idea for me to take a break from law enforcement. That's when I started my own pet-sitting business. Now that I'm somewhat socially acceptable again, I'm okay around guns, but I prefer working with animals to humans. Animals don't let you down, and they're always there when you need them.

Joyce said, "Come look at this, Dixie! I'm almost certain it's a resplendent quetzal!"

I brought Rufus close to my side and pulled up next to Joyce. There on the ground was a parrotlike bird with bright green wings, a red breast, a banana yellow beak, and a fluffy chartreuse crest that sat atop its head like a fringed helmet. Its green tail feathers were easily three times the length of its body and looked like two long Christmas ribbons, gleaming with a violet iridescence.

I said, "Huh."

Joyce said, "This may be the first resplendent quetzal ever seen in Florida!"

I said, "Huh?"

Rufus wagged his tail vigorously as if to make up for my ignorance.

Lord knows the Key has practically every bird known to man. They all touch down about the same time tourist season starts, so our little island's population increases tenfold with both feathered and nonfeathered globe-trotters. Pelicans, parakeets, terns, plovers, spoonbills, egrets, herons—and those are just the ones you see every day. It's a birder's paradise. There are probably at least two hundred species of birds that make their way through the Key at some time of the year, so we might as well have a few resplendent whatchamacallits too.

"Resplendent *quetzals*," Joyce said. "They're the national bird of Guatemala, and they're on the endangered species list. The ancient Aztecs thought they were gods of light and goodness, and it was considered a mortal crime to kill them."

Rufus made a snorting noise, and he and Henry the VIII exchanged a look.

I said, "Joyce, you do realize that bird is dead?"

"I know, but if there's one, there could be others. It looks like some kind of parrot, but that long tail and those shiny feathers are a sure giveaway. And see the yellow beak? No, this is a resplendent quetzal alright."

I scratched my left ankle with the toe of my right Ked. I admire and respect birders, but I'm not sure I understand their excitement when they spot something that for very good reasons probably does not want to be spotted. If I were a bird, I don't think I'd be very happy with hordes of giddy bird-watchers turning up and pointing their binoculars at me and scribbling in their little notebooks. Not to mention hunters with pellet guns and kids with slingshots. I'd much rather flit around behind a canopy of leaves and branches and hope nobody ever noticed me.

Joyce had pulled off a white bandanna tied around her neck and laid it on the ground beside the bird.

"What the heck are you doing?"

She gestured toward her house. "I'm going to put it in my freezer."

"Your *freezer*?"

"Yep. Then I'm going to call the ornithologists at the University of Tampa. They can analyze its stomach contents and tell whether it's been held captive or if it flew here. Maybe it got blown off course in a hurricane or something."

She rolled the bird into her bandanna and put it in her shoulder bag. Rufus pulled on his leash and pointed his nose at the brush beside the trail; he had probably had enough talk about dead birds.

I said, "Well, you know what they say, a bird in the freezer is worth two in the—"

Rufus and Henry the VIII both turned their heads toward the brush beside the trail. There was a short bleating sound, and for a moment I wondered if a baby goat had somehow wandered into the bushes. The sound came again, and Rufus bounded toward it. I was right behind him, but this time I knew: It was not a goat.

I circled the end of a line of bushy bougainvillea and jerked Rufus to a stop. A dark-haired woman lay on the ground looking up at us with terror in her eyes. She clutched a newborn baby to her chest. The baby's skin was bright

pink and glistening, its jet black hair wet with blood cling-
ing to its skull. A long umbilical cord trailed from the
baby into a dark red pile of blood-soaked leaves.

I said, "Joyce, come here right now."

The baby let out another cry, and the woman pulled it
close. Her arms were as thin as a child's.

Joyce ran to look, then silently tilted her head back and
closed her eyes.

While I rummaged through my backpack for my cell
phone, Joyce took Rufus and Henry the VIII over to a
stand of saplings nearby and tied them up. They sat side by
side without a whimper, as if they knew something very
important had happened in the human world.

As soon as I pulled my phone out of my pack, the young
woman on the ground started to cry. Her voice was a high
desolate keening, her mouth slewed so she looked like a
person on drugs, as if she hadn't had a decent meal or a
restful hour's sleep in a long, long time. Through the tangle of hair falling in front of her face, I could see that she
was much younger than I'd realized at first. A teenager.

I dialed 911 as I knelt beside her and put a gentling
hand on her shoulder. "It's okay, honey, you're gonna be
okay."

The 911 operator answered, "911, what is your emergency?"

"A young woman has just given birth in the woods. We
need an ambulance."

"Is the baby breathing?" the operator asked, as if she
had this conversation every day.

"Yes."

"Is the mother hemorrhaging?"

"I don't think so."

"How long has it been since she gave birth?"

I looked at the girl. "How long has it been since you had the baby?"

She flailed her head from side to side. "Please no, miss," she moaned. "Please no, no medicos."

I cringed. "Do you speak English?"

She hesitated. "A little."

The operator said, "What is your location, please?"

Joyce knelt down at the girl's side. "Sweetheart, do you have papers?"

The girl hesitated, then shook her head no. Even non-English-speaking immigrants understand the word "papers."

I clicked off the phone and looked more closely at the young woman. Her dark eyes stared back at me like a trapped animal's. Joyce knelt down beside the girl with her sweatshirt ready to swaddle the baby. Our eyes met.

Joyce said, "Don't tell me."

"We have to do this ourselves. Either that or let them take her to the ER, where she'll probably be arrested." The girl looked from me to Joyce. "Look at her. She's terrified."

Recently, in what had become a very famous incident, a local hospital had admitted a young man for emergency treatment, only to find out that he was an illegal alien. The man was treated, but instead of releasing him, the hospital contacted immigration and the man was deported back to his own country. He had a family here, and a job, but none of that mattered. His life was destroyed, and his family was left to fend for themselves.

For a second, Joyce looked as devastated as I felt. Then

every fiber of her body seemed to firm up, and I remembered that in her former life Joyce had been a marine.

"Okay," she said. "Let's do this."

Her tone was so authoritative that I was happy to let her take charge. She stood up and brushed off her shorts decisively. For a split second, my mind wandered off, probably to avoid what was about to happen. *I should really keep a former marine with me at all times,* I thought to myself. *They're quite handy.*

Joyce said, "We need to get her inside, but . . ."

At first I didn't realize she was talking to me. But then my eyes followed her gaze from the tiny newborn down the umbilical cord to the dark mass of blood and matted leaves lying on the ground.

"That's gotta be cut."

I raised my hands up and cupped them over my ears like a "hear no evil" monkey. In the police academy, I'd learned how to deliver a baby and how to cut the cord, but I'd never actually done it.

With just a touch of desperation I said, "Maybe we could leave it? People do that, don't they? It eventually just falls off, right?"

Joyce shook her head. "Sometimes, but in this case it will be impossible to move them safely. We have to."

She was right, and I knew it. We sat there for a moment as if frozen in time. Three women brought together by some perverse twist of fate, huddled over a tiny wriggling bloody baby, with no one to witness but the squirrels, the birds, and a couple of dogs tied to a maple sapling. Rufus and Henry the VIII lay side by side, watching our every move with rapt attention, like spectators at a tennis match.

Joyce said, "My shoes have Velcro. Give me your shoe-laces."

I snapped to and pulled the laces from my Keds and handed them to her. She was studying the still-pulsating umbilical cord closely.

"Don't want to do this too soon," she said. "Do you have a knife? Or scissors? Or I can run to the house."

"Pet sitters always have scissors," I said and dove into my backpack. "I use them for clipping kitten toenails or cutting any number of things stuck in matted dog fur. And here's a box of baby wipes. I use them for cleaning my hands when I'm traveling, and a bottle of rubbing alcohol and some cotton swabs."

I realized I was rambling on nervously, but I couldn't stop myself. I laid everything out in a row on Joyce's sweat-shirt.

Joyce looked at the scissors and sighed. "They're not very big, are they?"

"They're razor sharp, though. And we can anesthetize them with the rubbing alcohol."

Joyce raised one eyebrow. "You mean sanitize?"

"Yeah, that."

The young woman was watching us with mounting fear. When she saw the scissors, she whimpered and began scooting backward, trying to get away from us.

Joyce laid a hand on the girl's ankle. "It's okay. Trust me, honey, it's okay."

But the girl didn't trust either of us, all she knew was that we were bringing out sharp instruments we might be intending to use on her.

I tried my rudimentary high school Spanish. "*Es neces-*

sario que . . . um, to cut"—I made scissoring motions to illustrate—"*la* umbilical." For the first time, I glanced at the baby's sex. "*La niña* will not have *dolor*. No pain, *te prometo*."

The girl looked at the umbilical cord and then at me. She didn't look as if she believed my promise, but something in her eyes told me she understood.

The cord had stopped pulsating. I moved closer to the baby and tied one of my shoelaces around the cord a couple of inches from the baby's body. The girl watched me intently.

Joyce said, "*Por favor*."

With greater trust, the girl laid the baby down so I could more easily tie the other lace closer to the baby's body. I dabbed alcohol on the cord between the shoelaces, then dipped the scissors' blades into the bottle of alcohol and swirled it around.

Joyce looked sternly at the young mother. "Hold her steady."

She seemed to understand. Her hands pushed against the baby's sides gently to keep the baby from wriggling too much. I slid the blades over the cord.

As if she were giving a demonstration to a medical school class, Joyce said, "The cord is very tough. It's hard to cut."

I was glad she said that because it felt to me as if I was putting enough force on the scissors' handles to cut through a Goodyear tire.

I said, "Get ready to blot up the blood. There won't be much."

It took a moment for Joyce to realize I was talking to

her. She let out a nervous giggle and jumped to hold tissues under the scissors just as the blades broke through the cord. Some blood spilled out, but most of the blood in the cord had traveled back into the bodies it had linked. Joyce blotted at the nib attached to the baby before she let the end connected to the placenta fall.

I looked at Joyce, and we both let out a sigh of relief. Then we smiled at the young woman.

I said, "It's okay. Your baby is fine."

But the words were a lovely lie, because the baby wasn't fine at all. She had been born on the ground, in the dirt, to a mother who was alone and far from home and nearly a baby herself. There was no promise of security or safety, only a dismal future, riddled with uncertainty. Joyce wrapped the baby in her sweatshirt, and the girl lifted it to her chest and crooned while the baby nuzzled at her thin shoulder blades. The baby looked as worn-out as her mother, and Joyce didn't look much better.

I couldn't blame her. It wasn't even 7:00 A.M. yet, and the day felt like it had already lasted several years.

2

We were all sitting in the brush beside the trail. Me, Joyce, and the young girl holding her newborn baby. I think we were all just trying to get our bearings. Rufus and Henry the VIII were still watching from their post a few yards away.

I said, "What the hell are we going to do with her?"

Joyce looked away. We both knew what we should do. We should call the sheriff's office and report an illegal alien in our midst. We should report that she had given birth and now there were two people who needed our care, our food, our medical treatment. In time, if the young mother wasn't deported, her child would need education, and all that would have to be paid for by our tax dollars. We should have been outraged at the young woman for stealing our money.

Joyce said, "Florida has a safe haven law, you know. A mother can leave her baby anonymously at a hospital or fire station within seven days of its birth without prosecution."

We looked at the girl, who seemed to understand what Joyce had said. She pulled the baby tighter and looked as if she was about to scramble to her feet and run away.

I said, "Would you leave your baby with strangers?"

I thought of how precious my daughter, Christy, had been to me from the moment she was born. I would have fought like a rabid badger if anybody had tried to take her away from me. I had a feeling this young mother felt the same way about her daughter.

Joyce sighed. "I can't keep her indefinitely, but I have a spare room where she can stay for a while."

I said, "I'll bring some clothes and some diapers and things. And some food."

Joyce knelt down and picked up a leather handbag that was on the ground. "Is this yours?"

The girl nodded.

"You can come to my house. To my *casa*."

The girl nodded, and her eyes welled with tears. Joyce shouldered the bag and tipped her chin at a large cardboard box under a tree. The box was dented and broken, and rain had disintegrated it in places.

She said, "I suppose that's where she's been living."

I got up and walked over to the box, my Keds flopping without their laces. Kneeling at the opening, I pawed through the jumble of clothes and trash, looking for anything else the girl might want to keep, but there was nothing.

Joyce said, "I hate to make her walk, but I don't know how else to get her home."

I said, "Fireman's carry, but first I'll get the dogs."

While Joyce helped the girl to her feet, I ran over to

Rufus and Henry the VIII and untied them. I gave them both a good scratch behind the ears to let them know that everything was going to be okay, even though I wasn't sure of it myself.

The young mother was swaying slightly with the newborn tight against her chest. I slipped the leashes around my wrist, and Joyce and I stood behind her and crossed our arms in the classic fireman's carry, but the leashes got in the way. Rufus had circled around Joyce's legs, and Henry the VIII looked like he was about to bolt, his tail wagging so vigorously that his little rump was jiggling back and forth. I was holding one leash in my mouth while I tried to untangle the other from Joyce's legs when the young girl giggled.

"*Aquí,*" she said.

She gently shifted the baby to her other shoulder and held out her open hand.

I passed her the leashes, and she sat down gingerly on our crossed arms. With the dogs leading the way, we shuffled down the street in the pale morning light like a slow-moving parade. Rufus let out a few commanding *wufs!* as if he wanted to clear the road. *Move it, people! Newborn coming through!*

The girl wasn't heavy, but carrying her was awkward and unpleasant. I could feel her warm blood wet on my arms, and it brought a combined feeling of disgust and awe. Disgust at having another human's blood on my arms, but awe at the miracle of life asserting itself in all its direct, honest reality.

I started humming an old hymn, "Bringing in the Sheaves," but I sang it the way I thought it went when I was a little girl: "Bringing in the sheets, bringing in the sheets, we shall go to Joyce's, bringing in the sheets." Seemed appropriate at the time.

At Joyce's house, we carried the girl directly to the shower and undressed her. Her ribs were like piano keys on her thin body. She was too weak to stand, so she slid to the floor and sat under a warm shower with her face tilted back to receive its blessing. Joyce scurried to fetch a clean nightshirt and cotton underpants that she lined with a makeshift pad.

While Joyce took care of the girl, I cleaned the baby at the bathroom sink where the mother could see me. She was a beautiful baby. A little underweight, but healthy otherwise. She had a mop of jet black hair on her head and the biggest blue eyes I've ever seen on a baby. Joyce brought me a roll of paper towels and some masking tape.

"See if you can make diapers out of this."

"I'll get some pads when I get diapers and the other stuff."

"Better get several boxes. She's bleeding a lot."

"The 911 operator asked me if she was hemorrhaging."

Joyce shook her head. "No. Just heavy bleeding. She'll be okay as soon as she has some nourishment and rest."

We led the girl over to the edge of the bed and sat her down. I laid the baby next to her, and Joyce made a barrier out of pillows and blankets along the edge of the bed. I brought a towel from the bathroom and started to pat the girl's hair dry.

I said, "Your name . . . *como se llama?*"

She smiled weakly. "I am Corina."

I patted the side of her face. "I am Dixie, and this is Joyce."

Tears made her dark eyes shine. "Thank you, Dixie and Joyce," she said. *"Ustedes son hijas de Dios."*

We helped her lie down, and within seconds she had fallen asleep, the baby nestled in her arms. We pulled the sheets up over her and laid a blanket over her legs.

I whispered to Joyce, "I've got pets to check on, but I can come by after with supplies."

"Okay," Joyce said. "I'll stay here with her while she sleeps, and if anything changes I'll call you."

I hoisted my bag over over my shoulder and tiptoed across the room. At the door, I turned and looked back. Joyce had lain down on the bed next to Corina with one hand resting lightly on the baby's tiny outstretched arm. It looked like she had fallen asleep, too.

"Joyce!" I whispered.

She raised her head. "What?"

"What the hell is a sheave?"

She smiled and laid her head back down. "Dixie, I have no friggin idea."

The sun was coming up now, and there were a few early birds on the path. A couple of retirees rolled by on a matching pair of bright yellow bicycles. A man in red sweatpants and a Mets baseball cap walked by, briskly pumping his arms up and down to the beat of the music playing through his headphones.

Rufus and I made our way back to his house, both of us feeling a bit shell-shocked. I left him with a peanut-butter-filled chew toy, and, with a kiss on the nose, assured him that our afternoon walk would be a little less dramatic.

3

I thought about the morning's proceedings as I made my way over to the Suttons' house at the opposite end of the Key. Most of the time my work is pretty predictable. I check the food and water, I let the dogs out to do their business, I clean the litter boxes, I brush the fur, I give some hugs and kisses, I wave around a peacock feather or a piece of cheese, and then it's on to the next pet. I have it down to a very smooth routine, and that's the way I like it.

Taking on the responsibility of a young if not underage illegal alien with a newborn baby is not routine. It's crazy. The best that could happen was Joyce and I would give the girl a little comfort for a short time. The worst was that when we sent her on her way she'd have tasted a better life and would hate her old one even more. When I tried to imagine how bad it must have been in her home, so bad that she felt compelled to risk her life and the life of her unborn child to go to a foreign country and live in a box . . . my mind skittered away in guilt and shame and helplessness. I was born in a country that allows me enormous advantages, and I was no more deserving than that poor girl was. I was just luckier.

I pulled into the Suttons' driveway and flipped through my keys, which I keep on a big ring like a French chatelaine. Their Sophie is a tuxedo cat, mostly black with white boots, a white bib, and just a dip of white at the end of her tail. She met me at the door with some serious tail choreography and an excited *thrrrip!* to let me know I was late. While I prepared her breakfast, she purred and circled around my feet.

I have always prided myself on being a good citizen. I pay my taxes, I vote, I don't litter, and I don't speed . . . much. I get mad when I see a flag flying in the rain, and I feel a surge of pride when I sing "The Star-Spangled Banner." But if I helped this young mother I would be breaking the law. I would be aiding an illegal alien, which is wrong. At least, it's wrong in the eyes of the law.

I took Sophie out to the back porch overlooking the bay and brushed her. Or, to be precise, I held the brush steady and Sophie did all the work, cooing and purring as she pressed the full length of her body through the brush, first one side and then the other. I had never given much thought to the immigration brouhaha, but now I thought about the poem at the Statue of Liberty that epitomizes what it means to live in a democracy: "Give me your tired, your poor, your huddled masses yearning to breathe free . . ." I thought about what Jesus said to his followers: "Inasmuch as ye have done it unto one of the least of these my brethren, ye have done it unto me." I'm not very religious or political, but some things are either right or wrong, and you don't need to belong to a certain church or party to know which is which. Sending a homeless young woman with a newborn baby out into a world that was all too ready to label her a pariah was just plain wrong.

When I finished up my morning rounds, I headed over to the Village Diner, which is practically my home away from home. Like most of my pet clients, I am a creature of habit. Pretty much every day of the year, I go to the diner and have basically the same breakfast. Two eggs over easy with extra crispy home fries and a hot biscuit. There are a couple of booths in the front that have a nice view of the street, but I usually take one of the booths in the back. My friend Judy is the waitress there, and by the time I'm sliding into my usual spot she's sliding a cup of coffee in front of me. It's a well-choreographed dance we've been doing for I don't know how many years.

Judy is long limbed and quick, with honey brown hair, piercing hazel eyes, and a sprinkling of freckles on her nose. She's left a line of no-good men in her trail—all bums, cheaters, liars, losers, and sons of bitches, or as Judy calls them, dicks. I've held her hand through almost every one of them, and she held mine when I hit that bump in the road I mentioned before. Although I rarely see her outside the diner, she's probably my closest friend in the world other than my brother.

This morning, while Judy was pouring my coffee, I slipped into the restroom first. Normally there's maybe a little cat hair and some dog slobber to wash off, but not today. I pulled a few towels from the dispenser and wadded them up into a makeshift sponge. I scrubbed between my fingers and under my nails. I scrubbed my arms up to the elbow. I scrubbed like a sailor swabbing the deck of a shrimp boat. I'm sure I'd gotten it all off before, but there's something about having blood on your hands that makes you feel a little panicky, like the lady in that Shakespeare play—"Out! Out! Damn spot!"

When I felt like a certified clean freak, I tossed the towels in the trash pail and smoothed the wrinkles out of my shorts. I studied myself in the mirror. I don't know if it's a blessing or a curse, but it seems like I'm always getting mixed up in stuff I probably shouldn't be.

Judy was waiting for me at the table. She was twirling a pencil in her hair and had a particularly mischievous grin on her face.

"Your boyfriend was here earlier," she said.

I slid into the booth, feigning ignorance. "I have no idea what you're talking about."

"Uh-huh." She shifted her weight to the other hip. "You know, he left me an extra big tip and was giving me all kinds of smiles. I think he might be a little sweet on me, just so you know."

"Oh, really?" I asked, cupping my hands around the coffee mug. "You should hop right on that." I wasn't taking the bait. I know Judy far too well.

She went on. "Well, I'll tell you, it was distracting. And I think he's just so damn tired of waiting for you he's ready to settle for little ol' me."

"That must have been very upsetting for you," I said.

"Oh, don't worry, I'd settle with him any day of the week. In fact, I'd settle with that boy *every* day of the week!"

She flipped her hair off her shoulders and sashayed back toward the kitchen, swaying her hips for extra effect.

I had to admit, Judy was probably right. Ethan probably

was tired of waiting for me. And why I kept him waiting, I had no idea. Ethan Crane is an attorney in town, and he happens to be one of the most devastatingly beautiful specimens of man you could ever hope to lay eyes or hands on. He could carry around one of those numbered ticket machines, like the ones they have at deli counters, and women would line up for blocks. We've had a sort of on-again, off-again flirtation going, but something's always gotten in the way. And that something has always been me.

Five years ago—five years, six months, and a couple of days, to be exact—I lost the two most important things in the world to me: Christy, my little girl, and my husband, Todd. A ninety-year-old man plowed his car into them in a grocery store parking lot. He later said he meant to step on the brake pedal, but instead he stepped on the gas, and they were both killed instantly, or so I was told.

Christy was three, and Todd was thirty.

It's funny how it takes just a few seconds to tell the story of what happened, because it feels like it goes on forever. At first I spent a lot of time in bed or staring at the wall. I didn't eat and I barely slept—to be honest, I was a slobbering, filthy mess. Certainly, as anyone around here will tell you, I was unfit to be a police officer, let alone carry a gun.

I'm okay now, except that sometimes I feel like it's all been a terrible play, and then the curtain comes down and the lights go up and I realize I'm not in the audience, I'm on the stage. And you don't need to be Sigmund Freud to know that I'm a little commitment-phobic. That tends to throw cold water on the fire whenever somebody comes along that I might want to get a little committed to. Somebody like Ethan Crane.

I know Todd would want me to be happy and be with someone, and I know Christy would want the same. For a while I was happy, with Guidry, a local homicide detective I fell very hard for. But then he took a job in his hometown of New Orleans, and I didn't want to follow him there, or I was afraid to. And that was that.

Judy returned with the coffeepot, and Tanisha, the cook, came out with my breakfast. Tanisha is built like a linebacker but has the heart of an angel. We're good friends, even though we only see each other at the diner, mostly because she works nonstop. The thought of going away and letting anyone else in her kitchen drives her crazy. She runs a tight ship, and she doesn't want anybody messing with it.

"Tanisha, when are you going to take a vacation?" I asked. "I don't think I've ever been in here when you weren't cooking away in that kitchen."

"Oh, Lord," she cried. "Plenty times I think I'd like to just walk out of here and keep on walkin'. Go to Tahiti or some fancy island somewhere and never look back." She crossed her massive arms over the back of the booth and looked at me dreamily. "Lord knows they ain't nobody gonna stop me. But you know what my problem is?"

"You'd miss me too much."

She grinned. "Nope. I'm too nice. I'd be scared I'd hurt y'all's feelings if I up and disappeared."

"It's true," I said. "You're about the sweetest person I know."

"Oh, honey, I know it," she continued. "You know if

there's even a fly in my kitchen, I don't go swattin' after it. I move him out the back door like a goddamn fool, like a dog steerin' a herd of sheep!" She shuffled across the floor back to the kitchen, dodging around an imaginary fly. "Come on, mister fly sweetheart," she said. "Get yo ass back home. Your fly friends is all worried 'bout where you been!"

I wanted to tell Judy and Tanisha what had happened that morning, but I was afraid they'd just tell me I was nuts to get involved, and I already knew that. Anyway, by the time I left the diner I had made up my mind. I couldn't live with myself if I didn't try to help Corina. I might be arrested, but I didn't care. I had to look into my own eyes when I stood in front of my bathroom mirror, and I wouldn't be able to face myself if I turned her in. I'm not sure what that made me in political terms, but I wasn't thinking politics. I was thinking of all living beings and the fact that we're all part of one enormous family. If we don't help raise one another up, we will all go down together.

The question was: How could I help her?

4

I pulled my Bronco into the parking lot at Walmart and made a few slow circles before I found a good spot. I always get a little nervous in parking lots. Usually I'm totally unaware of it until I see my knuckles whitening on the steering wheel, the same color as those painted lines on the asphalt.

As I walked across the lot, I tried to imagine myself in Corina's shoes. She had probably suspended any fear of being taken into a stranger's house when faced with the alternative: alone in a strange world with a newborn baby, no medical help, no money. What could she possibly have been thinking? Where would she live? How could she hope to fend for herself and a newborn? I tried not to think of the possibilities as I pulled out a cart and headed over to the baby supplies aisle.

It suddenly occurred to me that I had no idea what to get. Before Christy was born, Todd and I had read every baby book under the sun. We could tell you which diapers were the most absorbent, and what brand of baby slings

were 100 percent cotton and why you shouldn't give a paci-
fier to a newborn. Surely I'd gone out and bought all this
stuff before, possibly in this very store, but I couldn't remember it to save my life. It's as if I'd blocked it all out.

There was a woman balancing a package of disposable
diapers and a can of powdered infant formula in one arm
and a towheaded baby boy in the other. The girl was young
and pretty, in pale-washed jeans and a light pink tank top,
with straight blond hair and clean skin. On her shoulder
was a tattoo of a bird, perched atop a cross of thorns.

"Excuse me," I said. "I was wondering if you could help
me a bit?"

"Yeah," she said, shifting the baby to her other arm, "if
you'll get *this*."

She lifted one leg up to reveal a white paper napkin
stuck to the inseam of her jeans just above the ankle.

"Just realized I've been walking around like this all day,"
she said. "It's stuck on there like glue, and if I put him
down now he'll start wailing."

I peeled the napkin off her leg and tried to brush away
as best I could whatever had held it there. I hoped it was
baby food.

I said, "My friend has a baby, and I want to help her out,
and I was wondering if you could help me with what kind
of stuff she needs."

The girl wrinkled her nose, stuffing the napkin into her
back pocket. "You mean, like food stuff? Or clothing
stuff?"

"Well, what would be the basics?"

"Depends," she said. "Boy or girl?"

"Girl."

"How old?"

I hesitated. "Well, my friend is one of those health-nut types, you know, so she hired one of those home birth people and—"

"A doula," she said.

"Yes, that. And she had the baby at home, because she . . ." I cleared my throat. "Because she doesn't really believe in doctors and everything."

The girl tilted her head. "Uh-huh. And how old is the baby?"

"Ummm, an hour?" I said, looking at my watch. "Two hours tops."

The girl pursed her lips together and looked at me with one cocked eyebrow, like I was perhaps the most moronic creature she had ever laid eyes on.

"Oh," she said. "Wow."

I raised my shoulders as if to say "What are you gonna do?" and made a face that was half apologetic smile, half tormented grimace.

She sighed. "Go get a cart."

You wonder how anybody ever had a baby before the invention of Walmart, plastic, and the assembly line. Disposable bottles, wet wipes, pacifiers, panty shields, rubber nipples, baby powders, booties, syringes, gas drops, burp cloths, Onesies, crib pads, cotton swabs, nursing bras, diaper pails, bottle warmers, breast shields, bottle brushes, bumper shields—the list goes on and on. I nearly had one whole cart filled and was ready to go get another when the girl finally said we were done.

Since I wasn't sure if Corina would choose to breastfeed her baby, I had to cover all my bases and get some powdered formula as well, not to mention eye drops, aspirin, rash cream, a bulb syringe, and an aspirator. I could barely remember what half the stuff was for, but between me, Joyce, and Corina I was sure we could figure it out.

"You can use this as a crib for now," the girl said, sliding a bright pink car seat onto the rack under the cart. "And you can never have too many baby blankets."

She handed me a fleecy pink blanket. As I tossed it on top of the basket, I was about to thank her for all her help when she said, "You know, it's not my place to say, but your friend should see a doctor."

For a second I thought I detected some quotation marks around the way she said *your friend*. She had definitely avoided asking any more questions, and I was pretty sure she was convinced I was either a kidnapper or was running some sort of illicit, black-market baby-supply company.

"No insurance, right?"

I shook my head. "She's going through a pretty tough time right now."

"Yeah, here." She held out her baby. "Take him."

Before I could think of a reason to protest, my arms were reaching out and taking the baby from her. He immediately howled in utter despair.

"I told you." She pulled a pen from her purse and the napkin from her back pocket and started writing on it. "This is my pediatrician. Kind of a dork, but total sliding scale and no questions asked." She handed the sticky napkin to me with a poignant look. "Watch out for the oatmeal."

I laughed. "I was wondering what that was. I'm Dixie, by the way."

The girl looked at me expectantly, and for a moment I thought she might be waiting for me to give her a tip.

She said, "Can I have my baby back?"

"Oh my gosh, of course!"

She laughed and took the baby. His head smelled sweet, like talcum powder and clean sweat. As soon as he was back in his mother's arms he stopped crying and turned around to look at me accusingly.

"I could use a break," she said, "but I figure you've already got enough babies to deal with for today."

Just then my cell phone rang.

"Well, I'm out of here," she said. "This monster's due for his nap. Cool?"

"Oh my gosh, yes. Thank you so much for your help," I said, fishing my phone out of my bag. "I would have been shopping for hours!"

"I know," she said as she disappeared around the end of the aisle. "Call that doctor."

I pulled my phone out and flipped it open. My heart skipped a beat when I saw it was Ethan Crane. I held the phone to my ear with one shoulder and swung the cart around to head for the checkout lanes.

He said, "Hey, it's Ethan. What are you doing?"

I thought for a moment. Just the sound of his voice made me a little weak in the knees.

"I'm shopping."

"What for?"

I wondered how he would react if I said I was at Walmart buying a cartful of baby supplies for an illegal alien and her newborn baby that I found this morning behind the bushes in a bed of blood-soaked leaves.

"Hats," I said.

"Fun. Listen, my friend just opened a restaurant down-town, and I was wondering if you might want to go down and check it out this Friday night."

I stopped the cart in the middle of the aisle. "With you?"

"Yes, with me."

"Oh, sure," I said. "I can do that."

"I'm asking you to go with me. Like a date."

"Yes, I got that."

"Just making sure."

I said, "No, I'd love to."

I couldn't think of anything I'd rather not do. Not that I hadn't been thinking about Ethan a lot lately, and not that I don't find him completely irresistible, but the idea of going on a date with him made me so nervous that I wanted to stick my head in a hole.

"I have a meeting at six," I lied. "So I'll meet you there?"

"Excellent. Eight o'clock?"

Eight o'clock seemed horrible. "Perfect. See you then!"

As I clicked the phone off I heard him say, "Dixie, you don't even know where—"

The D-word, I said to myself as I rolled my cart into the checkout line. Ethan had used the damn D-word. I'd known it was only a matter of time before he asked me out on a date, but I still wasn't ready for it. Did this man think we were going to be a couple now? Did he think he was just going to drop in and sweep me off my feet? Did he know things were over with Guidry? *Were* things over with Guidry? And did he not realize I had absolutely nothing cute to wear?

Then I caught myself. There was that voice in my head again—telling me to run away, to hide, to stay *safe*.

I decided for now I wouldn't think about it. Six bags and three hundred and seventy five dollars later, I was back in the Bronco on my way to Joyce's when the phone rang again. It was Ethan, but this time I let it go to voice mail. Ethan had used the D-word. . . .

At Joyce's, I carried the first two of the bags up the front walk and was about to set them down on the mat when Joyce slipped out the front door and pulled it closed behind her. She looked a little bit flustered.

"How is she?" I asked. "How's the baby?"

"They're fine, they're fine," she whispered. "They're just waking up. But I have two things to tell you."

"Oh, no," I said. "What happened?"

She looked over her shoulder and then leaned in with a whisper. "There's ten one-thousand-dollar bills in Corina's purse!"

I put the bags down.

"What?"

She said, "I know, I know. I shouldn't have been going through her purse, but she was asleep and I thought I might be able to find a phone number, somebody I could call and let them know she was okay, a relative or something, and that's when I saw the money. It's just loose in her purse. Ten thousand dollars!"

"Does she know you found it?"

"No no no, she's still resting and I put it right back. Oh,

Dixie, why on earth would she have that kind of money in her purse?"

I said, "Now, let's don't jump to any conclusions. For whatever reason, she has a lot of money. It could be her life savings for all we know."

"You'd think with that kind of money if she knew she was going to have a baby, she'd at least have gotten a hotel room."

"I'm sure it's nothing to worry about, and plus it's none of our business."

Joyce didn't look convinced, and to tell the truth I wasn't too sure either. It did seem strange. Why would a young girl who apparently had nothing but a cardboard box and the clothes on her back walk around with so much cash? I had heard that illegals often come into the country with every penny they own. They need money to pay the people who help smuggle them in, and they have to pay for everything with cash. *Still* . . .

We decided to let it go. For whatever reason, Corina had a ton of money in her purse, and it wasn't our place to ask why. Although I did wonder if I shouldn't give her my Walmart receipt.

I said, "What's the second thing?"

"What second thing?"

"The second thing you wanted to tell me."

She nodded. "Oh yeah. You know that dead bird?"

"Yes?"

"Well it's not dead!"

. . .

Joyce's handbag was sitting on the coffee table in the living room. It had exploded. There were bits and pieces of tissue thrown about, a scattering of crumbs from what looked like a granola bar, a couple of lipstick cases, loose change, and a few fluffy chartreuse feathers. Proudly perched atop the handbag in all its multicolored glory was the resplendent quetzal, clutching a ring of keys in its bright yellow beak and eyeing us curiously.

I said, "Joyce, that bird is not dead."

She said, "Nope. In fact, it is very much alive."

The bird cocked its head to one side, flicked the ring of keys onto the table, and chirped what sounded like a cheerful *cool!*

Joyce said, "I was in the bedroom with Corina and the baby, and I thought I heard you out here unpacking things. I came out and there he was. He looks a little groggy, but other than that he seems perfectly fine. Do you think he got sick and just passed out?"

"Could be something he ate," I said, "or just plumb exhausted. Do you have a box or something we can put him in?"

"I can do better than that. I have an old antique birdcage in the garage."

I kept an eye on the bird while Joyce went out to the garage. He did seem a little out of sorts. Occasionally his eyelids would droop and he'd list to one side for a split second, but since I'd never spent a lot of quality time with a resplendent quetzal, for all I knew that was perfectly normal behavior.

Joyce returned with a beautiful handmade wire cage,

about three feet tall. It had a gabled roof and several swinging perches, a couple of wooden feeding boxes, and a hinged door just big enough for the bird to fit through.

"Now all we have to do is catch him," Joyce said.

I got down on my knees so my eyes weren't higher than the bird's and then shuffled slowly toward him. He hopped to the far end of the handbag and eyed me warily.

"We could use the pool net," Joyce said, "or I can throw a blanket over him and you grab him."

"I have a feeling it's going to be a lot easier than that."

Looking away from the bird, I moved my arm toward him with my palm down and two fingers extended. He hopped right off the bag and onto my hand with a high-pitched *cool!* and started pecking at my watch.

Joyce said, "Oh my gosh! Who are you, the bird whisperer?"

"His flight feathers are clipped," I said. "This little guy didn't blow in with a hurricane. He's somebody's pet."

Joyce set the cage down on the coffee table and opened its little hinged door. Moving my hand as slowly as possible, I ferried the bird up to the cage and held him level with the doorway. He flicked his long tail a couple of times, looked at me with one eye and then the other, and then hopped right in without so much as a peep.

There was a sharp intake of breath behind us, and we both started at the sound of it. I turned to see Corina standing in the doorway of the bedroom, her eyes as big as dinner plates and her jaw hanging wide open. She reached out to the door frame to steady herself.

We both jumped up and helped her to the couch. I got a pillow to put behind her back, and Joyce went into the kitchen to get a glass of water. Corina was staring at the bird like it was a ghost.

"*El pájaro,*" she said, shaking her head. "*Ay dios mío.*"

Joyce came back with the water and handed it to Corina. "She must have seen it lying dead on the path."

"She probably thinks it's a sign," I said. "I know that's what I'd be thinking if I were her."

I sat down on the couch next to her and pointed at the bird.

"Uh, the bird . . . *no es muerte. Es muy bueno!*"

"Yes," Corina said and nodded. "It is good."

"Joyce found it on the path this morning, uh . . . *esta mañana,* right before we heard the baby . . . *antes de la niña.*"

"Yes, yes," Corina said. She couldn't take her eyes off the bird.

"It's very exotic," I said, trying to think of the Spanish word for rare. "It's not from here. *No es de aquí.*"

"*Dios mío,*" she said, shaking her head. "*Dios mío, dios mío, dios mío.*"

I decided to take this opportunity to ask Corina again about seeing a doctor. I had the number that the young mother had given me at Walmart, and if anything was a sign, it was that a random stranger had given us a doctor that supposedly wouldn't ask too many questions. I didn't want to risk anyone turning Corina over to the immigration officials, but I didn't see how it was possible that we could let her go much longer without at least having the baby looked at by a pediatrician—and this seemed like my only chance.

"Corina," I said, taking the crumpled napkin with the doctor's number on it out of my pocket. "*Es necessario . . .*"

I paused to make sure I was using the right words.

She looked at the napkin and said, "Yes?"

"Es necessario . . . el médico."

She was silent.

"Es muy importante, for the baby."

She nodded. "Yes, yes I know."

I tried to figure out a way to tell her that I had a doctor that would probably not report her to immigration, but I just couldn't do it. All I could do was look Corina in the eye, woman to woman, and tell her with my voice that everything was going to be okay.

I said, *"El médico es bueno."*

I could see a little note of doubt in her eyes, but it vanished. She seemed to understand.

She said, "Okay, I can go."

"I promise nothing bad will happen," I said, even though I knew I couldn't honestly make that promise, and I'm sure Corina knew it as well, but we had no choice.

I said, "I'll call the doctor and make the appointment. *Comprende?"*

"Yes, I understand. *Gracias,* Dixie."

Joyce handed me the phone, and I dialed the number on the napkin.

A woman answered the phone. "Doctor's office, how can I help you?"

I said, "Hi, I wanted to know if I could talk to the doctor? I just have a few questions for him before I make an appointment."

She said, "What can I help you with?"

"Well, it's a little personal, actually. I really would feel better if I could speak to him directly."

"Alright," she said, "hold on while I get the doctor."

"Thanks very much." I nodded to Joyce and Corina. "She's getting the doctor."

There was a slight pause, and then the same woman said, "Hello, this is Dr. Harper."

"Oh no," I said. "I am a complete fool."

The woman laughed and said, "No, no, it's my fault, I should have told you when I answered the phone. My receptionist is out today with the flu, so I'm wearing a variety of hats and it's making me a little bonkers."

I knew right then and there that I could trust this doctor. I can relate to bonkers.

"A friend gave me your number," I said. "I have a newborn that needs to see a doctor right away."

"Alright, when would you like to come in? And congratulations, by the way."

I nearly shouted, "Oh, it's not mine! It belongs to a friend, but she doesn't speak English so I'm calling for her."

"I understand. I happen to have a cancellation tomorrow afternoon at three. Can you bring the baby and the mother then?"

"Oh, that would be great, thank you so much."

"And the name?"

"Corina . . . uh, hold on one sec."

I covered the phone and turned to her. "What is your last name? Corina . . ."

She hesitated. It was clear she didn't want to tell me, but she must have known there was no sense in trying to hide anymore. We were clearly here to help her.

"Flores."

"Corina Flores," I said into the phone.

"And the baby's name?"

I sighed. This was going to be tricker than I thought. I covered the phone again and turned to Corina.

"*La niña?* What's her name?"

Corina folded her hands in her lap and smiled.

"Dixie," she said. "Dixie Joyce Flores."

Joyce laughed, and I rolled my eyes in disbelief.

"Seriously, Corina, they'll need to put something down for the records, and you can always change it later. What's the baby's name?"

Just then the baby started crying softly in the other room. Corina stood up and looked at me with big, un-blinking eyes.

"Dixie. Joyce. Flores."

5

Some of the bathrooms in my clients' houses are so big and luxurious, you sort of want to run down to the local gas station and clean up before you step foot in them. Roy and Tina Harwick's master bathroom was like that. It was hands down the most flamboyant bathroom I've ever been in. You might even say it was a little crazy, but in their own way, so were the Harwicks. They lived in a huge, ornate mansion off Jungle Plum Road at the north end of the Key. They were driving to Tampa later in the afternoon, and I had gone to their house to meet their cat and to finalize our pet-sitting agreement.

The bathroom was just what you'd expect from people that have more money than they know what to do with: a gleaming marble floor, gold-laced wallpaper, a crystal chandelier dripping with thousands of twinkling diamonds, a gold-plated toilet with matching faucets, and a vaulted ceiling painted with harp-toting cherubs flying around in fluffy pink clouds. At one end of the bathroom were two multicolored stained-glass windows that glittered like a kaleidoscope, and between them was a cozy little nook and a peach-colored velvet bench where a person could sit and contemplate her navel, inspect her tan lines, or make a call from the gold-plated antique telephone sitting in its own little alcove in the wall.

But the focal point of the bathroom was a fish tank. And I don't mean a nice little tank on a stand with some goldfish and a couple of snails. I mean a humongous aquarium that took up an entire wall from floor to ceiling, with fish of every size, shape, and color swimming around in wide, slow circles, opening and closing their mouths in that eerie way fish do.

Artfully arranged around the inside of the tank were pieces of coral almost as tall as me, and holding court at center stage was a life-sized, brightly painted, porcelain mermaid. She had violet eyes, light pink skin, and flowing red hair, with a turquoise bikini top over melon-sized breasts, and a long blue-and-green tail that spread out across the floor of the tank. She was sitting on a gold-and-black treasure chest looking over her shoulder with a coy purse to her lips, like a pin-up movie star.

"These are goldflake angels," Mrs. Harwick said, pointing out a group of slender, butter-colored fish congregated at the base of the mermaid's tail. "And that sinister-looking creature hovering around the treasure chest is a dragon eel—very rare species, my son had it brought over from Japan. Priceless! And there's a dozen butterfly fish, seahorses, rabbit fish, damsels, a porcupine fish, ten albino tangs . . ."

She turned and gave me a meaningful look. "*Anybody* can get yellow tangs. These are *albino* tangs. I'd say there's at least three or four hundred thousand dollars' worth of fish in this tank. Roy thinks I'm out of my mind to spend so much money on them, but they make me happy, and that's what it's really all about it, isn't it?"

I must have still been staring openmouthed at the life-sized mermaid, because Mrs. Harwick laughed and said, "Isn't she fabulous? We found her in the islands. Roy, what island was it again?"

Mr. Harwick was standing in the bathroom doorway staring blankly at the tank. He wore a black, three-piece, pin-striped suit and a wide maroon tie. He must have been at least a foot shorter than Mrs. Harwick. He had thin hands and a balding pate, which he had skillfully camouflaged with jet black hair combed over from the back of his head, but I could tell that in his younger days he had probably been quite handsome. He wasn't a big man, but he had the air of someone who is accustomed to getting his way, a man with power and money.

"Barbuda," he said without blinking.

"Oh, Dixie, Barbuda is fabulous. Have you ever been?"

I had to bite my tongue to keep from laughing out loud, not just because the idea of traveling to some far-off exotic island was not exactly in my budget, but also because I had absolutely no idea where Barbuda was. "No," I mumbled, "but I'd love to go sometime."

"Honey," Mr. Harwick growled, "why don't you show her how you feed the fish?"

The aquarium was flanked on either side by two large pocket doors that slid open to reveal a hidden walkway around the back of the tank. There was a built-in cabinet with an impressive assortment of aquarium supplies: fish food, water testers, medications, and dozens of different-colored bottles filled with all sorts of chemicals and water conditioners. On the wall directly behind the tank was a collection of nets of various sizes, as well as a couple of long poles with hooks on one end to move shells and things around inside the tank. Mrs. Harwick led me up several narrow steps to a platform at the back of the tank and slid open a panel on the top.

"Sprinkle it," she said, gracefully waving her heavily bejeweled fingers over the surface of the water, "from one end to the other. You don't just take a handful of food and plop it down in one place like a fool. It has to be spread across the surface to mimic the way it is in nature."

I was pretty sure there wasn't a single creature in this tank that thought it was living free in the open ocean with a golden toilet, a crystal chandelier, and a tarted-up mermaid nearby, but I didn't say a word. From our vantage point, I could see down the mermaid's cleavage. There was a tiny hermit crab nestled there, snug as a bug in a boob.

"I've written out the feeding instructions for you," Mrs. Harwick said, stepping down off the platform. "It's really quite simple, so I'm sure you'll do fine. I probably don't need to tell you this but, if you do have to put your hands in the water for any reason, I'd recommend taking any rings or bracelets off first, the water is probably not the best thing for . . ."

She trailed off as she glanced down at my hands, which of course had no rings or bracelets of any kind. She blushed a little, and I got the feeling that in her world a woman whose hands aren't decked out in gold and jewels is a woman to be pitied.

As if she were trying to make up for some indecorous offense, she extended her left hand out to me. There was a sparkling wrist cuff about an inch wide around her wrist.

"This one's got about two hundred diamonds on it, and I promise you that Japanese eel will swallow just about anything!"

She laughed, and I nodded enthusiastically. *How true!* I thought. The last thing a girl needs is a Japanese eel eating her diamonds.

Mrs. Harwick closed the pocket door, and I followed her out of the bathroom and down a short hallway lined with mahogany dressers that led to the master bedroom. There was a king-sized canopy bed, draped in folds of yellow and red silk, with white tassels at each corner the size of overfed guinea pigs and an arrangement of pillows leaning against the headboard that can only be described as epic. The second-floor hallway was wide enough to drive through in a Cadillac, and everywhere I looked the walls were covered with big, expensive-looking paintings, the type I'd only ever seen in school trips to the museum. There was a wide curving staircase of white marble that led down to the main entry, where two life-sized statues of Roman gods guarded the arched entrance to the sprawling living room. If I didn't know better, I'd swear there were even a couple of Picassos hanging over the sofa.

Mr. Harwick was standing at the bar, pouring himself a drink. There was a cat circling his feet and rubbing itself against his ankles.

"And this," Mrs. Harwick said, waving her arm at the cat dismissively, "is Charlotte."

I've always had a special place in my heart for Siamese cats. They're smart as a whip and intensely loyal, and their origin is steeped in mystery. Some historians believe they were a favorite of the kings and queens of ancient Siam, where their name meant "moon diamond." All it took was one look in Charlotte's sparkling azure eyes to know why. She was long and sleek, with a dark, silver-tipped chocolate coat.

"We call her Queen B," said Mrs. Harwick.

I knelt down and held out the back of my hand for Charlotte to sniff—my standard cat greeting. She took one step back and hissed.

"The *B* does *not* stand for beautiful."

I grinned. "Are you saying Charlotte has a bit of an attitude?"

"That's one way of putting it."

Mr. Harwick said, "Don't take it personally. She's that way with everyone."

He scooped Charlotte up in his arms and cooed to her, "And the *B* stands for baby, because that's what she is, my baby."

I had to chuckle at the sight of a grown man in a business suit babbling like a little girl at a fluffy Siamese cat. Animals have an uncanny way of bringing out the sweet side of even the most hard-edged customer.

Mrs. Harwick shuddered like a minister finding a roach clip in the collection plate. "That cat is not your baby."

Charlotte chose that moment to hiss again. She squirmed out of Mr. Harwick's arms and ran into the kitchen without so much as a "nice to meet you." I feel that way myself sometimes, so I didn't take offense.

"Bit of an attitude problem," Mr. Harwick said. "I'll show you where we keep her food."

The first thing I noticed about the kitchen was that it was twice the size of my entire apartment. There was a center island as big as the king-sized bed upstairs, made out of what looked like one solid piece of snow white marble. Dangling over it was a pair of crystal chandeliers, these twice the size of the one in the bathroom, and there were two ovens set side by side in the wall. I barely know what to do with one oven, but apparently the Harwicks needed two.

As I looked around the kitchen, making small sounds of delight like I was at a fireworks display, I realized there were actually two of everything: two refrigerators, two ovens, even two dishwashers. It was the Noah's Ark of kitchens. At one end of the island were two stainless-steel sinks, and dozens of gleaming copper pots of all shapes and sizes were hanging everywhere.

"My brother is a cook," I gushed. "He'd love your kitchen."

"Well, Tina here is the chef in the family," Mr. Harwick said as he pulled up a stool and spread several official-looking files across the island. "Although these days she only uses the kitchen for special occasions."

I said, "Special occasions, you mean like holidays?" I wondered if there wasn't another kitchen somewhere that Mrs. Harwick used for nonspecial occasions.

"No," Mr. Harwick said, "I mean like when the pool boy is hungry."

He pushed one of the files toward me. "This is the emergency file. It has numbers for my office and my secretary's home number, along with the telephone number and address of the hotel where we'll be staying and my personal cell phone number. You'll find contact numbers for the alarm company, the housekeepers, the plumber, the electrician, and so forth. Of course, if there's anything wrong, you'll call me directly first."

I wondered why, if I was supposed to call him first, he wanted to give me all this information, but I could tell Mr. Harwick was the kind of man that liked to cover all his bases. I could appreciate that kind of thoroughness. In my police training, I'd been taught to anticipate danger before it happens, and that comes in handy every once in a while. In fact, it's not a bad way to operate in any situation. In Mr. Harwick's case, though, it did seem a little over the top.

"This is Charlotte's file. It has a copy of her medical history and all her records, as well as the numbers of her veterinarian, her backup veterinarian, and the emergency animal hospital. Her eating schedule is there, too, just in case you forget, along with a list of all her vitamins and supplements."

He stood up and crossed over to a wall of cabinets, opening one to reveal row upon row of cans and boxes of cat food.

He said, "It's her choice. She eats both wet and dry. She'll let you know what she wants. And there's yogurt in the refrigerator. She gets one teaspoon diluted in warm water mixed in with every meal. Please don't forget that, otherwise her irritable bowel syndrome kicks in. Everything you need to know is in the file, except for the alarm code. You should write that down."

I reached for my backpack. Mrs. Harwick had moved

out to the living room just off the kitchen, and I could see her through the arched doorway, looking at the pool just outside a pair of large sliding glass doors. I opened my pack and took out the notebook I keep with information on all my pet clients and any medications they take or special dietary requirements. I even make a note of their favorite toys and where they like to hide.

Mr. Harwick was pleased. "Ah, a fellow note taker, I see."

I said, "Mr. Harwick, I run my pet-sitting business with the same professional attention to detail that I devoted to being a police officer. I always take notes and keep records of everything I do. That comes in handy sometimes."

"I bet it does."

"I can assure you that Charlotte and Mrs. Harwick's aquarium will be in good hands while you're away."

He snorted. "Oh, I don't give a rat's ass about the fish. But you should write down the alarm code. It's my wife's birthday: ten nineteen."

"Ten nineteen," I repeated as I wrote in my notebook.

"Nineteen is the day, by the way, not the year."

"Very funny," Mrs. Harwick said.

She was leaning in the doorway to the kitchen now, and for the first time I noticed she was really quite beautiful. With one hand resting on the side of her neck, she looked like she was posing for the cover of *Cosmopolitan* magazine. She had silver hair piled casually on top of her head, and her body was long and graceful like a dancer's. I said a little silent prayer that I looked half as good as she did when I was her age.

I wasn't sure if Mr. Harwick's teasing banter was just a game they played—you can never really know what goes on in the vast world of two people in love—but she seemed genuinely hurt by his joke. She was watching him out of the corner of her eye, and I could tell she was trying to come up with some stinging retort. Mr. Harwick, on the other hand, seemed to barely notice her.

He said, "The password is Tiger. Every window on both floors is tied into the system as well, so if you open anything while you're here you have to make sure you close it before you go. The lanai is wired, too. We keep the alarm on at all times when we're not here. You should do the same. The only people that know the code and the password are the housekeeper and the pool man. And the kids, of course."

"The kids?"

"Becca and August, but I doubt you'll see them very often."

"Oh, they live here?"

"They do," he said, "but Becca's started her freshman year at college, and August just got a job at the golf club, so they won't be in your way."

I wrote both their names down in my notebook and tried not to look mystified as to why Becca and August couldn't just take care of the pets themselves.

"You may be wondering what the hell we need you for when we have two grown, perfectly capable adults living in our house."

"Oh, no." I blushed. "I completely understand."

"Good," he said. "Perhaps you can explain it to me one day. They came as a package deal with Mrs. Harwick, so my DNA's got absolutely nothing to do with it." He handed me the files. "The pool boy's name is Kenny Newman. His number is there should you need him."

A little too excitedly, I said, "Oh, I know Kenny! I mean, I used to look after his cat."

I didn't say it, but Kenny also worked for me sometimes as an overnight dog sitter. We had met when he hired me to take care of his elderly orange tabby, Mister T, who was a very sweet old guy. I was the first person Kenny called when Mister T died, and we had been friends ever since.

And now I knew exactly why Mrs. Harwick might think it was a special occasion to whip up a snack if the pool man was hungry. Kenny looked like he fell off the cover of a men's fashion magazine. He was tall and broad shouldered, with long sandy-blond hair and eyelashes any woman would kill for. A bit scruffy, perhaps, and a little rough around the edges, but that only made him even more irresistible to women. He lived in a rickety old houseboat behind Hoppie's Restaurant on the south end of the Key. In exchange for doing odd jobs around the place, Hoppie let him live on the boat for free. The occasional dog-sitting gig at night was perfect for him—it provided a comfortable bed and a decent shower every once in a while. He parked his small truck in the client's driveway, which was a good signal to would-be burglars that somebody was home. It was great for me because he provided company for the dogs at night, and he fed and walked them before he left in the morning, saving me a trip.

Mrs. Harwick was studying me closely. She had a curious look on her face. "Kenny never mentioned he had a cat. What kind of cat is it?"

"An orange tabby, but unfortunately it passed away a while ago."

"Oh, no. What was his name?"

"Honey," Mr. Harwick said, "I think Miss Hemingway probably has better things to do than stand around talking about the pool boy's cat."

Before I could answer, there was a loud clumping sound from upstairs. I turned around half expecting to see the chandeliers over the kitchen island shaking.

Mrs. Harwick said, "Oh, that's our daughter."

She went out to the front foyer and called up the marble staircase.

"Becca," Mrs. Harwick called. "Come and meet the cat sitter."

There was a short pause, and then the clomping sound started again, growing louder and louder until finally a young woman dressed almost entirely in black appeared at the top of the stairs. From the sound of it I had expected her to be a linebacker-sized Amazon, but instead she was a petite wisp of a thing. She wore a short black shawl wrapped around her narrow shoulders, with a faded pink T-shirt and a tight black miniskirt over black tights, and black lace-up army boots with two-inch-thick rubber soles. Her hair was jet black, too. It fell across her forehead, half hiding her face. She looked like every sullen, angry teenager in the world, and I wondered if Christy would have gone through a similar stage had she been given the chance.

"Becca, this is Dixie. She'll be taking care of Charlotte while we're away."

Becca came stomping down the stairs in her boots and

shook my hand limply, mumbling something that sounded like "hello." Her green eyes were framed in magenta eyeliner, and her lashes were thick with black mascara. She had her mother's thin figure and pale skin, but where Mrs. Harwick was polished and confident, Becca was all sharp angles and angst-ridden. I immediately liked her.

I leaned toward her and said, "Love your boots."

Becca peered up from behind her curtain of black hair and smiled, but before she could say anything Mr. Harwick handed me the stack of files and said, "Thank you for coming by, Miss Hemingway."

I nodded. "Well, it's been a pleasure meeting all of you. If there's anything else you think of, please feel free to give me a call, twenty-four/seven. I keep my cell phone with me at all times."

I extended my hand to Mr. Harwick, but he stood still with his arms folded over his chest. "No questions?"

Mrs. Harwick smiled tensely and said, "Roy . . ."

He shot her a look. "No, I'm just curious. Not a single question? We've given you a lot of information here, Dixie. I'm a little surprised you wouldn't have at least one or two questions for us."

Becca was standing motionless at the bottom of the staircase looking down at the floor. I know men like Mr. Harwick. I had encountered a lot of them in the police force. He was the kind of man that liked to be in charge, and he liked to be in charge *all the time*, especially around women. In extending my hand to him, I had basically signaled that our meeting was over, and that had obviously made his testicles shrink up a couple of sizes. Had I been a little bit more on my toes, I would have made up a couple of lame-ass questions just to stroke his ego. He was, after all, a client. But I'd had a long day, and I didn't feel like playing along.

"Mr. Harwick," I said, "I've been pet sitting for quite a while, and I'm pretty good. I promise you there won't be anything to worry about. Charlotte and I will have a great time while you're away. She's in good hands."

He frowned slightly. "So not one question."

With a sweet smile, I said, "Nope. If I had a question I would ask it. Was there something in particular you were thinking of?"

He paused, but his expression didn't change. "Good for you. And no, I think that about covers it."

He shook my hand firmly and walked back into the living room with a nod at Mrs. Harwick.

She said, "I'll see you out."

We walked to the door in silence. I looked back to wave good-bye to Becca and caught her staring at me in awe. I don't think she'd ever seen a stranger stand up to her father. I had to admit it was not the most professional thing to do, but when a kid has an asshole for a parent, it sometimes feels really good to point it out to them.

Outside on the winding cobblestone driveway, Mrs. Harwick brightened. "Oh, Dixie, I almost forgot!"

She pulled a notecard out of her pocket and handed it to me. It was written with the most precise, miniature handwriting I'd ever seen.

"It's the feeding schedule for the fish, and there's also instructions for checking the water chemistry. I doubt you'll need to adjust it, but it's important that you check it at least once a day. Fish are funny creatures, you know.

They seem so strong and invincible, but introduce just the slightest chemical imbalance and the next thing you know they're belly up at the bottom of the tank. When my Reggie died, I thought I'd never get over it."

"Oh, what kind of fish was Reggie?"

She frowned and looked off in the distance. "That's funny. Reggie was my first husband. I have no idea why I just said that."

As I pulled my Bronco out and headed down the driveway to the front gate, Mrs. Harwick watched from the porch. I wasn't sure if it was the day or the Harwicks' craziness or both, but my head was swimming and I felt a little more loopy than usual. I waved as I turned south to head home, and Mrs. Harwick waved back and went inside the house. I felt such a rush of sympathy for her, an almost immediate bond. I glanced over at Mr. Harwick's files stacked neatly on the passenger seat.

If I had known what was good for me, I would have tossed the whole stack right out the window and never set foot in that house again.

6

I drove down Midnight Pass at about twenty miles per hour. Nobody honked or drove right behind me shaking their fists and yelling at me to drive faster. They were all driving slowly, too. It was the time of year when clouds of lovebugs swarm the air, and the more slowly you drive, the more gently the lovebugs splat into your car. The more gently they splat, the easier they are to clean off.

Lovebugs are small black flies with long, narrow wings. They come out of their vegetative hiding places every May and September with an urgent need to copulate. They give the term "hooking up" a meaning even the smallest child can understand. The male attaches to the female, and then they fly around crazily in a cloud of other copulating lovebug couples until they fall dead of exhaustion or smash into a moving vehicle. They leave the windshields smeared with gunk, corrode the paint on the cars, and occasion many a raunchy schoolboy joke. On the other hand, birds like to snack on them, and a lot of car wash businesses would go bankrupt if they disappeared, so we just leave them alone and drive at a snail's pace a couple of times a year.

Siesta Key is long and narrow, eight miles north to south. On a map, it looks like a fish skeleton, with Midnight Pass Road running down its center like a spine, and smaller lanes like fish bones leading off at regular intervals to the Gulf on the west side and Little Sarasota Bay on the east. The head is at the wider, northern end of the Key, where the main village of shops and restaurants is, and the southern end of the island tapers off like a fishtail. Only about seven thousand people make their home on the Key year-round, but another seventeen thousand or more come here during "season." People with homes on the bay have boat docks, but there are no docks on the Gulf side, just gentle surf lapping onto a crystal white sandy beach.

I live on the more deserted tail end of the Key in a two-story frame house that faces the Gulf. My grandfather ordered it out of the Sears, Roebuck catalog when he was a young man and land here was cheap. It's a weathered two-bedroom house at the end of a meandering drive of crushed shell, surrounded by palms, sea grape, pines, and mossy oaks on which night-blooming cereus twine to the top like secret floodlights. Flocks of parakeets nest in the treetops, and wild rabbits forage through the grasses. The drive ends at the Gulf's edge, so I've gone to sleep almost every night of my life with the whispering sound of the surf kissing the shore. That pulse of the sea is like a lover's heartbeat to me.

When I rounded the last curve in the drive and pulled into my slot in the four-car carport, a huge orange sun was already sliding down the sky toward the horizon. My brother, Michael, and his partner, Paco, were on the deck with their tanned legs stretched out in sturdy Adirondack chairs my grandfather built decades ago. Ella Fitzgerald was with them, sitting in Paco's lap. Ella is a true calico-Persian mix originally given to me as a kitten, but it didn't take her long to realize that the good stuff was in Michael's and Paco's kitchen, not mine. She likes me well enough and stays with me when the guys are working, but her heart belongs to them.

When I joined them on the deck, Michael took one look at me and said, "You need a beer." He got up and went into the kitchen, and I dropped into the chair next to Paco. He raised his beer in greeting and gave me a lazy grin.

He said, "Long day?"

"Is it that obvious?"

Paco is the kind of man that women fantasize about turning straight. He's of Greek American descent, but with his dark good looks and facility with languages he could pass for any nationality in the world. In his line of work with the Special Investigative Bureau, that comes in handy. His family name is Pakodopoulos, but nobody in the world can pronounce that, so he's called Paco.

Michael returned with a beer for me and a plate of cheese twists still hot from the oven. Michael is blond and blue eyed and just as handsome as Paco. He's a fireman like our father was and also the firehouse cook. To Michael, food is almost holy, and to feed people is second only in importance to saving their lives. Our mother didn't have a domestic bone in her body, but he's made up for it in spades. He's been feeding me and taking care of me since I was about two years old and he was four. When I was nine, not long after our father died in the line of duty putting out a fire, our mother ran off, so we moved in with our grandparents in the house that Michael and Paco live in now. I live in the garage apartment above the carport. Michael has created our own kind of domestic bliss here. Funny how life curves in on itself like that sometimes.

I decided not to tell them about Corina and the baby, at least not for now. Michael and Paco are both crazily protective of me, and since Paco is part of the Special Investigative Bureau, illegal immigration falls directly under his jurisdiction, and I might be telling him something that he might not be able to ignore. Michael has always felt responsible for me, mainly because he's my big brother. There's no changing that, and I know it. There was a time when it really bothered me, and it still does sometimes, but I know it's in his DNA, just like being a fireman is in his DNA. In his eyes, I will always be the little sister that he has to look out for. So keeping a few things to myself every once in a while makes it easier.

I also decided not to mention my prospective date with Ethan. Not because I thought Michael would object to it, but because, being the little sister, I get a delicious thrill keeping secrets from him every once in a while.

Paco gave Ella Fitzgerald a nibble of cheese twist, and we all watched the sun continue its slide down the sky. Sunsets on Siesta Key are spectacular, even the ones with cloud cover. Every day brings different colors, different shapes of streamers in the sky, different shadows on the water. Even the birds seem to grow silent as the sun hovers for a moment above the sea, toying with it before giving in completely. It always seems to disappear into the water too soon, and we continue to watch for it to show an edge of itself. But it only sends up ribbons of undulating light, cerise, magenta, aquamarine, like favors from an invisible party to which we're not invited. Every day we're awed and inspired and vaguely disappointed because we want more.

When the lights had drifted away, Michael waved away some lovebugs and said, "I have chowder inside."

I said, "Can I take a shower first?"

"Dixie, if you don't take a shower, we'll hose you down on the deck."

Nobody wants to share a meal with a person covered in cat hair. It's an occupational hazard for pet sitters. I handed him my half-full beer bottle and tried to think of a smart comeback, but I was too tired. I felt like I'd had one of the longest days in the history of my life, so instead I punched him in the arm before I climbed the stairs to my apartment.

Behind me, Paco strolled to my car with a big dripping sponge to wipe away the lovebugs.

Dinner was Florida red chowder made with fresh fish Michael had caught the day before on a fishing trip. With it we had hot buttered French bread, a green salad dressed with a Florida grapefruit vinaigrette, and a fruity white wine. Ella Fitzgerald sat on her appointed stool and watched us with the lazy look of disinterest that only a well-fed cat can manage. The rule for Ella is that she can sit on her stool at the dinner table as long as she's polite and doesn't call attention to herself.

We were just finishing the last crumb of bread when my cell phone rang with the tone reserved for business calls. It was Kenny Newman.

I said, "I better take this. It's my overnight dog sitter, and he's on a job tonight."

Michael's left eyebrow quirked in disapproval as I rose quickly to take the call out on the deck. In our family, it's a hard and fast rule that phones are not allowed at the table and dinner shouldn't be interrupted with business. But Kenny was spending the night at the Daltons' house with their two German shepherds, George and McGee, and I knew he wouldn't call unless it was something important.

Kenny said, "Hey man, sorry to bother you, but I need a little help here. This girl just came to the door asking if she could take George and McGee out for a walk. She said she's a neighbor and she walks the dogs all the time, but like, nobody told me anything about a neighbor kid, so I said no. She looked totally pissed off, so I hope I didn't do the wrong thing."

"You were completely right. If anyone has permission to walk them, we'd need it in writing from the Daltons. They'll be back in the morning, so I'll be in touch with them. If there's any problem, I'll take care of it."

He thanked me, and we rang off before I thought to mention that I was pet sitting at the Harwicks' house, where he cleaned the pool. I slipped back into my spot at the table and took a sip of wine.

Paco said, "Was that your beach drifter guy?"

"That was Kenny. He had a minor problem that we straightened out. And he is not a drifter."

"He lives on an old dilapidated boat."

I sputtered, "Paco, there's nothing wrong with living on a boat."

"Yeah, especially if you don't want to leave behind a trail of those pesky things called mailing addresses."

Michael said, "Wait a minute, what does he do if it gets cold at night?"

"It never gets that cold here, plus he has a little wood-burning stove."

Paco rolled his eyes. "Or he sleeps in his car."

Michael said, "What? Are you kidding me?"

I waved my hand like I was waving away a fly. "He has a truck for his pool-cleaning supplies. He may sleep in it occasionally if the weather's bad or he doesn't have a house-sitting job."

Michael said, "Seems pretty suspicious to me."

"Maybe he's just saving up his money. I like that in a person."

Paco raised one eyebrow. "Or maybe you just like the sexy blond surfer type."

I said, "Please. He's a good worker, and he's honest, and he's always been fair with me. People can fall on bad times. That doesn't make them criminals. Anyway, you should have seen how much he loved that old cat of his. In my book, anybody that loves a cat can't be all bad."

Michael didn't look convinced, but I wasn't worried. I think I'm a pretty good judge of character, and I knew Kenny was a good guy, even though I had to admit, you could see how they might think Kenny was a bit sketchy. I chalked it up to one of the many occupational hazards of being in the line of work they're in. When you're in close contact with danger or criminals on a daily basis, you tend to look for the negative in everything and everyone.

To change the subject, I said, "I got a new job today. At a house with a mermaid in a tank in the bathroom."

Michael grinned and said, "The toilet tank?"

"No, you doofus. I'm talking a *huge* mermaid. Nearly life-sized. The aquarium is so tall you have to climb up a flight of stairs to feed the fish. Mrs. Harwick said combined the fish are worth hundreds of thousands of dollars."

Paco said, "Wait a minute. *The* Harwicks? Roy and Tina Harwick?"

"Yeah, do you know them?"

He shook his head. "Not personally, but Roy Harwick is one of the top executives at Sonnebrook."

He had a tone in his voice, as if saying the word "Sonnebrook" explained everything. Unfortunately, it kind of did. Sonnebrook is the Oklahoma-based company that inevitably comes up whenever there's a conversation about war, or oil, or consummate greed. It's one of the largest oil-drilling and construction companies in the world, not to mention one of the biggest private employers in the country. In the last twenty years, they've raked up billions of dollars in no-questions-asked government contracts to maintain military bases or help rebuild war-torn countries. Along the way, they've been exposed countless times for corruption, illegal practices, and worse.

Michael said, "It's all over the papers today. He's giving a speech in Tampa tomorrow at a conference on earth-friendly energy. Do you believe that? The head of one of the biggest oil-manufacturing companies talking about how we can make the planet greener! That guy is hated all over the world. Sonnebrook has probably bumped off more potentates in those little Middle Eastern countries than the CIA and MI6 combined."

Paco and I rolled our eyes. Michael's sense of morality is more highly tuned than ours, and he has a tendency to see conspiracy and skullduggery around every corner. It doesn't take much to get him going about all the underhanded things done by the world's biggest corporations and governments, including our own. He can get himself pretty worked up.

"They've been implicated in propping up despots just to make a dime and bribing senators to get their way in Congress. I mean, you name it, they've done it. They're all cutthroats and thieves. And of course you can't touch them with a ten-foot pole because their money is spread all over Washington. The whole operation smells worse than dog shit."

Paco chuckled and said, "Alright now, calm down."

Michael laughed. "Well, I'm sorry, but I can't help it, and I read they have a world-class art collection, too, all of it bought with dirty money, of course. I'm guessing they live in a huge mansion on the water, right?"

I said, "Yep. And they have a gold-plated toilet."

Michael practically jumped out of his chair. "See? I told you! What kind of person wants to sit on a gold toilet?"

Paco and I both burst out laughing. Paco has a knack for disarming Michael. No matter how worked up Michael gets, Paco can flip his mood like tossing a coin, but I'm good at pushing all his buttons, so together we make a pretty good game of mercilessly teasing him up and down like a yo-yo.

"Yeah, very funny," Michael said. "We'll see if you two get any dessert tonight."

Michael's desserts are nothing to joke about. He makes the most amazing pies and cookies. You haven't lived until you've had a slice of his key lime pie, which he makes from actual key limes he collects from a wild tree, the whereabouts of which he won't tell a living soul.

I said, "Okay, okay. No more talk about the Harwicks. They do, however, have a beautiful little Siamese cat named Charlotte that I'm trying to win over. She's a big grump."

Michael turned to Ella and smiled. She slitted her eyes and gazed at him with rapt adoration.

He said, "You'd be a big grump too if you lived with murdering thieves."

Paco and I exchanged grins, but we didn't say a word because Michael reached over and took the key lime pie off the kitchen counter and set it in the middle of the table.

"Mmmm," I said. "What were we just talking about?"

Paco said, "I have no idea. Pass the pie!"

All in all, it had been a normal, ordinary end to a long, surreal, and crazy day. I helped clean up the kitchen, kissed Michael and Paco on their handsome cheeks, nuzzled the top of Ella Fitzgerald's head, and staggered up the stairs to my apartment, drunk on good wine, good company, and good key lime pie.

Just before I drifted off to sleep, I heard a little voice in my head say, *Well, at least tomorrow can't be any crazier than today!*

Sometimes that little voice in my head is dead wrong.

7

My morning routine is pretty much written in stone. I get up, stagger to the bathroom to splash water on my face, brush my teeth, and twist my hair into a ponytail. I stumble into the kitchen for a glass of orange juice, and then I'm out the door in my regulation cargo shorts, white sleeveless tee, and a fresh pair of clean white Keds. The secret to being a good pet sitter is having good shoes. I'm on my feet about as much as a big-city mailman, so I have a row of clean Keds drying on a rack at all times. The minute a pair starts getting even the slightest bit raggy, out they go.

On my porch, I took a minute to inhale the clean salt air and to nod good morning to the glossy sea. At that hour, only a few early birds are walking along the shore's edge picking up the choicest goodies brought in on the overnight tide. There were a couple of snowy egrets standing perfectly still, watching a small team of piping plovers that were running back and forth in the sand to the rhythm of the waves rolling in. Some sleepy chirping sounds came from the trees as other birds opened an eye and nudged one another awake, but mostly I had the fresh new day to myself. I need that moment of connection to life, need to pull it into my lungs and feel it climbing from the soles of my feet up my bones.

When I was fully aware, I clattered down the stairs, shooed away a brown pelican who had roosted on my Bronco overnight, and turned on my headlights for the drive down my twisty lane. I went slowly so as not to wake the parakeets, but they're so sensitive they rose from the treetops in agitated flutters that made me feel guilty. At Midnight Pass Road, where a line of mailboxes stand guard, I turned left and headed off to bring food, fun, and frivolity to all the pets that were home alone and waiting for my arrival.

As always, morning or afternoon, my first stop is the Sea Breeze, a big pink condo building on the Gulf where Billy Elliot lives. Billy Elliot is a greyhound that Tom Hale rescued. Like most race dogs, once Billy Elliot stopped winning races, he wasn't much use anymore and his days were numbered. Tom is a CPA, and in exchange for his handling my taxes and anything else having to do with money, I go over to Tom's and let Billy Elliot drag me around the parking lot a couple of times a day. It's a perfect arrangement. I'm not good with money, and Tom can't run because he's been in a wheelchair ever since a wall of lumber fell on him in a freak accident at a home-improvement store.

I rode the mirrored elevator up to Tom's floor and then used my keys to open the door. Tom was sitting at the kitchen table with a computer in front of him as usual, probably working on someone's taxes. He spends a lot of time in front of a computer, and since I have no interest in computers at all, he is my sole connection to the Internet. He looked up and waved, and I waved back. He has a sweet, round face with warm eyes behind steel-rimmed glasses and a head of curly black hair. He looks like a slightly pudgy Harry Potter.

Billy Elliot came trotting up to say good morning, his tail wagging like an out-of-control whirligig. I patted him on his head, and he snuffed and snorted in that way dogs do when they're happy to see you. I didn't want to interrupt Tom's work, so I snapped on Billy Elliot's leash and headed out for our morning session.

A lot of older greyhounds suffer from all manner of long-term side effects from the way they were treated during their racing careers. Broken toes are common, torn ligaments, fractured bones, chronic arthritis. Most retirees are happiest when they're lying on a nice soft bed at the feet of their humans, but Billy Elliot is different. He likes a good run at least twice a day, and that's where I come in.

The Sea Breeze has a circular parking lot with an oval spot of grass in the middle that makes a perfect practice track. After Billy does his morning business and pees on every bush in sight, he starts out at a slow trot around the lot. This is completely for my benefit. He's learned over the years that he can't wear me out too fast or I'll collapse from exhaustion after just a couple of laps. Gradually he works up to a good jogging pace, and we keep that up for about fifteen minutes. Usually it's so early that we're the only ones out. Sometimes I'll let him off the leash and he'll race around the track a few times at warp speed just to prove he's still got it. Then we ride back up in the elevator, both of us panting happily.

Billy Elliot is like my own personal fitness guru. If Tanisha is the little devil on my shoulder trying to plump me up with her scrumptious cooking, Billy Elliot is the angel on my other shoulder, cheering me on as I burn off all those fat calories.

Tom was still working when we got back, so I hung up Billy Elliot's leash, gave him a good scratch under the ears, and left quietly.

It was about seven thirty when I got to the Harwicks' house. From the outside, it looked like a Mediterranean castle from some far-off country that had been uprooted and flown across the sea. It just didn't fit, as impressive as it was. The long paved driveway sloped up to the grand entrance, lined on either side with palms and oak trees and bougainvillea in full bloom, scenting the air with their bubble-gum and cherry blossoms. There were turrets around the upper balconies of the house, where there were more flowering plants spilling over: trumpet vine, jasmine, honeysuckle, flame vine. There were ruby-throated hummingbirds and yellow butterflies flitting about everywhere. I felt like I was strolling through a postcard of a quaint Italian village as I walked up to the big wooden double doors. I pulled out my ring of keys and my notebook with the alarm codes written on it, turned the key in the lock, and opened the door. A loud beeping sounded throughout the house. I opened the cover to the little keypad on the side of the entrance and punched in the private code.

Charlotte was waiting for me at the bottom of the

marble staircase, sitting in a sphinx posture and gazing straight ahead as if she didn't notice I was in the same universe as she was, just as unfriendly as she'd been when I'd met her the day before. But she didn't fool me. If she'd really wanted to shut me out, she would have been hidden somewhere.

I knelt in front of her and extended the back of my hand for her to sniff.

I said, "Hi, Charlotte. Remember me? I'm going to make your breakfast today."

She didn't respond, just watched me as I stood up and walked to the kitchen.

Her food bowl was on the floor with some stale crumbs of dry cat food in it. I wrinkled my nose, threw away the stale stuff, and washed the bowl. I don't like to leave cat food sitting out because it affects a cat's appetite the same way it would affect a human's if the same food was always sitting on the table growing stale and unappealing. *Yuk.* When I feed a cat, the food is left out for fifteen minutes, then it's tossed. Cats learn they'd better eat up when they have the chance. That way they look forward to mealtime and their appetites never become jaded. I leave them a kitty treat to enjoy between meals, but only one. I'm not sure how long they wait to eat their treats, but I imagine them sitting and watching the clock, thinking they'll wait just a few more minutes before they pounce on it.

While I washed out her food bowl, Charlotte came into the kitchen and walked around with her tail swishing and little growls coming from her throat like a chef getting ready to shout obscenities at the kitchen staff because they're too slow.

I said, "Oh, you're so right. Yes, it is a lovely day. And did you see that moon last night? Beautiful!"

Charlotte stopped talking and stood with her front paws spread apart, ready for a showdown. She obviously did not suffer fools gladly.

I washed her water bowl and gave her fresh water. She watched me with a highly suspicious look on her face. I opened up the pantry and surveyed the rows and rows of cat food.

I said, "Which do you prefer, wet or dry?"

She swished her tail some more. Not in a friendly way.

Since I approved of the dry food more than the canned, I put a couple of scoops in Charlotte's bowl and set out a kitty treat for later. When I put the food bowl down on the floor, Charlotte waited a few seconds before she crept forward to sniff at it.

I said, "Oh, were you thinking I would bring a taster for you to make sure your food isn't poisoned? Sorry, Queen B. Eat up while I go check to see if you've committed any royal offenses."

I scurried through the house on the lookout for overturned wastebaskets or chewed paper, upchucked hairballs, or flowerpots used as litter boxes. Everything seemed okay. In a spare bathroom, I hurried to empty the litter box, wash it, spritz it with my ever-handy mix of hydrogen peroxide and water, then rinse the heck out of it with scalding hot water. Cats like their toilets to be as clean as their food dishes. I'm like that myself, so I understand.

The big canopy bed in the master bedroom had indentations on the pillows suggesting Charlotte had slept there. I didn't smooth them out or vacuum up the cat hair because

I figured those spots gave Charlotte comfort while the Harwicks were gone. I could clean and straighten them later before they returned. Now it was time to feed the fish.

Still looking side to side for signs of things to clean up, I loped down the short hallway lined with mahogany dressers and swung open the door to the master bathroom. I came to such a quick stop that my Keds squeaked on the marble tile.

There on the floor, curled up in a ball, was the Harwicks' daughter, Becca.

I gasped as she jumped to her feet, wiping her hair away from her face with the back of her hand. Her eyes were puffy and red, and there were wet trails of mascara streaming down her cheeks.

I said, "Oh my gosh, I'm sorry!"

She said, "Hello? Ever heard of knocking?"

I turned to leave. "I didn't realize anyone was here. I'll come back later."

"Wait wait wait," she said. "I'm sorry. I'm having a really bad day. Please don't go."

She was wearing the same clothes and big black boots she had on when I'd met her the day before. I wondered if she hadn't spent the entire night on the floor in front of the fish tank crying.

She said, "After my parents left, I had a huge fight with my boyfriend. Well, he's not really my boyfriend but he kind of is, and now he's not talking to me and . . . and . . ."

She dropped down to her knees and started whimpering softly. I remembered what it was like to be her age, when hormones are raging through your body like flames through a fireworks stand and your brain can't keep up with the tsunami of emotions that wash over you every minute. Every little thing feels like it's the absolute end of the world.

"It's going to be okay," I said. "I think you just need some food and a little rest."

"No," she wailed. "You don't understand. I'm pregnant!"

She collapsed in a heap on the floor, sobbing hysterically. I don't know why, but people are always telling me their deepest, darkest secrets. I can be minding my own business in a grocery store, picking out an avocado or reading the ingredients on a cracker box, and suddenly a perfect stranger will strike up a conversation. The next thing I know they're blurting out things they wouldn't tell a priest in a confession booth.

I knelt down beside her and patted her shoulder while she cried. In this situation, there's nothing to do but wait for the tears to work themselves out. Then all you can do is listen. When a man pours his problems out to you, he wants you to give him solutions. He wants you to fix it and make it all better. A woman already knows how to fix it. She just needs you to listen.

"We've been dating for a few months, and my parents don't even know about it, and if they find out they'll kill me. And he came over last night and I told him I was pregnant. And then he started saying that I don't really know him and there are things in his past that nobody can change and he isn't any good for me . . . and now everything is just *ruined*!"

I patted her back some more while she sobbed and snuffled and blew her nose into a tissue.

"I just want to get out of here! And he won't even answer his phone and I don't know what I did to him. What did I do to him? Why would he treat me like this? Why won't he just tell me what's wrong?"

She looked up at me with big brown eyes welling with tears. The angels in the overhead mural were all flying around with their harps and flutes, gazing down at me too, waiting expectantly for me to say something brilliant and comforting. I couldn't think of a single thing to say except "love sucks," and I didn't think that would go over too well.

"I think it might be a good idea to talk to your mom about this."

"I can't talk to my mother about anything! And she already told me I was spending too much time with him and not to talk to him again. But of course it's okay for her to talk his ear off every time he's here."

"Your mother knows him?"

She threw her arms out with her palms up, as if to say *That's all, folks!* but instead she rolled her eyes at me. "Duh? It's Kenny!"

I tried not to let my jaw hit the floor.

"Kenny Newman? The pool boy?"

"He's not a pool boy. He just cleans pools for money. He's an artist and he's the most amazing guy I've ever known! Nobody knows him like I do."

Now it was me that felt like falling to the floor in a heap. Not because I felt sorry for Becca (although I did; this was certainly a pickle she was in) and not because I was mad at Kenny for putting her in this situation (it takes two to tango, after all), but because it was just so stupid and irresponsible on Kenny's part. How in the world could he allow himself to get involved with the daughter of one of his clients? A teenager, for God's sake! It made me wonder, too, if Paco and Michael hadn't been right about Kenny—that there was something suspicious about him, something he was hiding. And right this very minute, he was in the house of one of my clients, caring for the beloved pets of people who trusted me implicitly. Perhaps I had made a huge mistake in hiring Kenny. Perhaps he wasn't at all who I thought he was.

Becca must have noticed I was a little distracted.

She stood up and said, "Ugh! You think I'm a total idiot, don't you?"

"No, I just think you're in over your head and maybe your mom could help."

She put her hands on her hips. "You know, I'm not a little girl. I'm in college. I don't need help from anybody."

"Becca, that's not what I meant at all. This wouldn't be easy for anyone. You're in a very difficult situation, and of course you're upset. You just have to think about what's best for you."

"Oh, really? No shit, Sherlock!"

She threw her sodden tissue at the trash can and stormed out of the room. Before she even got to the door she was crying again and was only about halfway to the bedroom when she turned around. With her head hanging down, she clomped back into the bathroom, tears streaming down her cheeks.

She said, "I'm sorry."

"It's okay, honey."

She stepped into my arms and hugged me. I suddenly

felt like I was hugging a younger version of myself, remembering what it was like to feel alone and helpless. When our mother left, as young as I was, I knew she was never coming back and I knew my life would never be the same. But my brother was there for me. He filled in the holes that my mother made. I couldn't have survived without him. Everybody needs someone there to help pick up the pieces when the world comes shattering down.

She said, "I'm sorry, I'm a total mess. I just love him so much. He's the sweetest thing I'll ever know."

"It's okay. We all have our moments."

She stepped back and looked at me. "Please don't tell anybody about this."

"Becca, if you can't talk to your mother, maybe your stepfather could help."

Her pale cheeks flushed with rage. "Yeah, right. Guess what? We're rich! Do you have any idea why my brother had to get a job at that stupid golf club?"

I shook my head.

"Well, I'll tell you why, because my stepfather talked my mother into completely cutting him off when they found drugs in his room! What do you think they'll do to me when they find out about this? You have any idea what will happen if the press finds out? My stepfather would probably kill me! 'Sonnebrook Heiress in Pool Boy Scandal.' I can just see it now!"

"Honey, they're going to find out sooner or later."

The anger fell from her face, and her eyes welled with tears. "I know."

While she cried some more, I held her in my arms and looked around the bathroom in all its glory: the tank with its quiet world of fish floating about in peaceful bliss, completely unaware of the human drama just on the other side of the glass. The mermaid looking coyly over her shoulder, staring into the distance, her expression frozen forever. The golden toilet, the crystal chandelier, and all the angels flying about. It suddenly seemed so odd to spend so much money on a room where basically waste gets flushed away. Like throwing money down the toilet, my grandmother always said.

Hugging always makes me think of my grandmother. She was quick to give me a smack on the butt when I deserved it, but whenever I needed a little tender loving care, she was just as quick to snatch me up in her arms and hug me back to myself.

There's no better medicine than that.

8

Tanisha is the Martha Stewart of biscuits. I don't know what kind of magic she works back there in her kitchen, but her biscuits have a special power over me. They're the second-most-delicious thing in the world, the first being her bacon. As Tanisha puts it, "So good you wanna smack yo momma!" I eat one of her biscuits just about every day of my life, but I only allow myself bacon on very special occasions. I was sitting in my regular booth at the diner, thinking about ordering another biscuit, when Judy put a side of bacon down on the table and said, "Well?"

"Well wuth?" I asked, my mouth full of biscuity goodness.

"Oh, please. You don't order bacon unless there's something big happening. What is it?"

I sighed. Judy could read me like a book. "I'm just a little nervous is all. There's a lot going on."

She slipped her notepad in her apron and sat down opposite me. "Let's hear it."

I sighed. "Okay, but you can't tell a living soul."

"Got it."

"Okay. So yesterday morning, right around sunrise, I was walking along the nature preserve with Rufus and we ran into Joyce Metzger, she was—"

Judy interrupted. "Whoa, whoa, whoa, slow down there, Don Juanita. Who is this Rufus and what were you doing with him at sunrise?"

"Rufus is a dog! He's one of my clients, I was walking him."

She looked disappointed. "Oh. Okay, go on."

"We found a woman in the bushes. She had just delivered a baby."

Judy's jaw fell wide open.

I said, "I know. A young girl, eighteen or nineteen. She doesn't speak English, and I'm pretty sure she's here illegally."

"What the hell?"

"Yep, that's how my day started yesterday."

"Was she okay? What about the baby?"

"They were both fine, considering what they'd been through, but she was terrified, and she didn't want to go to the hospital. She was living in a cardboard box hidden in the brush, so . . . we took her to Joyce's. She's there now."

Judy's eyes widened. "She's homeless?"

"Well, technically, not anymore."

Judy cocked her head to one side. "Wait a minute. This was yesterday?"

"Yep."

"Yesterday, at sunrise?"

I nodded as I slid the plate of bacon over in front of me. She slid it back. "But you were here yesterday after that, and you didn't order bacon. What happened between then and now?"

Tanisha's big round face appeared in the kitchen window, and she rang the pickup bell on the counter.

I grinned. "You've got an order ready."

"Oh, dammit to hell. You're not getting off that easy. I'll be back."

She slid out of the booth and went scurrying back to the kitchen. I reached over and delicately picked up a slice of Tanisha's bacon. She had cooked it exactly the way I like: extra crispy, with no yucky white spots. I was taking my first glorious bite of it when Ethan Crane walked in the door.

With his long, wide-shouldered body in a dark pin-striped suit, thick black hair falling over the collar of a baby blue dress shirt, he could have been on the runway of an international fashion show. As he strode down the aisle toward me, an estrogen-induced hush descended on the room and the dopamine level of every female in the diner bumped up a little bit. A woman across the aisle from me froze with her mouth open and squirted lemon juice in her coffee.

Ethan has that effect on women.

He said, "I thought I might find you here."

"Have a seat," I said, dabbing a napkin at my lips just in case they were coated with grease and biscuit crumbs. "I'm glad you found me."

He grinned. "Me too."

"I actually have a question for you."

Judy appeared with a cup of coffee and silverware rolled in a napkin. As she laid them on the table, Ethan said,

"Were you wondering which restaurant we're going to Friday night?"

Judy shot me a sly look and then turned to Ethan. "Can I get you anything, sir?"

"Not for me. I just stopped by on my way to work, thanks," he said.

"Oh, you're welcome, sir." She turned to me and arched her eyebrows comically. "And for the young lady?"

"Nope, I'm good."

"Another platter of bacon?"

"No. Thank you," I said.

She smiled sweetly at Ethan and shrugged her shoulders. "Alright then, just the one today."

On her way back to the kitchen she looked over her shoulder and mouthed *Oh my God!* at me. I had to pinch the inside of my arm to keep from giggling out loud. Ethan didn't even seem to notice. He was probably accustomed to women acting like complete and utter fools around him.

I said, "First I have a kind of legal question for you."

"Okay, shoot."

"Well, I have a friend who recently had a baby. Well, it's not my friend that had the baby, but she knows somebody who had a baby and this friend is sort of homeless, so she's letting her stay in her house and helping her out until she can get back on her feet. But the thing is, this girl, the one that had the baby . . . well, she's an illegal immigrant, or I'm pretty sure she is. So here's the question: Is my friend doing anything against the law?"

Ethan listened intently, sitting forward with his fingers laced together. I could feel myself getting a little lost in his eyes, and the insides of my palms were getting sweaty.

He said, "Well, does your friend live in Arizona?"

"No."

"Alabama?"

"No, she lives here in Sarasota."

"Then she's perfectly fine. In Florida, it's not against the law to offer help to a fellow human being, no matter what their legal status. Next question."

I smiled. Any other man would have wanted to know more. I had expected to get a stern warning and a lecture about getting involved in other people's business or fraternizing with criminals. But not Ethan, he just sat there, ready for whatever was next, like a puppy waiting for a treat. I liked that he trusted me, that he thought I was smart enough not to go around getting involved in things I shouldn't. Stupid man.

"Was there anything else you wanted to know? Anything at all?"

I laughed. "Yes, that was going to be my next question. Where are we having dinner Friday night?"

He grinned. "It's called Yolanda. It's just next to the bookstore, where the old bakery used to be. You sure you don't want me to pick you up?"

"No, no, it's fine. I'll see you there at eight."

"Sounds good."

"And it's kind of dressy. So . . . you know. Dress up."

I rolled my eyes. "Yeah, I think I know what the word 'dressy' means."

He touched my hand briefly as he stood up. "I'm looking forward to it."

"Me too."

I surprised myself, because I meant it. He looked at me for a second before he turned to go, and the little hairs on my neck stood up and I could feel myself getting lost in his eyes again. If I was going to start spending more time with this man, I'd have to come up with some tricks to stay in focus, like counting backward or reciting the state capitals.

I watched him cross the street at the corner and then head uptown to his office. I tucked a twenty-dollar bill under my coffee cup, and while Judy was busy clearing off a table at the other end of the diner, I snuck out the front door. That was a rotten thing to do on my part, but I knew she was going to ask if Ethan and I were getting serious, and I did not want to know the answer. . . .

Joyce opened the door with a smile. *"Buenos días!* Corina's teaching me Spanish, and I'm teaching her English. Come on in, we're all ready to go to the doctor. Oh, and by the way, Corina has a new friend."

I followed Joyce into the living room, where Corina was sitting on the couch. The baby was sleeping soundly on her lap, swaddled in a pink blanket, and Henry the VIII was dozing on the couch next to her. Perched on Corina's shoulder, just as happy as could be, was the resplendent quetzal.

Apparently, Corina had a way with birds. Joyce explained it had only taken Corina a couple of hours to get the bird to eat fruit out of her hand, and now it followed her around everywhere she went.

Corina smiled proudly and said, "Hello, Dixie. How are you today?"

I said, "I am *muy bueno*! How is the baby?"

"The baby is very good. I am happy we go to the doctor."

I sat down next to her, and the bird hopped around behind her neck to the opposite shoulder.

I cooed at the baby, "Your mama's English is very good!"

Corina nodded at Joyce. "Joyce is my teacher."

Joyce beamed at her. I could tell these two were going to become good friends. Their lives could not have been more different, but it's amazing how people can be drawn together in the strangest of circumstances.

Joyce said, "We were wondering if you might be able to take René to see your vet friend."

I said, "René?"

"Oh, the bird! It was Corina's idea. Dixie, did you know that Kermit the Frog is called René in Spain?"

I shook my head.

"Well, he is. Corina told me. So that's what we named the bird, because of his green feathers like Kermit."

I turned to Corina. "You're from Spain?"

She nodded and smiled nervously. "Yes, Spain."

I had just assumed Corina was one of the tens of thousands of people that flee Cuba every year, literally risking their lives to get to American soil. If they have the money, they'll take a plane to Mexico and then try to come into the country from there, but more often they'll hire a smuggler to ferry them across the stretch of ocean between Cuba and Florida's southernmost beaches. It's expensive, though, and in a country like Cuba most people don't walk around with a lot of cash in their pockets. The only other way is by boat, raft, dinghy, or anything else that floats. It's a hundred miles from the coast of Cuba to Florida, but people have been known to set out on an inner tube if that's all they can get their hands on.

Of course, it was entirely possible that Corina was lying. If she had crossed the ocean on a smuggler's boat, she might have tried to escape without paying the smuggler's fee, which would explain the cash in her purse, and there'd be some very nasty people looking for her. Plus, Cuban immigrants are blamed for nearly every ill in the state of Florida, from the shortage of jobs to limited housing to the shortage of fresh water, so either way she'd be smart to make up a story about where she was from.

I usually know when someone is lying. Sometimes I can tell by the way a person looks to one side while they're talking, or maybe they blink a couple times more than normal. It's a skill I picked up at an early age. Whether my mother was drinking or not, what came out of her mouth was sometimes the truth, or a jumbled version of it, and sometimes it was just outright lies, so I got pretty good at recognizing the difference. It was hard to tell with Corina. I didn't think she was lying exactly, and it might just have been the language barrier, but something didn't seem quite right, like she was hiding some part of herself from me.

I helped them out to Joyce's station wagon, and Corina lowered the still-sleeping baby down into the car seat. It took nearly all of my brain cells operating at full capacity to remember how to decipher all of its belts and straps and buckles. While we were trying different combinations, the baby opened its eyes and squinted at me.

Joyce said, "This is going to be Dixie Joyce's first ride in a car!"

I rolled my eyes. "Joyce, don't call her that."

She and Corina exchanged smiles. "Until Corina tells me different, that baby's name is Dixie Joyce."

When we finally had the seat figured out, Joyce started the car while Corina slid into the back next to the baby. I walked around and tapped on Joyce's window, and she rolled it down.

Speaking low so Corina wouldn't hear, I said, "I'll split the cost with you."

"No," Joyce said. "You already paid for all the baby stuff, I'll get it."

"That was nothing compared to what this will be. I'll pay half."

"I pay," Corina said.

She was looking down at the baby, which had fallen back to sleep. There was a distant look in her eye, but her voice was steady. Joyce and I both looked back at her.

"I have money," she said. "I pay."

For a brief moment we both nodded dumbly, as though it were perfectly reasonable that a person who'd been living in a cardboard box in the woods yesterday could easily afford to pay an expensive pediatrician bill today.

Joyce said, "Well, that's settled."

I watched them back out of the driveway. Joyce and Corina both waved as the car pulled around and headed up the street.

I didn't know what to think. Neither of us had wanted Corina to know that we'd seen the money in her purse, because that would only have destroyed the trust she was beginning to have in us. But I was worried. I was worried about who that money was for. If there was somebody out there looking for it, what would they do to Corina when they found it? Or me? Or Joyce?

Sooner or later, we'd have to get the real story out of Corina. If we were going to help her, we'd need to know exactly where she was from and why she had so much money. I cringed to think what could have been so horrible in her home country, wherever it was, that would drive her to run away, and with a baby due any minute. I decided I'd ask Paco. He speaks Spanish fluently, and I knew he'd want to help.

I carried René out to my Bronco and put him in the back, wedging some rolled towels around the cage so it wouldn't rattle around too much on the drive over to the veterinarian's. Normally I would never show up without an appointment, but I wanted to see the look on Dr. Layton's face when I showed up with a creature as exotic as this.

When I walked in with René, there was a collective "oooo" from the people in the waiting room, like it was the Fourth of July. I set the cage down, and Gia, Dr. Layton's assistant, slid open the little window in front of her station.

"Hi, Dixie, what can I do for you?"

"Well, I have a bird rescue and I was hoping Dr. Layton could take a look at him, but it looks like you're super busy today."

She winked. "Well, I'll let Dr. Layton know you're here and we'll see."

René hopped from one perch to the other and said, "Cool!"

I couldn't agree more. One of the perks of being a

professional pet sitter is you get to feel like a celebrity sometimes. I buy so many treats at the local pet supply shop they all know me by name, and if there's a line I just lay my money on the counter and leave. No one even raises an eyebrow. I admit that may not sound as exciting as riding around in a limousine all day and eating bonbons, or whatever it is celebrities do, but it's good enough for me. I've referred so many clients to Dr. Layton, she could easily have an examining room named after me.

I took a seat next to an elderly woman with a tiny ball of fluff in her lap that turned out to be a miniature poodle. He sat up and eyed René curiously, along with everyone else in the room.

The woman leaned over and said, "That is quite the bird you've got there."

I smiled proudly, as if I'd created him myself. "Oh, thanks. He's a resplendent quetzal."

She smiled back. "He certainly is. What kind of bird is he?"

"No," I said, raising my voice a bit. "That's what they're called: resplendent quetzals."

"Well, what a pretty bird. He looks like a pigeon in drag."

I laughed. "I'll take that as a compliment."

She scratched the top of her poodle's fluffy white head, and he looked up at her lovingly.

"Monty here got his toenails painted green on St. Patty's day last year, and I knitted him a little green sweater, but he wouldn't wear it, would you boy?"

I said, "Sometimes they have to try it on a few times before they'll accept it."

"Well, it's too late now. I gave it to my next-door neighbor's new baby."

I wanted to ask if the neighbor knew her baby was wearing a miniature poodle's hand-me-downs, but Gia slid her glass panel open and said, "Dixie, you can come on back now."

Dr. Layton is a comfortably plump African American woman with a head of glossy black curls. She was already in the examining room when I got there, peering over her half-rimmed glasses and making notes in a big blue binder. She was wearing black patent-leather heels, a fitted coffee-colored linen skirt that fell just past her knees, and a white brocade blouse with tiny mother-of-pearl buttons. I almost didn't recognize her. I was used to seeing her in the standard getup: white slacks, teal lab coat, and sensible loafers.

I lifted the cage up and set it down on the examination table with a flourish.

She glanced up briefly and said, "Oh, a resplendent quetzal," and then went back to writing in her notebook.

This was not at all the reaction I was hoping for. I had always admired Dr. Layton for being a no-nonsense kind of woman. A veterinary office can have a lot of drama, and she always keeps her cool, no matter how crazy it gets. But surely she didn't see a bird like this every day.

"Oh. I thought you'd fall to the floor when you saw this."

She looked up with a mischievous grin. "I might have, but Gia warned me. Dixie, what the hell kind of animal is that and where in the world did you find it?"

I laughed. "Now that's more like it!"

"Sorry, I'm in a mood. Dr. Prawer is filling in for me today, and I've been going over some of the patients' files with him, and I'm making last-minute notes for a speech I'm giving tonight at the Vet Council and I'm scared to death! But when Gia said you were here . . ."

She trailed off as she studied René more closely. As he hopped around from perch to perch, a varied mix of emotions played across her face: wonder, sadness, delight, resignation. I told her all about how Joyce had found him, and how we were certain he was a goner, how Joyce had wrapped him in a bandanna, and then how he'd risen from the dead a couple hours later.

She said, "Well, I think I can safely say he's in good spirits. Normally I might guess he'd been blown off course in a hurricane and wound up here, but I guess you noticed his primary flight feathers are clipped—so I think it's safe to say that more than likely someone's lost their pet. His coordination looks good, his eyes are bright, and I don't see any signs of a respiratory problem, which is common with exotics like this. They're taken out of their native habitat and their immune systems get quite a shock. It's possible he might have ingested something toxic. How's his appetite?"

"It's good. We've just been feeding him fruit and birdseed. I wasn't sure what else to give him."

"I can help you with that, but I think it might be a good idea to keep him here for the night. The first thing that comes to mind is trauma. Birds routinely fly into buildings or windows. You'd be surprised how many birds knock themselves out for a bit, and then wake up later completely unharmed. Still, just to be safe I'd like to do some X-rays. We can also run some blood tests and check for a cardiac event, like a stroke. It could be he was simply exhausted and dehydrated, but I'd feel better if we covered all our bases. Any idea who he belongs to?"

I shook my head.

"I'll ask Gia to call around and see if anyone reported a missing bird. In the meantime, are you busy this afternoon and would you like to give a speech for me?"

I assured her that I was a disaster in front of a crowd, although the topic of her speech, the overpopulation of animal shelters and how pet stores should be regulated, if not done away with entirely, was a topic I am keenly interested in. But I was not meant for a life on the stage. When I was in fifth grade, my class put on a production of "Puss 'n Boots." I barely remember what part I played because the moment the curtain went up on opening night, I vomited all over the stage. That was my last appearance in front of an audience, and I plan on keeping it that way.

Dr. Layton took René out of Joyce's cage and transferred him into a state-of-the-art number with an automatic water feeder and all kinds of rings and mirrors for him to play with. I said good-bye and promised him I'd be back bright and early tomorrow morning to pick him up, and thanked Dr. Layton for seeing me.

As I was putting the empty cage in the back of the Bronco, I noticed the weather had changed dramatically. There was a mountainous black cloud lurking out at sea, and the air had grown still and damp—perfect conditions for a lovebug orgy. They were out in full force now, frolicking unabashedly in the air, so I drove down Midnight Pass toward home at a snail's pace. I still had my afternoon rounds, but I needed a shower and a nap first.

On the way I couldn't stop thinking about Becca and what she must have been going through. I wondered if she'd worked up the courage yet to call her parents. I wondered how they'd react when they learned that Kenny had been working on more than their pool.

I was going to have to talk to Kenny, even though there were lots of reasons not to. First, it was none of my business who he slept with; his employment with the Harwicks had nothing to do with me. Second, he was a grown man, and Becca was childish but not a child. Still, I felt an obligation, if not as his employer then as his friend, to try to set him straight. I knew he was a good man, and whatever reasons he had to be afraid of becoming a father, I couldn't imagine he wanted to hurt Becca. Maybe he just needed a little push in the right direction.

When I pulled into my spot under the carport, I could see Ella Fitzgerald waiting for me in the window of my apartment, which meant both Michael and Paco were probably at work. She flicked her tail excitedly as I climbed up the stairs. When I unlocked the door and opened it, she hopped down and ran up to greet me. I gave her a little scratch on the top of her head and she scrunched up her shoulders with a high-pitched *thhrrrip!* and then padded into the bathroom behind me. I was out of my clothes and under a strong stream of hot water in seconds. There is nothing in the world as wonderful as a shower. I don't care how bad things get, if a person can still take a long, hot shower, life is good.

I fell naked into bed, and Ella Fitzgerald circled herself into the crook of my arm and purred softly. I soon found myself in a dream. I was standing in front of a huge crowd of people. They were all raising their hands, waiting for me to call on them. I pointed at a young man, and someone handed him a microphone. He said, *Hi, Dixie, my question is about string theory: If you rotate one dimension so that its trajectory is opposite to its original path, do the strings then fold in on themselves?*

I had no idea what the hell he was talking about, but I knew I had to come up with some sort of answer. All I could think to say was *no*. The man looked surprised at first, but then softened. He said, *I'm sorry for what's about to happen. I should have been honest with you from the start, but I was scared, and now it's too late. I hope you'll understand that I didn't have a choice.*

I woke with a start. Kenny was leaving a message on my answering machine. I frantically reached for the phone and pressed the TALK button, but he'd already hung up. I pressed the NEW MESSAGES button, and Kenny's familiar voice came out of the speaker.

"Dixie, it's Kenny. Listen, I should have told you, but I couldn't. Something's about to go down and . . . it's big. I can't tell you what it is, and probably by the time you hear this I'll be gone. I just wanted to say I'm sorry for not being honest with you from the start. I was scared, and now it's too late. I hope you'll understand that I didn't have a choice."

There was a slight pause, and then he sighed softly before the machine beeped off. I laid my head back down on the pillow and stared up at the ceiling. My first thought was that he was running away. Becca had worked up the courage to tell him she was pregnant, they had fought, and now he was abandoning her, throwing everything away to join the deadbeat dad club. But it wasn't like Kenny to be so dramatic. He was a pretty straightforward, shoot-from-the-hip kind of guy, and for a brief moment my nap-happy brain toyed with the notion that it was just Kenny trying to be funny.

I reached for the phone and dialed his number. By the tenth ring I knew he wasn't going to pick up. When his voice mail didn't kick in, I knew he wasn't joking. I wondered if he hadn't already had his phone shut off and had called from a pay phone. I looked down at Ella Fitzgerald, curled up and purring in the crook of my arm. I had the distinct feeling I'd been in this exact place and time before: Warm and cozy, curled up in bed without a care in the world, while dark clouds were looming all around me.

9

When I arrived at the Harwick house the next morning, I fully expected to find Becca in hysterics on the floor of the bathroom again. Kenny had probably called her the night before to say he was leaving town and she'd never see him again, or for all I knew he might have sent her a text message. That seems to be the primary mode of delivering important information for young people these days. Either way, I had a feeling Becca was going to need a lot more shoulder-crying time, and I already had a full day as it was. I certainly didn't want her to go through this alone, but the bottom line was I barely knew her, and it wasn't my job to shepherd her through the hazardous terrain of love and heartbreak. I decided that if she hadn't talked to her parents by now, I'd try my best to convince her it was the right thing to do.

The house was completely quiet. This time when I opened the door, the alarm panel didn't beep, and Charlotte wasn't waiting for me at the bottom of the stairs. I called out to announce my presence, expecting Charlotte to come slinking around the corner to give me the stink-eye, but no one answered. I went into the living room, where there was a half-empty liquor bottle and a couple of glasses on the coffee table, but no Charlotte. For the first time, I had a funny feeling that something wasn't quite right.

Every house has a particular scent to it, a very subtle mixture of the people and animals that live in it, as unique as a fingerprint. The Harwick house had a clean, earthy scent: a combination of cooking aromas from the kitchen, chlorine from the pool, the salty air off the ocean, and a note of lavender, perhaps Mrs. Harwick's perfume. But now, something was different. I told myself that the Harwicks had been gone for almost two days, and it was only natural that the scent of the house would change in their absence.

But I couldn't find Charlotte anywhere. She wasn't in the kitchen or the dining area. I even looked under the couch in the living room and behind the dryer in the laundry room off the kitchen, both popular feline hiding spots, but she was nowhere to be seen. I went up the marble staircase and tiptoed down the main hall toward the master suite. The doors to Becca's and August's bedrooms were both closed, and I didn't think it would be right to go snooping around in there. At least not yet, especially since I wasn't completely sure they weren't home and I didn't want to barge in on them if they were. Hell hath no fury like a teenager awakened at dawn.

The pillows on the big bed in the master bedroom had the same indentations where Charlotte had slept the night before, and the bedspread was a little mussed. Maybe she had slipped under the bed when she heard me open the front door. I felt around the pillows for signs of warmth, but there was nothing. I looked under the bed anyway, hoping I'd see her emerald eyes sparkling mischievously at me, but there were only a couple of dust bunnies and the foil wrapper from a piece of chewing gum.

I was beginning to get a little concerned as I made my way down the short hall toward the master bathroom. As grumpy as Charlotte was, it didn't make sense that she would hide—especially since cats are such inquisitive animals. She would have at least been curious enough to find out who was in the house before she gave them the cold shoulder, and it certainly wasn't possible that anyone else had fed her this early in the morning. I tried to form an image in my mind of where I might be if I was a snarky queen in a sprawling mansion, and that turned out to be quite easy: that peach velvet bench in the bathroom opposite the aquarium, next to the gold-plated telephone.

I flicked on the light switch by the doorway, and the overhead chandelier lit up to reveal the bathroom in all its over-the-top glory, but no Charlotte. There was a damp towel draped over the counter next to the sink, but otherwise everything looked normal.

I leaned into the little alcove and peered behind the velvet bench just in case Charlotte was hiding there and thought, *This is getting serious.* I was out of ideas. I sat down on the bench and put my hand on the gold-plated phone, wondering if it wasn't time to call the Harwicks and ask them if there were any other places she might be hiding. That's when I had a feeling I was not alone.

I looked up at the aquarium, fully expecting to see the

mermaid staring serenely back at me, and instead locked eyes with a bloated hedgehog, floating motionless in the middle of the tank. It took me a couple of seconds of shock to realize that it wasn't a hedgehog at all but a porcupine fish.

Porcupine fish are pretty cute in their natural state. They have gloppy, rounded bodies with drooping eyes and a goofy smile, like drunken Pillsbury Doughboys with fins. But when frightened, they fill their bodies up with water, pumping to twice their normal size and extending their sharp, quill-like scales out in every direction. If that's not enough to scare off a would-be predator, a naturally occurring chemical in their body that's about a thousand times more poisonous than cyanide usually does the trick.

While the porcupine fish and I stared blankly at each other, my mind did a little wheelie inside its skull. The alarm was off. Charlotte was hiding. The porcupine fish was in a full state of alarm. I glanced about the room looking for anything else out of place. I could hear myself telling Michael and Paco how valuable the fish were, and then I could see Mrs. Harwick pointing at the painted dragon eel and whispering, "Priceless!" I looked back at the tank. Now there were two pairs of eyes on me: the porcupine fish's and the mermaid's. She was staring directly into my eyes, like she was trying to tell me something, and I suddenly thought, *A burglar is in this house and I've just interrupted him.*

I was still sitting on the velvet bench. I tried to look as casual as possible. I shrugged my shoulders.

"Well, Charlotte," I said out loud, "you're not hungry, and I don't have time to look for you all day."

I walked out of the bathroom, flicking the light switch off with a trembling hand as I passed, and steadily made my way downstairs to the front door, talking to myself the entire way, certain I was about to be jumped by an intruder.

"Charlotte, you'll just have to wait and have breakfast later, because I have other things to do and I don't have time to go looking around every nook and cranny whenever it's time to eat. You'll just have to learn that if you want your breakfast, you have to eat it when it's served. So I'll just be back after lunchtime, and maybe you'll decide you're hungry by then."

I pulled out my ring of keys and jangled them loudly so whoever was in the house, if they were still there, would hear them and know I was leaving.

"See you later, Charlotte!" I yelled and pulled the front door closed behind me. I walked down the winding driveway on rubbery legs, feeling like there was a target on my back. As soon as I was in the Bronco, I put the key in the ignition with one hand and pulled my cell phone out with the other. I rolled down to the front gate, and by the time I'd pulled out onto the road I had already dialed the number. Not 911, as I probably should have, but the number of my old superior when I was a deputy, that of Sergeant Woodrow Owens.

As shaken as I was, I had to smile when he answered the phone. Sergeant Owens and I have a long history together. I served under him when I was a deputy with the sheriff's department, I cried in his arms when Todd and Christy were killed, and when I laid down my gun and my badge, it was on Sergeant Owens's desk. Since then I'd stumbled across more than my share of crime cases, and I was beginning to feel like an adjunct private investigator for the local law. Sergeant Owens had once told me I was too fucked up (his words) to carry on as a police officer, but I imagined he had an entirely different opinion of me now. Or at least, that's what I hoped.

Even when he's being his official police self, Owens can't keep from sounding like he's about to sit down to crisp catfish and hush puppies that his mama just fried up for him and thirty-nine of his closest kinfolk. Owens is six-three, slow and lanky to look at, but lightning fast when he thinks. He sets high standards for himself and his subordinates, and he's quick to let you know when you're being a dumb-butt. Believe me, I know.

I said, "Sergeant, it's Dixie Hemingway. Sorry to bother you, but I've got a bit of a situation here, and I think you might want to send somebody over."

His voice warmed as if he was smiling. "What you got, Dixie?"

I said, "I'm pet sitting for the Harwicks on Jungle Plum Road, and they have a huge saltwater aquarium full of fish in their bathroom. Valuable fish. When I arrived, the alarm wasn't on, which is unusual, and the cat is missing, or hiding, I'm not sure which. I went into the bathroom where the aquarium is, and one of the fish is in a state of alarm. I'm not sure, but I think there's been some kind of crime."

After a pause Owens said, "A cat is hiding, and a fish is alarmed?"

"Yes."

"And where are you now?"

"I'm parked on the side of the road a little ways down from their driveway."

After a moment, Owens drawled, "Are any of the other fish alarmed?"

Okay, maybe he still thought I was a bit loopy. I sighed. "I know it sounds pretty flimsy."

"Dixie, flimsy is not the word I was thinking."

"I just don't have a good feeling about it."

"Well, could be that cat ate one of them fish, and now he's trying to make a run for it. You want me to shut down all the roads out of the city?"

"Alright then, maybe I'm overreacting a little bit."

"Could be. Give me a call if you got any more nervous critters."

"Sorry to bother you."

"Not a bother at all, Dixie." I could feel him grinning over the phone. "Good to hear from you."

Just as I hung up, a shiny black sports car pulled into the driveway. There was a young man behind the wheel, and I knew it had to be the Harwicks' son, August. I jumped out of the car and flagged him down. He rolled down his window as I came jogging up alongside the car.

I said, "Hi, I'm the cat sitter. Are you August?"

He smiled, looking me up and down, and said, "I am. What's up?"

"Look, I know this is going to sound crazy, but I was just in the house, and I think there may be someone in there. I can't find Charlotte anywhere, and . . . well, one of the fish is alarmed."

His smile faded a bit. "Is my sister in there?"

"I don't know, I didn't see her. I know it sounds ridiculous, but I just had a feeling something was wrong."

He looked up at the house and said, "Okay."

He shifted his car into park and turned off the ignition. I stepped back as he opened the door and got out. He was tall, at least six feet, with dark stubble and shaggy hair. He had the awkward swagger of a teenaged boy trying to come off like a man. I could smell liquor and cigarettes on his breath, and I wondered if he hadn't been up all night partying and was just now getting home. No wonder the Harwicks needed me.

He said, "I'll check it out. Maybe you better wait in your car."

"I'm not sure you should go in there alone."

"Look, I already got ripped off once this week. I'm not letting that happen again. You wait in your car and I'll be back."

As I turned to go back to my car, he leaned over and pulled something out of his glove compartment. At first I couldn't quite make it out, but then I saw the familiar glint of black metal and realized it was a pistol. Why in the world this rich kid drove around with a pistol in his glove compartment was beyond me. Every bone in my body told me to get in my car, drive away, and never look back, but I wasn't about to go anywhere until I knew Charlotte was safe.

I got in my car and locked the doors and hunkered down low in the seat, just in case there was about to be an all-out gun battle in the driveway. In the back of my head, I knew I was probably letting my imagination run away with me, but all I could see were those big mermaid eyes staring into mine and that porcupine fish's engorged body covered in sharp needles. One thing you can say about animals: They never lie.

After what seemed like an eternity, August came sauntering out of the driveway and up to the car. I rolled down the window, and he leaned in, his cigarette and alcohol breath flowing over me.

"The coast is clear. Charlotte's out by the pool."

I let out a sigh of relief. "How did she get out there?"

He grinned and looked me up and down again, his eyes lingering on my breasts. "No idea."

For a moment I considered punching him in the nuts, but I had to remind myself that the combination of alcohol and raging hormones never brings out the best in anybody, so I did my best to forgive his blatant leering, and since I was almost old enough to be his mother, I'm ashamed to admit I was kind of flattered by his lame, schoolboy flirting.

I followed him up the cobblestone driveway past his fancy black sports car. He looked the car up and down with about the same degree of smarminess he'd looked me up and down, and I could tell he was hoping I'd be impressed. I was, a little bit—it actually was a pretty cool-looking car—but I certainly wasn't about to let him know I thought so.

"How do you like my new wheels?"

I shrugged and kept walking. "Cars aren't really my thing."

If it actually had been a gun that he pulled out of the glove compartment, he must have stashed it inside the house, because I didn't see any sign of it in his pockets.

I considered asking him about it—being alone in a rambling mansion with a gun and a half-drunken teenager is not exactly my idea of a good time—but I told myself if there had been some perverted fish burglar lurking around inside, a gun might have come in handy.

We went out to the lanai. I dropped my backpack by the door and walked over to Charlotte, who was busy cleaning her face using her paw as a napkin. She barely acknowledged my presence.

August propped himself up in the doorway. "You need anything else?"

"No, but thanks, it was nice meeting you. Thanks for finding Charlotte."

"Yeah man, I totally came to your rescue, huh?"

"Well, I'm sorry I got a little spooked back there. I have a very active imagination."

He flashed that stupid grin again. "I bet you do." He pulled out an off-white business card and slipped it into one of the pockets of my backpack. "Here's my digits."

I raised an eyebrow. "Your digits?"

"Yeah, my phone number. We should hang out sometime."

One of the many skills I acquired as a police officer is the ability to put an expression on my face that says "I'm tired of your bullshit, take it down a notch." It's useful in a variety of situations, like at the return desk at Marshalls or in a movie theater surrounded by rowdy teenagers on spring break. I put my hands on my hips and looked him squarely in the eye.

"Well, August, it was nice to meet you."

His grin flattened, and he faked a yawn. "Yeah, well,

I'm gonna go crash now—party all night, sleep all day. Catch ya later."

He disappeared inside, and I rolled my eyes at his back. What kind of teenager carries around a business card? Charlotte stood up and rubbed her cheek into my ankle. I looked down and grinned. I knew she'd come around sooner or later—I can usually win over even the grumpiest customer. Humans are trickier. Of course, by now her breakfast was a little late, so it was possible she was just pretending to love up against me so I'd feed her. Either way, I had other pets to tend to, and it was already getting late. I went over to the glass-paneled door and slid it open.

"Come on, Queen B, let's go get some breakfast."

Charlotte swished her tail and strolled over to the edge of the pool. Now that she'd gotten my full attention, it was apparently time to play hard-to-get. I know from experience that the best way to get a cat's attention is to pay no attention to it whatsoever, but I didn't have time for Charlotte's shenanigans.

"Let's go, Your Highness. It's now or never."

She stretched an arm out over the pool and tapped nonchalantly at the water a couple of times with one paw, as if to let me know my powers were useless here. I stepped up behind her and was leaning over to pick her up when something registered in the corner of my eye. It was a dark shape at the bottom of the pool. At first glance it appeared to be a big black suitcase or one of those black plastic liners for garbage barrels. I knelt down next to Charlotte to get a closer look, and she nuzzled herself in between my legs and swished her tail a couple of times.

Now I swooped her up in my arms. She protested a bit

as I rushed her across the lanai and back into the house. I put her down, slid the door closed, and walked back to the pool. I pulled out my phone and punched the REDIAL button.

Sergeant Owens picked up on the first ring. Smooth as butter, he said, "Well, hello, Miz Hemingway. Whatcha got for me now?"

I said, "I've got a goddamn body at the bottom of a pool."

There was a pause. I imagined the smile slowly fading from his face, then came his reply: four short, businesslike words.

"I'm on my way."

10

As soon as I hung up with Sergeant Owens, I dialed 911. I knew what I had to do, but I wanted somebody there while I did it. I punched the speaker button on my phone and laid it down by the edge of the pool.

"911, what is your emergency?"

"This is Dixie Hemingway. I'm at 57 Jungle Plum Road. There's someone at the bottom of the pool."

"Okay, are you able to get them out?"

Kicking off my shoes, I said, "I'm way ahead of you."

I plunged headfirst into the water and swam down to the bottom of the pool. It was eerily quiet. I felt as if I'd entered a whole new world. The chlorine water stung my eyes, but I could see dark pants and a dark jacket, with a blurry mass of black hair waving gently in the water like seaweed. I grabbed on to the back of the jacket and pulled the body along the bottom of the pool toward the steps at the shallow end. When I couldn't stand it any longer, I pushed off the bottom as hard as I could, bringing the body with me. I gasped for air when my face broke the surface. Reaching out for the edge of the pool, I pulled the body up the steps and onto the deck as far as I could. The water was cold, but there was so much adrenaline coursing through my bloodstream I barely felt it. I heard the 911 operator calling out from my cell phone.

"Hello? Hello?"

I shouted, "I have the body out. I'm going to perform CPR."

It's standard procedure to attempt revival of any drowning victim no matter how long they've been underwater, because the human body is an amazing thing. We come equipped with a mind-boggling kit of tools designed to help us through all kinds of dangerous situations. Our faces have sensors in them that fire off a warning signal to our brain the instant they detect water less than seventy degrees. Instantly, the heart slows down and blood flow to the arms and legs starts to decrease, saving precious resources for our two most important organs: the heart and the brain. People have been revived after being unconscious for more than half an hour underwater.

I could hear the 911 operator talking on her radio to the emergency crew as I rolled the body over and pulled the wet hair away from its face. Staring up at me, his mouth hanging open in a silent scream, was Mr. Harwick.

Without thinking, I turned his head to the side, dug my palms into his abdomen, and pushed with all my might, sliding my hands up toward his chest. I had expected a gush of water to come up out of his mouth, but there wasn't near as much as I'd thought there would be. I kept pushing until I was sure there wasn't any more trapped in his lungs, and then I laced my hands together, placed them in the center of his chest, and started pressing down firmly, allowing his chest to rise back to normal each time. I counted each compression until I reached thirty, then I tilted his head back and pinched his nose. I took a deep breath and blew air into his lungs. His chest rose and fell. I tried again, but there was no response. His eyes were glassy and vacant, and his lips were cold. I started again, this time pressing a little harder. I felt a popping in his chest under the weight of my body, but I didn't stop. Again I blew air into his lungs, repeating the whole procedure several more times, but there was nothing.

The 911 operator said, "Ma'am? What's happening now?"

I sat back, exhausted, and tried to remember my training, anything that I was forgetting, anything else that could be done.

I said, "There's no response. He's gone."

"An ambulance is on the way."

I dragged myself up and walked across the lanai to the sliding doors where Charlotte was waiting inside. I slid the door open and felt the cold air-conditioning envelop my soaked body. I picked Charlotte up and walked through the house into the main foyer. I knew any minute now the whole place would be swarming with police officers, crime-scene units, and forensic experts. Taking Charlotte away from the scene of the crime was probably not the smartest thing in the world, but I wanted her out of there. Since the Harwicks had hired me to be her guardian while they were away, she was coming with me. I'd already handled her so much that if by chance there was some piece of evidence on her, I had probably already contaminated it. And anyway, there was no way I was waiting for the police by myself. She could damn well wait with me.

I hesitated at the base of the stairs leading up to the second floor and considered waking August up, but something told me it was best to leave that to the detectives. My heart started racing. Despite the gun and his tough-guy swagger, August was just a kid. He was in for quite a shock. On the other hand, how did I know what his involvement was? When he showed up in the driveway, was he just coming home? Or had he fled the scene earlier, waiting for me to show up so he could arrive and pretend he'd been out all night drinking?

I took Charlotte and walked out the front door and down the driveway to my car, which was still parked on the side of the road just by the entrance. I opened up the hatch and pulled out a couple of towels and one of the cardboard pet carriers I keep in the back. I tossed them on the passenger seat in the front and got in on the driver's side. My eyes glazed over and I just sat there staring straight ahead, like I was in a movie. I didn't even try to dry myself off yet; I just held Charlotte in my lap and waited.

My head was spinning. Mr. and Mrs. Harwick were supposed to be in Tampa, more than an hour away, so what was Mr. Harwick doing here? I thought of the gun that August had, and how he'd reacted so nonchalantly at the suggestion that there was possibly someone in the house, almost as if it were something that happened every day. I could hear Michael's voice saying the Harwicks' world was filled with cutthroats and thieves and Mr. Harwick was hated all over the world. Then, the thing that I had been avoiding the entire time, the thing that I could hardly even thing about, hit me like a brick to the side of the head.

Michael had said it was all over the papers that Mr. Harwick was giving a speech in Tampa. That made his house a pretty good target, especially if someone was in the market for some priceless artwork. If Mr. and Mrs. Harwick had come home unexpectedly and walked in on a burglary in progress, it was entirely possible that the intruder could have killed them. But where was Mrs. Harwick? Barely a minute passed by before I saw a pair of flashing red and blue emergency lights coming up Jungle Plum Road.

I opened the pet carrier and gently maneuvered Charlotte inside.

"Okay, Queen B, you have to wait in the car for a little while. I'll be back to check on you."

I got out of the car and toweled myself off as the police cruiser approached. It pulled up alongside me, and the window rolled down. The man at the wheel was wearing mirrored sunglasses that hid his eyes, but I recognized his short-cropped hair and sharp cheekbones. It was Deputy Jesse Morgan.

He nodded at the house. "This it?"

I said, "Yeah, the owners are away, and I'm taking care of—"

He held one hand up like a school guard stopping traffic and said, "Stay right there, please."

Jesse Morgan is the Key's only sworn deputy, which means he carries a gun. I didn't know him when I was on the force, but I've gotten to know him over the years since. He's about as fun as a root canal, but he's an impressive figure: broad shoulders, buzzed military haircut, a chin so sharp it looks like you could peel an apple with it, and a diamond stud in one ear. I didn't think he was all that surprised to see me. In fact, it hadn't been that long ago that he'd been the first to arrive when I stumbled upon another crime involving a famous model and a pro football player, but that's another story. My work puts me in a lot of people's homes, so it makes sense that I might run into something fishy now and then, but I could tell Deputy Morgan was beginning to wonder what kind of hex I had that was always plopping me down in the center of a murder scene. I couldn't blame him. I was beginning to wonder myself.

He pulled the cruiser up in front of my Bronco and got out, leaving the emergency lights flashing, and walked over. He didn't seem one bit fazed that I was soaking wet. I knew the 911 dispatcher would have told him everything that had happened while she was on the phone with me.

He nodded. "Dixie."

I smiled weakly. "Deputy Morgan."

"You alright?"

For a moment, I thought I was going to burst into tears, but I stopped myself. I bit the inside of my cheek and looked away, waiting for the feeling to subside. Deputy Morgan had the grace not to notice. Instead he adjusted his belt, which was weighted down with all the tools of his trade: nightstick, handcuffs, flashlight and a 9 mm semi-automatic pistol, securely seated in a black leather harness.

When I had gathered myself back together, he turned and walked toward the front gate, pausing long enough for me to catch up. For a split second it felt like I was back on the force, and this was just another day on the beat. Two deputies checking out a crime scene. I had to remind myself that not only was I no longer on the force, I doubted seriously that Deputy Morgan was thinking anything along those lines. Not to mention the fact that I was as damp as a wrung-out mop from head to toe.

As we walked up the driveway he said, "So what's the story?"

I told him all about how the Harwicks were out of town, and how they had hired me to take care of their cat and their aquarium, and how I had noticed that the alarm was off, even though it was super early, and how I couldn't find Charlotte anywhere. I told him about the fish tank, and how one of the fish had been in a state of alarm, and how I'd gotten spooked and called Sergeant Owens.

We were almost to the front porch when he stopped abruptly.

"You called Owens *before* you found the body?"

"Yeah, I did."

He nodded. "Go on."

"So the Harwicks' son came home, and he searched through the house and didn't find anything out of the ordinary, and it turned out Charlotte was on the lanai. How she got out there I have no idea. But that's when I noticed something at the bottom of the pool, when I went out to get Charlotte."

"And where was the son?"

"He had gone upstairs. I think he was out all night."

He nodded. "Mm-hmm. And where is he now?"

"He's still up there. I didn't wake him."

"Why not?"

"I wasn't sure if I should."

He nodded again, silently acknowledging what I couldn't say out loud—that I wasn't completely sure August wasn't involved somehow.

I could hear the low, distant wail of a siren, and from the direction of it I knew it wasn't coming from the police station but from the north, which meant it was an ambulance dispatched from Sarasota Memorial Hospital. It had probably come over the bridge on Siesta Drive. I hoped Charlotte wasn't too freaked out by the noise, and then I remembered I hadn't yet fed her. It was too late to go into the kitchen and grab some of her food. The entire house was a crime scene now. Soon there'd be technicians covering every inch of the property, checking for signs of anything out of the ordinary, brushing every surface for fingerprints, looking for any clue that might shed some light on what had happened. A crime scene is a very delicate thing. A change to even the smallest, seemingly unimportant object can have catastrophic effects on the outcome of an investigation. I didn't want to tamper with any more evidence than I already had, so Her Highness would just have to wait a bit longer for breakfast.

We had stopped at the front door, and I realized Morgan was waiting for the other units to arrive before we went inside.

Finally, after a few moments of awkward silence, he said, "So, how you been?"

"Good. You?"

"Good."

I nodded. That was about the longest personal conversation I'd ever had with Morgan.

We watched as the ambulance came slowly up the

driveway and pulled up alongside August's black sports car. A green-and-white sheriff's van pulled in behind it, closely followed by two squad cars and finally an unmarked sedan. Sergeant Owens got out of the sedan and waited for the other deputies. There must have been at least eight of them. I wondered if Owens hadn't called up every unit in the county, trying to make up for not taking me seriously on the phone before. They met in a group in the middle of the circular drive and then followed Sergeant Owens up to where Morgan and I were standing.

Owens took off his sergeant's cap and said, "Well, Dixie, I suppose I owe you an apology."

I could feel myself blushing. "No, it's alright, sir. I probably wouldn't have believed me either."

"Well, then, I at least owe you a beer."

I smiled. "I'll take you up on that, sir."

He turned to the congregation of men behind him and said, "Gentlemen, this is Dixie Hemingway."

Just then, the front door opened to reveal August, bleary-eyed and shirtless in a pair of jeans. He looked around at all the deputies and the squad cars with their flashing emergency lights filling the driveway.

"What the hell?"

I said, "August—"

Sergeant Owens interrupted. "Sir, is this your house?"

August said, "I live here. It's my parents' house."

"And your parents are away?"

"Yes, sir, they're in Tampa."

Owens nodded thoughtfully. "Alright. You have a number where they can be reached?"

August looked at me. "Where's Becca?"

I said, "August, I called the police. I went out to get Charlotte and—"

Sergeant Owens stepped forward and said, "August, would you mind waiting out here while we have a look inside?"

August began to tremble slightly as he moved out on the porch. I wasn't sure if it was the cool morning air or the all-night drinking, but suddenly all the color seemed to drain from his face. I felt a pang of guilt for not having woken him up earlier to warn him that something was wrong, even though I knew I'd done the right thing. Now, all his swagger had fallen away. He looked like a little boy, wide-eyed and lost in the woods.

Owens glanced over at one of the deputies and said, "Kendrick, would you please get this young man a blanket while we have a look inside?"

The deputy nodded and motioned for August to follow. They walked down to the squad van.

When they were out of range of hearing, Owens turned to me and said, "Who's Becca?"

"She's his sister, but I don't think she's here."

He nodded. "Okay, where is it?"

I said, "By the pool. Go through the archway on your right and through the living room to the big sliding glass doors. I can show you."

Owens pointed at another deputy. "Hanson, take Dixie down and wait by the cars, and keep an eye on the front. The rest of you lock down the grounds and let me know right away if anything looks out of place. Morgan, Lyle, you're with me."

He pulled out some blue rubber gloves and booties and

passed them to Deputy Morgan and another officer. They
all slipped them over their hands and feet. Rule number
one at any crime scene is to ensure the safety of both the
witnesses and the responding officers. I knew Owens was
going in to search every single inch of the house, not just
for evidence, but for anything else that might be hiding
inside. Like another victim. Or a murderer.

I shuddered at the thought that there could still be
someone lurking inside. Deputy Hanson motioned to me,
and I followed him down to the squad van, where August
was waiting with a blanket wrapped around his shoulders.
I looked back to see Owens, Morgan, and the other deputy
moving slowly through the front door and into the house.

I turned to Deputy Hanson and said, "I have the cat in
my car. Is it okay if I just check on her?"

Hanson had jet black hair cut close to his ears and a
little bit of stubble on his chin. He couldn't have been
much older than August.

He said, "Where's your car?"

"It's on the street, just down by the gate."

"Let's walk down there."

I walked down to the gate with August and Deputy
Hanson close behind me. We went around to the passenger side of the Bronco, and I opened up the door. Charlotte hissed from inside her cardboard prison, just to make
a statement, not with any real ferocity behind it.

Deputy Hanson turned to August. "This is your parents' cat?"

"Yeah," August said. "She always acts like that."

I said, "I think she's probably not too happy cooped up
in this box."

Hanson walked around the back of my car, and August turned to me. "Dixie, what the hell is happening?"

"August, I'm sorry, but I really think you should let the sergeant tell you."

Hanson had noticed Joyce's antique birdcage in the back of the Bronco. He raised one eyebrow. "You always travel with a birdcage?"

I said, "No, sir, I was walking with a friend yesterday morning and we found an exotic bird in the woods. I'm picking it up from the vet this morning."

August stared at the birdcage without blinking, like he was studying it with every cell in his body, but I knew better. He wasn't stupid. I was soaking wet, and there were cops and ambulances everywhere. He was bound to have figured out by now that something very bad had happened in the pool, and I knew he must have been thinking it had something to do with Becca.

Sergeant Owens came out on the front porch and called out to Deputy Hanson, who turned and motioned for us to follow him. I could tell he didn't want to leave me alone with August. And then I realized: For all he knew it was August that needed protecting, not me.

Until it was ruled otherwise, August and I were not only witnesses. We were suspects.

11

The scene of a murder is like the inside of a beehive. Everyone has a job to do, a job for which they are specifically trained. The body lies at the center, en-shrouded in perfect stillness, while all the crime specialists buzz around it in ever-widening circles, performing their one particular skill with single-minded concentration, seemingly oblivious to everything and everyone around them. Together they operate as one efficient organism, all in service of answering a deceptively simple question: What happened here?

Sergeant Owens had asked me to wait in the living room, and even though I'd been in this kind of situation before, I felt about as out of place as if I actually was inside a bee-hive. I was sitting on the couch, wrapped in towels with a blanket over my legs, trying to stay warm. My hair was still damp, and my clothes reeked of chlorine.

I had a partial view of the proceedings out on the lanai. The paramedics had moved Mr. Harwick's body onto a blue plastic tarp and were huddled over it. A photographer was circling around the edge of the pool, taking pictures from every angle. Beyond the lanai, deputies were stringing up a line of yellow police tape to seal off the entire property and more than likely the adjoining properties as well.

Sergeant Owens was talking to somebody I didn't recognize, a rangy, long-boned woman in her midforties, with sorrel hair and skin threatening to freckle. She wore a knee-length skirt approximately the same reddish brown color as her hair, with a beige blouse that was ruffled down the front and a dull gray scarf tied in a knot around her neck. The next thing I knew she and Owens were walking up to me.

With a firm handshake, she said, "Samantha McKenzie, homicide."

"Dixie Hemingway. I'm the pet sitter. You're Guidry's replacement?"

A defensive blush rose in her cheeks. "So they tell me."

"I'm sorry. I'll bet you get that a lot."

"I'm used to it. Miss Hemingway, I was wondering if you wouldn't mind answering a few questions?"

"Sure, except it's almost nine, and I have other pets waiting for me."

She nodded. "We won't be long. I understand you have the owner's cat in your car?"

"Yes, I took her with me after I tried to revive Mr. Harwick."

"And why is that?"

I looked at the scene outside on the lanai. "I didn't want to leave her here alone with . . ."

McKenzie nodded. "And how long have you known August?"

"You mean Mr. Harwick's son? I only just met him this morning."

She looked down at a clipboard and read from the police report.

"That's right, he arrived when you were waiting in your car with the cat."

"No, he came home before I found the body."

She looked up at me. "Oh? You just told me you didn't want to leave the cat alone in the house after you revived the body. Where was August when that happened?"

My mind was beginning to feel buttery. Detective McKenzie was frumpy and plain on the outside, but she was sharp as a razor on the inside. She was testing me. Deputy Morgan had obviously told her everything I'd said when he arrived, and now she was deliberately trying to trip me up, looking for any inconsistencies in my story. I could feel my entire body getting warm, and my armpits felt slippery.

I took a deep breath. "I didn't want to be alone after I discovered Mr. Harwick, so I took Charlotte with me. August was asleep upstairs."

"Why do you say that?"

"He said he was going to bed. I think he'd been out all night."

The corners of her mouth rose slightly in a smile. "No, I mean why do you say you didn't want to be alone? August was here, wasn't he? Why didn't you go up and get him when you saw a body in the bottom of the pool?"

I said, "Detective McKenzie, I'm an ex-cop . . ."

I paused to see if that got a reaction, but it didn't. Either she'd already been briefed on my sordid past or she didn't care. Either way, she didn't even blink.

"I'm trained in CPR, so at that moment I wasn't thinking about August or anybody else. I was thinking I needed to get the body out of the water, and I needed to get it out fast, so that's what I did. I tried to revive him, and when that didn't work I just needed to get out of the house. I took Charlotte with me because I've been hired to take care of her."

Her expression didn't change. She stared at me with milk-paint gray eyes and waited. She knew I was leaving something out, even before I knew it myself.

I went on, "When I first got here, I had a strong feeling something was wrong, like somebody was in the house or something. That's when I called Sergeant Owens. And then August came home, and before he went inside he pulled something out of his glove compartment. I think it was a gun."

She nodded. "You were afraid to be in the house alone with August."

"I don't know. Possibly."

"Were you aware that the Harwicks' Cadillac was in the garage?"

I said, "I didn't even know there was a garage."

"Yes, it's off the service driveway at the far end of the house."

"No, I didn't think to look there, but Mr. Harwick did say that they were driving to Tampa."

"Okay. And how long was August inside the house while you waited in your car?"

I said, "Less than five minutes, I think."

"And how would you describe his mood?"

"His mood?"

"Yes. Was he happy, sad, nervous, angry?"

I was starting to wish I hadn't said anything. I should have known the minute I revealed that August had a gun she'd latch onto him as a key suspect.

"I would say drunk and horny."

She suppressed a smile and made a note on her clipboard. "Sounds like a typical teenager."

"Yes."

She paused for a moment and then looked me squarely in the eye. She said, "I was with the FBI for twenty-five years. Dallas office. My husband was murdered nine years ago. I have a sixteen-year-old daughter. Her name is Eva."

I didn't have to wonder anymore if Owens had told her about me. I figured he'd also told her I'd lost my husband and my child and been dismissed from the force for "mental instability." It wasn't that she probably thought I was a nutcase that made me want to melt into a puddle at her feet right then and there. It was hearing her daughter's name that broke me open. Hearing her name made me want to lay my life out for this detective, tell her about my own daughter, whose name was Christy and who had died when she was three, about my husband, Todd, who'd died at the same time, tell her how my life had ended that day and how I'd built a new life from scraps and shards I'd clawed from the rubble of the old. I wanted to ask her if it had been that way for her, too.

But before I could say anything, my cell phone rang. It must have fallen out of my pocket down into the cushions of the couch. I fished it out and flipped it open, realizing before I could stop myself that it wasn't my phone at all— it just had the same ringtone as mine.

Awkwardly, I said, "Uh, hello?"

A woman's voice said indignantly, "Who is this?"

"Uh, this is Dixie."

"Dixie? Dixie Hemingway?"

I said, "I'm sorry, I thought this was my phone."

The woman cleared her throat. "This is Tina Harwick. I just woke up, and my husband isn't here. What the hell is going on?"

My mouth fell open, and Detective McKenzie looked up from her clipboard. I stammered, trying to think of the right thing to say.

"Mrs. Harwick, I'm in your house right now . . ."

Detective McKenzie immediately snapped on a pair of blue rubber gloves and thrust her hand out in front of me. I laid the phone down in her open palm. I could hear Mrs. Harwick's voice rising, "Dixie, what the hell are you doing with Roy's phone?"

Sergeant Owens led me out of the living room. As we passed the two Roman statues flanking the archway, I heard Detective McKenzie say, "Mrs. Harwick, my name is Samantha McKenzie. I'm with the Sarasota Police Department. Is there someone there with you?"

I felt a stab in my chest, as if an arrow had hit me full force in the back and plunged all the way to my heart. Mrs. Harwick had called her husband's cell phone only to find herself talking to a homicide detective. Of all the tricks that fate can play on a person, that had to be one of the dirtiest.

I felt a little weak in the knees, and I think Sergeant Owens knew it. He walked me all the way down the driveway to my car and even opened the door for me. Charlotte peered through one of the holes in her cardboard penitentiary with one accusing eye.

I said, "I'll see that their cat is taken care of until the crime units are done with the house, but if Mrs. Harwick is still in Tampa tonight, I'll need to come back to feed the fish."

"Not a problem," Owens said, his words thick as syrup. "I'll let the deputy on watch know you're authorized to enter the premises whenever you need to."

There was a note in his voice that caught my attention. He cocked his head to one side and squinted at me. "Anything else?"

I said, "I know what you're thinking."

"I'm not thinking anything, Dixie, except for some reason you seem to have a remarkable talent for stumbling upon dead people."

I sat down in the driver's seat and sighed. "That's what I thought you were thinking, and I would *not* call it a talent."

"You did a good job back there, Dixie. You did the best anybody could've done."

I stared down at my hands folded in my lap. "If I had looked out on the lanai in the very beginning, it might not have been too late to save him."

"You don't know that, and you can't blame yourself."

I nodded mutely. I could feel my cheeks getting hot. Sometimes it felt like Sergeant Owens had a twenty-four-hour security camera aimed right at the center of my brain.

He smiled and knocked on the hood a couple of times.

"Alright, go home and get some dry clothes. Detective McKenzie will probably want to see you down at the station later."

I pulled out onto the road, flashing him a pained grimace at the thought of having to spend another moment under Detective McKenzie's magnifying glass, but in truth I didn't want him to see the tears that were forcing their way out of my eye sockets. At the very core of any cop's heart, any cop worth a grain of salt, is a burning desire to help people. I guess that's true for ex-cops, too, because I felt like I had failed Mr. Harwick.

As for Detective McKenzie, I knew Owens was right. There was a lot more she would want to know, and there was a lot I hadn't told her.

12

The Kitty Haven is a boarding kennel on Avenida del Mare, just a block from the beach in an old Florida-style house with lemon yellow siding and peeling white shutters. There's a big bay window in the front overlooking a shady porch with a pair of white rocking chairs. Inside, it's all burgundy velvet, overstuffed pillows, and lace curtains. I always feel like I've walked into the front parlor of an old-timey brothel whenever I go there.

Instead of some scantily clad ladies of the evening lounging about, there were four cats stretched out on a big puffy sofa and two more sleeping blissfully on the windowsill. One of them raised its head when I came in and squinted at me the way cats do when they can't be bothered. The others barely moved a whisker.

A little bell over the door announced my arrival, and from the back of the house I heard Marge's assistant call out, "Be right there!"

Marge Preston is a plump, white-haired woman with a soft voice and the patience of an angel. She started the

Kitty Haven almost by accident. A stray cat had taken up residence under her porch, and Marge, being a softie through and through, decided to rescue it. She started putting out little pieces of cheese and tins of tuna to seduce the cat, whom she named Albert. Eventually Albert was sitting at the breakfast table in Marge's kitchen and eating kibble out of the palm of her hand, although it turned out she hadn't picked the best name in the world, since within a few weeks Albert gave birth to nine beautiful calico kittens. Marge decided to raise them all herself and find good homes for them, and in no time at all she was known all over the Key as "that cat lady." Perfect strangers would knock on her door with cats they'd rescued, asking if she could take them in and offering donations.

The Kitty Haven is Marge's one true passion. In all the years I've known her she's never had a single vacation, and she'll take any cat, no questions asked. In fact, business had been so good in the past few months that she'd recently hired a new assistant.

"Dixie!"

"Hi, Jaz!"

I put Charlotte's cage down, and Jaz wrapped her arms around me in a big bear hug. When I first met Jaz, she was an angry, confused teenager who'd fallen in with a crowd of hooligans and gotten herself into all kinds of trouble. But now she'd grown into a beautiful, mature young woman, and all that anger had disappeared.

She had coffee-colored skin and a head of long black curls. There were still a few telltale signs of her "questionable" past—nails painted jet black, a dagger tattooed on her ankle—but she had the biggest smile on her face, and I could tell all those days were long forgotten. She had always been a fierce animal lover, so when Marge mentioned she was looking for someone to help out at the Kitty Haven, I knew Jaz would fit in perfectly.

She said, "Marge isn't here. Some lady called, said she'd seen a box of kittens on the side of the road, so of course Marge ran off to save them."

Charlotte had poked an arm out of one of the air holes in her crate and was frantically waving it around trying to get our attention.

I said, "That's okay, I'm just dropping off a temporary orphan."

"Awww, what's her name?"

"Charlotte, or sometimes she's called Queen B."

I unfolded the top of the crate. Charlotte poked her head out and hissed, but I could tell her heart wasn't really in it.

Jaz knelt down. "Oh my goodness, she's not in a very good mood, is she?"

"Well, don't take it personally. She's grumpy even on a good day, and so far she has not had a good day."

Jaz picked Charlotte up out of the box and cradled her like a baby. "Poor Queen B, did you have a bad morning?"

I cringed, waiting for Charlotte to go ballistic, but instead she buried her face into Jaz's armpit and started purring like a miniature jackhammer.

I said, "Wow, I think she likes you, which is good because she could definitely use some extra TLC today, and she hasn't had any breakfast."

"Oh, I think we can take care of that. We have all kinds of goodies around here that nobody can resist, no matter how big a grump they are!"

I gave Charlotte a little scratch between the ears. "Okay, well, tell Marge I'll give her a call. It should only be a couple of days."

Jaz flashed me a big smile. "Don't worry, she's in good hands."

I winked. "I know she is."

I barely remember the rest of my morning. I had a few more pets to check in on, and then I must have switched into autopilot, like a homing pigeon drawn to her coop, because the next thing I knew I was dragging myself up the stairs to my apartment. Michael and Paco were both at work, which was a relief, because I knew if they saw me they'd know right away something was wrong, and I just didn't have the energy to explain it to them. Plus, I didn't think I could even if I tried. My brain felt like cold mush, and I needed some time to sort it all out. Not to mention the fact that I was absolutely starving.

I didn't even say hi to Ella Fitzgerald, who was napping in a little shaft of sunlight from the kitchen window. I headed straight for the refrigerator and reached for half a grapefruit, but just behind it was a chocolate brownie calling my name. I slapped the grapefruit aside and went for the brownie, practically devouring it in one gulp. Clearly I needed some comfort food. I found a bag of corn chips in the cabinet and was about to rip it open and down them, too, when I remembered my date with Ethan the following night. The last thing I needed to be worried about was fat hips. I stopped myself, put the grapefruit in a bowl, and glumly carried it out to the porch with one of the silver-plated grapefruit spoons my grandmother left me.

I sat down on the hammock and looked out at the waves

lapping up on the beach. Ella Fitzgerald followed me out and rolled around at my feet, scratching her back on the rough wood flooring.

Where could I even start? My head was spinning with questions. Why had Mr. Harwick come home, and why had he left Mrs. Harwick in Tampa? Perhaps they'd had a fight. Given the way they treated each other in front of me, I had a feeling things could get a lot nastier when they were alone. Had he just gotten up in the middle of the night and snuck out of their hotel room? And if so, what did he think would happen when Mrs. Harwick woke up in the morning and discovered he wasn't there? Maybe it was just one of the stupid games they played, goading each other on, each of them trying to get under the other's skin. But I knew that wasn't right. When I answered Mr. Harwick's phone, there had been a note of desperation in Mrs. Harwick's voice. She was genuinely worried.

Then I think I actually said out loud, "No!"

I shook my head like a salt shaker, literally trying to empty it out, and took a bite of grapefruit. I decided it was time to give myself a good talking-to.

I told myself enough is enough. How Mr. Harwick got in that pool, and who put him there, was none of my damn business. He had a wife and two grown children and an entire police department to help figure it out. He didn't need me. I wasn't his wife or his daughter, and I'm certainly not a homicide detective. I'm a cat sitter. Besides, maybe he hadn't even been murdered at all. I thought of the liquor bottle on the coffee table—I hadn't noticed that the night before. Maybe he'd just gotten drunk and fallen in the pool all by himself. Although, there had been *two* glasses.

No. I shook my head again.

If what Michael had said was true, Mr. Harwick traveled in circles that I did not want to get mixed up in: cutthroats and thieves and oil potentates and foreign dictators. He was a principal figure in one of the largest companies in the world, a company synonymous with greed and wealth. There were probably people all over the planet that would jump for joy at the news that he'd been found dead at the bottom of a pool, and probably just as many that would have pushed him in themselves. I didn't want to be involved any more than I already was. And anyway, Detective McKenzie seemed like a perfectly capable detective. I was sure she didn't need my help.

Except . . .

It was hard not to compare McKenzie to her predecessor. Guidry had probably been the finest homicide detective Siesta Key would ever know. Everything about him was smooth and flawless, from the way his mind worked right down to his fine Italian shoes and imported linen slacks. Okay, I might or might not have been in love with him, but any fool could see that Samantha McKenzie was his polar opposite. She was obviously intelligent, but she was about as stylish as a sack of wet rats. I couldn't imagine her wearing expensive Italian shoes any more than I could picture Guidry wearing a beige blouse with ruffles, although it made me giggle a bit to try.

I'd almost put the whole thing out of my mind. I had even started to swing a bit in the hammock, absentmindedly eating my grapefruit and imagining Guidry in a skirt and high heels, when it hit me.

I jumped off the hammock. Poor Ella scattered out

from under me like it was a bomb raid. I raced inside to the answering machine and hit the PLAY button. There were no new messages, just the one Kenny had left me the day before:

"Dixie, it's Kenny. Listen, I should have told you, but I couldn't. Something's about to go down and . . . it's big. I can't tell you what it is, and probably by the time you hear this I'll be gone. I just wanted to say I'm sorry for not being honest with you from the start. I was scared, and now it's too late. I hope you'll understand that I didn't have a choice."

The machine beeped and clicked off. I sat down on the edge of my bed and cradled my head in my hands. This whole time I had assumed he was planning on telling Becca he couldn't handle having a baby, that he was running away, moving on to another town and starting all over again. Was it possible he'd planned on something else? Detective McKenzie would need to hear about this, but before I could jump to any conclusions, I picked up the phone and started dialing.

I hadn't even thought what I would say if he picked up, but I was relieved this time when I got Kenny's voice mail. At least that meant he hadn't canceled his phone service.

I said, "Kenny, this is Dixie. You need to call me. Right away. I don't know what you've done, but I just need to talk to you before . . . before things get out of hand. I'm not mad at you, I just need you to call me the minute you get this, okay?"

I paused for a second, as if he might answer, and then hung up. I peeled off my clothes, tossed them on top of the washer, and stepped into the shower. I stood there for a few blissful moments and let the hot water stream down my body. When Becca had first poured her heart out to me, she had said she was completely afraid of telling her mother she was pregnant by the pool man. Could Becca have turned to her stepfather for help? Perhaps he'd snuck out and driven home in the middle of the night. Tampa is only a little more than an hour away by car. Maybe he'd come home to console Becca, only to find her in the house alone with Kenny . . . and then what? Had there been a fight?

I knew there were things in Kenny's past that he wasn't proud of. Michael and Paco were right, why else would he live on a boat and only work odd jobs for cash? Even so, I couldn't imagine him hurting a flea. And yes, Becca was impetuous, immature, and an emotional disaster, and she didn't seem too fond of her stepfather, either, but she couldn't be a murderer. She just couldn't. I started to feel a little knot at the center of my chest. It was just a small tightening of the muscles there.

I toweled myself off and put on a clean pair of shorts, a sleeveless white tee, and a fresh pair of Keds. I sat down at my desk, and Ella hopped up and curled into a purring ball in my lap. I ran my hand down the length of her spine and thought, *If only she could talk to Charlotte in whatever secret language cats speak, then we'd have some answers.* I shuddered at the thought that poor Charlotte must have witnessed everything that had happened.

Forget it. I opened some mail and paid a few bills, trying to think about anything else. I left a message for a prospective client, a woman with a Yorkshire terrier that lives out on South Coconut Bayou, and then I tried to

balance my checkbook, but it was no use. I had given myself a good talking-to, but apparently my self hadn't been
listening. My mind kept flashing back to one particular
moment. When I had pulled the body up on to the edge of
the pool and moved the tangle of black hair away, I hadn't
for one second considered the possibility that it might be
Mr. Harwick.

But I wasn't surprised when I saw his face. I wasn't surprised one bit.

13

Some afternoons on the Key can be as hot as blue blazes, especially in the summer when the sun reaches its highest point in the sky. The crickets and birds and frogs all take a break, finding cover in the shade and giving their voices a well-deserved rest. Afternoon clouds sneak in off the shore all demure and innocent, but before you know it they let loose with a torrent of rain and lightning bolts, sending golfers and beachcombers dashing for cover. Then, just as quickly as they rolled in, the clouds roll out. The sun shines through again, the leaves all sparkle, and the crickets, birds, and frogs start warming up for their evening performance, which usually begins about the same time the sun starts her slow descent into the Gulf.

It was a little after two o'clock when I headed out for my afternoon rounds. I called Dr. Layton to let her know I'd be late picking up our feathered friend. I didn't tell her why. I was itching to talk to somebody about what had happened, but I knew I couldn't, especially since there hadn't been an official announcement from the police yet and I didn't want to do anything that might compromise the investigation. Instead, I told her I'd had a "client-related mishap" and left it to her imagination. She told me not to worry, that René was doing fine. He was in his cage on Gia's desk by the front window, basking in all the love and attention he was getting from everybody in the clinic.

I imagined that by now Mrs. Harwick was on her way back from Tampa, and somebody had probably gotten hold of Becca and told her what had happened. Becca's relationship to her stepfather seemed complicated, but I knew it must have been devastating for her, especially when she was already in such emotional turmoil. I hadn't heard from Detective McKenzie yet, but I knew it was only a matter of time before I'd get the call to meet her at the station. I was dreading it. Being back at that station brings up all kinds of memories that I long ago figured out how to suppress.

At the Suttons' house, Sophie had knocked over a potted palm in the living room, which wasn't all that surprising. On the outside, Sophie looks like a sweet, domesticated house cat, but inside she's a tiger, and a very frisky tiger at that, so she's always on the prowl for mischief. There was so much dirt scattered around I think she must have spent half the day engaged in a mighty battle with an imaginary mouse, or at least I hoped it was imaginary. I righted the palm and vacuumed up the dirt while Sophie watched me from the back of an armchair with a mildly disdainful look, as if I was spoiling all the fun. But I didn't feel too guilty. I had something else in store for her.

I like to get all the grooming out of the way in the

morning so afternoons are free for playtime. Sophie must have known what was coming next, because after I put the vacuum away and headed for the kitchen, she ran ahead and raced around the center island a couple of times, slipping and sliding on the tile floor. That's her warm-up.

I pulled a white Ping-Pong ball out of my pocket and held it out at arm's length. "Ready?"

She made a sound that was less like *meow* and more like *ackackack!* and twitched her whiskers with pure, unadulterated excitement.

I let the ball drop, and then both Sophie and the Ping-Pong ball went bopping and bouncing all over the kitchen for a good five minutes. That gave me the opportunity to check the house for any other mayhem she might have wreaked, and it gave her the opportunity to unleash some of that boundless kitty power. She was still at it when I came back, so I even had time to fill her bowl with fresh water and get her dinner ready. If I ever come up with a way to harness the energy created by a cat and a Ping-Pong ball, we won't need to dig any more oil wells and us cat owners will all be billionaires.

I still had a couple more clients to check on, but first I wanted to stop by Dr. Layton's office. I knew Joyce and Corina were waiting to hear how René was doing, and I was eager to get him back to Joyce's so I could get the news on Corina's appointment with the doctor. I prayed her baby had gotten a good bill of health—things were already hard enough as they were, and Corina didn't need any more problems on her plate. Thinking about Corina and her baby made the wings of my heart flutter a bit and the corners of my mouth sneak up in a little smile. It made me feel good to know we'd at least given Corina a safe place to stay while she got her bearings. That was one less thing she needed to worry about.

I parked outside Dr. Layton's office and grabbed René's cage from the back. Before I went in, I fished my cell phone out and dialed Kenny's number again. It went straight to his voice mail. If Ken knew what was good for him, he would've called me back by now. I figured he probably didn't like the idea that I was trying to track him down, but he certainly wasn't going to be any happier when he started getting calls from the homicide department—and if he didn't talk to me first there was a pretty good chance he'd wind up at the top of the suspects list.

Inside, René was in a cage on Gia's desk with a view of the waiting room, where there were four or five people watching him with the attention normally reserved for a good TV show, like he was their own personal nature channel. They all looked up at me when I came in, waiting to see my reaction to such a rare and splendid thing. He was clearly the star of the clinic.

Gia waved and said to René, "Here's your mommy!"

I felt a little blush of pride, as if I'd hatched René myself. Sometimes I like to stand out from the crowd. Having everyone think I was the lucky owner of such an exotic bird made me feel a little special. Gia signaled for me to come on back while she ran to fetch Dr. Layton, and René let out a high-pitched *cool!* as I came around to the side of his cage. He was swinging on one of the perches, using his long tail feathers for balance. He looked at me with one eye and then the other and then went back to pecking at a slice of fresh orange.

Dr. Layton said, "He's very talkative today. He's been entertaining everybody with all kinds of whistles and calls."

I wanted to say that I'd only heard one or two, but I didn't want anyone in the waiting room to know I was just the bird chauffeur, so I nodded dumbly.

"He's still a little tired though, so I'd say it's a good idea to let him rest as much as possible over the next few days. Whatever he's been through was pretty hard on him, but his appetite has definitely picked up since yesterday. He's probably already gained a few ounces. I sent some blood samples over to the lab for testing, but in the meantime, I don't think there's any reason to be concerned. He's a very healthy boy."

I let out a sigh of relief. With everything that had happened today, getting some good news felt like hitting the jackpot at a slot machine.

Dr. Layton looked me up and down. "On the other hand, you're looking a little beat. You okay?"

I nodded as I took out my checkbook. "It's been a very long day."

She wagged a finger at me. "First of all, go home and get some rest, and second, put that checkbook away."

"No, you have to let me pay you."

"No ma'am, you saved that bird's life, you don't owe me a penny."

I wagged my finger back at her. "What about the lab fees?"

"Oh no. Do not try to sass a sasser. That's a fight you are definitely not going to win. First of all, I always devote a portion of my work to charity, and if there was ever an animal in need of a little charity, this is it. And secondly, he's out of his normal environment and he's completely defenseless. If you and your friend hadn't taken him in he would've wound up somebody's supper. So you don't owe me a penny. Of course, it's a good thing you waited a bit before you stuck him in the freezer."

I nodded in agreement as I set René's antique cage on the desk. Gia helped me transfer him from his state-of-the-art number. He didn't look at all upset to be leaving his fancy modern digs, probably because he was eager to get back to Joyce's house—which I guessed was now what he thought of as home. I wondered if Joyce had considered the fact that she'd now taken in three boarders. She'd been living alone for so long, I think she was probably grateful for the company.

I thanked Dr. Layton, and Gia gave me a list she'd written up of all the foods that were safe for René. As I passed through the waiting room, everyone smiled and waved good-bye to René like he was George Clooney leaving the Academy Awards, and René called out a couple of *cools!* to let everyone know how honored he was to be there. He skipped and hopped around in his cage all the way to the Bronco, as if he actually had won some sort of award. I guess I'd be happy too if I found out I'd narrowly avoided being packed away in somebody's freezer. I loaded him into the back and wedged the towels around his cage to keep it from toppling over. The towels were still damp from my morning swim. I made a mental note to hang them up to dry when I got home.

Joyce's house is only about a block from where we found Corina, so on the way I turned down the side lane that runs along the the park where we found her. I slowed a bit to see if the box she'd been living in was still there, but there was too much foliage in the way to see from the street.

Corina and Joyce met me at the door, both wide-eyed with joy, and before you could say *buenos días* they had whisked René away. They put his cage down in the middle of the coffee table and huddled over it, cooing at René like two love-struck schoolgirls. Henry the VIII scampered and hopped around the perimeter of the table, wagging his tail and panting excitedly. I was beginning to get a little annoyed with all the attention René was getting.

I said, "Would anyone like to tell me how the baby is doing?"

Joyce said, "Oh, the doctor said she's in perfect health. What did you find out about René?"

"That's all she said?"

"Well, the baby's underweight. She said it was probably at least a month premature, but they didn't think it was anything to worry about. What did you find out about René?"

I sighed. These two were more excited about the bird than anything else. "He's totally fine, but he's supposed to rest up for a while, and he's also a little underweight, but otherwise she said he's a healthy boy. They gave me a list of foods."

Corina nodded expectantly. "So, the bird—he will not die?"

"No, not at all! She said he is very healthy."

I pulled out Gia's list of recommended foods and handed it to Corina. "He eats all kinds of things, but fruit seems to be the favorite." As I spoke, Corina looked down at the list and nodded. I could see tears welling up in her big brown eyes.

Joyce put her hand on Corina's shoulder. "Oh, Corina. It's going to be okay."

Corina started to cry softly. "The bird, she is okay. I am happy."

Joyce caught my eye, and we shared a look. Corina wasn't just crying because some crazy-looking bird had gotten a clear bill of health from the vet. She was crying because, at the heart of things, Corina and René had a lot in common. They were both far from their own homes, in a foreign land where they weren't completely understood, where they had to depend on the goodwill of perfect strangers in order to survive. They had both placed their trust in our hands. It was easy to understand how they might immediately form a tight bond.

Now Joyce started dabbing at her eyes with the corner of her blouse.

"Oh no, not you too!"

Joyce laughed through her tears. "Well, Corina's right. I'm happy the bird she is okay, too!"

I rolled my eyes and left the two of them together, sniffling and hiccuping. The baby was in the guest bedroom sound asleep in her bright pink car seat, which was situated in the middle of the bed, surrounded with pillows. Her cheeks were flushed pink, and her hands were balled into fists like two tiny cauliflower heads.

As I sat down on the bed, her eyes opened into narrow slits.

I whispered, "Hi, Dixie Joyce."

She tilted her head back a bit and her eyes widened a little, trying to focus on me. I laid my hand down over hers and softly kissed the top of her head.

"You know," I said, "there's a couple of crybabies in there."

14

I pulled up to the Harwick house not knowing what to expect. Sometimes investigators can take days to comb through the contents of a crime scene, and sometimes it can be over in hours. It all depends on the crime. The first thing I noticed was that the entire property was still cordoned off with yellow police tape, and now it was stretched across the front gate. Partially blocking the entrance were two white news vans with brightly colored logos splashed across their sides and big satellite dishes perched on top, casting long shadows up the driveway. The ambulance was gone now, but there was still a police cruiser next to August's sports car, and behind that was an unmarked sedan.

I parked behind one of the vans. There were a couple of reporters talking to some neighbors, and across the street there was a balding man, in boating shorts the same orange as Cheetos, pointing his phone at the scene. He was probably taking a video that would be on the Internet as soon as he went back inside his house.

I knew one of the neighbors must have made a call to the local television stations, because if Detective McKenzie had her way, word of Mr. Harwick's death would have been kept from the media until at least the initial investigation was over and all the family members had been notified. But I guess it's hard to keep things under wraps when ambulances and police cars start surrounding the home of a major figure in one of the biggest companies in the world. This little group of local reporters was just the tip of the iceberg. Once word started spreading, the whole neighborhood would be crawling with news teams and photographers from all over the place.

I took a deep breath. I don't get along too well with reporters. Anyone who knows me can vouch for that. So before I got out of the Bronco, I closed my eyes and started slowly counting to ten. With each breath, I imagined myself taking one step toward a gently babbling brook, with sparkling water softly gurgling over time-polished pebbles and blue and yellow butterflies flitting all about. Growing up the lush banks of the brook on both sides were cheery black-eyed Susans, sunning their yellow petals in the dappled sunlight and swaying gently in the warm, nectar-scented breeze. Just when I was at the fifth blissful step, I heard an obnoxiously loud rapping next to my head. I nearly jumped out of my seat, and there was Deputy Morgan's big face looming in the window next to me.

"Hey, Detective McKenzie is inside. She wants to see you."

I gulped out, "Okay, I'm on my way."

"Were you sleeping?"

I grabbed my bag and opened the door. "No, I was not sleeping. I was preparing."

"Preparing for what?"

"That."

I tipped my chin in the direction of the reporters, who were now making a beeline right for us.

"Ma'am! What's your connection to the Harwicks?"

Before I could even answer, another said, "Are you an employee here?"

A young woman in a Tampa University baseball cap stuck a microphone in my face. "Can you tell us in your own words what's happening here?"

I put my head down and concentrated on the heels of Deputy Morgan's shiny black boots as he led me past the news vans. The reporters ran alongside us like angry geese until we reached the front gate. Morgan lifted up the police tape and I scooted under, then we made a quick escape up the cobblestone driveway, leaving the gaggle of honking reporters behind.

Morgan grinned. "Well, that wasn't too bad."

As we walked away, I heard one of the reporters say, "I think I recognize that woman. She's a pet sitter."

I shifted my backpack to the other shoulder and nodded mutely. Detective McKenzie was standing in the doorway on the front porch with her clipboard of notes and police reports.

"Miss Hemingway, I'm glad you're here. I was wondering if you might show me that fish."

. . .

The master bathroom looked exactly the same, except now the wet towel I had noticed on the counter had a small yellow card lying next to it with the number 21 written in black ink. There was another yellow card next to the gold-plated phone, and another taped to the door above the handle. The cards were markers left by the investigative team, each indicating a potential piece of evidence. It gave me an eerie feeling to know they'd picked up my own fingerprints in the room, and that they were now part of the puzzle of clues.

The hermit crab I had spotted in the mermaid's cleavage on that first day I met the Harwicks was now perched precariously on the ridge of her nose. She looked a little peeved about it, and I completely understood. Who can look sexy with a crab on her nose? I pointed to a little fish that was hovering at the base of one of the coral towers, peeking at us from behind a gently waving frond of sea fern. He was creamy yellow from head to tail, with a russet jigsaw pattern tattooed down his sides and fins that seemed almost comically small for his plump body. He had big puppy-dog eyes and a wide goofy smile that looked painted on, as if he'd learned to apply it at clown school.

"It's that one right there. That's a porcupine fish."

Detective McKenzie said, "How did you know it was afraid?"

I said, "Believe me, you know. They puff up into a big ball. And see all those stripes going down his body? Those are spines. When he gets scared and puffs up, those spines stick out like needles in a pin cushion."

"Or a porcupine."

"Exactly."

She nodded thoughtfully. I felt a little secret twinge of pride, imagining her telling Sergeant Owens how brilliant it was of me to notice such an important clue.

"They're poisonous, aren't they?"

I nodded. "Yeah, big-time."

"And did you notice anything else out of place?"

I hesitated. "Not really, other than I couldn't find Charlotte. And I was a little surprised that the alarm system wasn't on when I arrived. The Harwicks made a point of telling me that they always kept it on when they were away. When I unlocked the door, it was the first thing I thought."

"The door was locked?"

"Yes, I'm positive. I know because I remember taking my keys out to unlock the door."

She sniffed. "Yes, except the use of a key to open a door doesn't necessarily mean that it's locked, does it? All it means is that you inserted your key in the lock and turned it. Did you try to open the door before you unlocked it?"

"No . . . I guess I just assumed it was locked."

She wrinkled her nose and flipped a page in her clipboard. "Tell me about Mr. Harwick. You've known him a while?"

"No, I never even heard of him before this week."

She looked up at me and tilted her head. There were a couple of tangled strands of mousy brown hair falling across her face, and I resisted the urge to brush them aside.

"Miss Hemingway, that's a little difficult to understand."

"Huh?"

"I said, that's a little difficult—"

I said, "Yes, I heard you, I'm just not sure what you mean. I know he's famous in the business world, but I really don't keep up on that kind of stuff."

"Well, what I meant is, your boyfriend cleans the pool here, doesn't he? I would assume you'd at least be familiar with the Harwicks through him."

I sputtered, "Kenny? He isn't my boyfriend! I don't have a boyfriend. I know Kenny Newman because he hired me to check in on his cat a few times, and he sometimes works for me doing overnight dog sitting. But I didn't even know he cleaned the pool here until Mr. Harwick told me himself."

She pulled a pen out of her clipboard and circled something in her notes. "So, you did not know Mr. and Mrs. Harwick before two days ago?"

"No, I did not."

"I apologize. Mrs. Harwick was under the impression that you and Kenny Newman were seeing each other."

This woman was smart. I couldn't be sure, but I had the distinct feeling she was testing me again. I considered the possibility that Becca had already spilled her guts to Detective McKenzie and told her everything: that she was secretly dating Kenny, that she was pregnant, that Kenny had left her when he found out. McKenzie probably also knew that Becca had told me everything that morning when I found her crying her eyes out in the master bathroom. McKenzie had laid out a little piece of bait, and now she was waiting to see if I would snatch it up. Would I tell her everything I knew about Becca and Kenny? Or would I keep some secrets to myself?

I said, "I don't know where Mrs. Harwick got that impression, but I think you should probably talk to Becca about Kenny."

"Why is that?"

"I don't feel right telling you things that Becca told me in confidence. If she hasn't already told you, I think you should ask her what's happening in her life right now. I'm not sure it has any bearing on the investigation, but it could."

"What's happening in her life right now?"

"Look. I'm sorry, but you're going to have to talk to Becca first."

"Miss Hemingway—"

She stopped herself and took a deep breath. There was suddenly a very distant look in her eyes. She glanced down at the floor and then absentmindedly smoothed away one of the numerous wrinkles in her drab skirt, which was sprinkled here and there with short white cat hairs.

She looked up and leveled me with her gray eyes. "Dixie, Becca never came home last night, and she didn't show up at her school this morning. At this point we have no idea where Becca is."

I stared at her blankly.

"If for any reason you feel that Becca might have been involved in the death of her stepfather, I need you to tell me right now."

I had no choice. I really didn't think it was possible, but if Becca had anything to do with what happened to Mr. Harwick, I needed to tell everything I knew, even if it meant betraying Becca's confidence.

I told McKenzie how I'd found Becca in a ball on the

bathroom floor sobbing hysterically, how she was terrified about what her parents would do if they found out she was pregnant, and how Kenny seemed to have gotten cold feet and was leaving town ASAP. Detective McKenzie listened patiently, occasionally nodding and making notes on her clipboard. If she was disappointed that I hadn't been completely up-front about Becca and Kenny from the beginning, she didn't let on.

She said, "When was the last time you talked to Kenny Newman?"

"A couple of days ago. He was dog sitting for me on an overnight job, and he called because a neighbor wanted to walk the dog, and he wasn't sure if they had permission."

McKenzie nodded but didn't say a word. She could tell there was more.

I said, "Okay. He left a message on my answering machine yesterday. I didn't want to say anything because I wanted to talk to him first, but I've been calling him ever since and he won't answer."

"What was the message?"

I sighed. "He told me there was something that he was about to do, and that he was sorry, and that it was big."

"He didn't say what it was?"

"No, I assumed he was skipping town. He said by the time I heard the message he'd be gone."

She nodded. "Had he ever mentioned any kind of tension with the Harwicks before? A dispute about money, perhaps, or anything else?"

She was doing it again. "No. Like I said, I didn't know he worked for the Harwicks until two days ago."

"Right. You did say that. Do you know where he lives?"

"Detective, there's just no way he could be involved. I haven't known him for very long, but I just can't imagine he would do something like this."

"I'm sure there's nothing to be worried about. I just need to talk to him. Can you give me his address?"

I sighed again. "No. He doesn't have one. He lives on a boat, and sometimes he sleeps in his car."

She nodded as if that was the most normal thing in the world, but I knew exactly what she was thinking.

"Do you happen to know where he keeps this boat?"

"Down at the dock behind Hoppie's Restaurant. They let him stay there in exchange for doing odd jobs."

As much as I didn't want to admit it, I knew deep down inside that I might have misjudged Kenny, and now I was beginning to see him from Detective McKenzie's point of view. What I saw was not pretty. An itinerant worker, a drifter basically, who lived on a houseboat and slept in his car, who disappeared with his pregnant teenaged girlfriend after her domineering father was found fully clothed at the bottom of the family swimming pool.

McKenzie said, "Okay. You've been very helpful."

I said, "I just need to feed the fish and then I'll be out of your way. Do you know how long it'll be before I can bring the Harwicks' cat back home? I have her in a kennel now."

"Mrs. Harwick is staying in a hotel for the time being. I'm not sure she's going to be able to come home anytime soon."

Her tone was unmistakable. The words spilled out of her mouth like dice on a game board, completely devoid of judgment or drama. I've grown to recognize that tone almost immediately. It's like a secret code, or a song that only people who've lost someone they fiercely loved can hear. She didn't need to tell me that Mrs. Harwick was distraught. More than likely she was in shock.

She murmured, "We've called a doctor in."

I nodded. We both knew how unprofessional it was for her to include that little detail, but I understood her need to tell me. After Christy and Todd were killed, I couldn't get out of bed. There was no doctor or sedative or antidepressant strong enough to bring me back to real life. I just needed time. I stayed wrapped in sheets for months, like a blithering lunatic in a cocoon. I barely ate or bathed.

And now here it was again, that crazy urge to pour my heart out to this woman, to tell her my whole tragic story. What in the world was happening to me? I had always been the silent, brave type, the one that held everything in, that did all the listening but none of the talking. Now all of a sudden I was chomping at the bit to open myself up to someone I barely knew, and all because she had lost her husband as well.

We stood there for a couple of awkward moments; then I grabbed my backpack and pulled Mrs. Harwick's fish-feeding instructions out of one of the side pockets.

Detective McKenzie cleared her throat and handed me her card. "I'll see you downstairs when you're done here. In the meantime, let me know the minute you hear anything from Kenny Newman, and please ask him to call me."

I slipped the card in my pocket. "Okay, I will."

"And Dixie, it would be helpful if you could be as brief as possible with him."

I knew what she meant. She didn't want me to tell Kenny what had happened or ask him any questions about the case. A good detective can learn a lot just by observing the way people handle themselves. Kenny's first reaction to the facts of the case could mean the difference between being a witness and a suspect, and McKenzie wanted to be there when he was given the news.

As she walked out I glanced over at the mermaid, who was staring off blissfully at some distant horizon. *Stupid bitch,* I thought. How nice it must be to sit on your porcelain treasure chest throne, encased in a silent wall of water without a care in the world, while fish serenely circle around your empty porcelain head.

I slid open one of the big panel doors on the side of the tank and shuffled around to the back, trying to focus in on Mrs. Harwick's tiny handwriting. The instructions for the evening feeding were simple enough, six tablespoons each from two different cans of dried fish food. The first looked like tiny multicolored snowflakes, and the second were BB-sized pellets, half of which sank to the bottom of the tank the moment they hit the water. The fish seemed to know right off the bat which food they preferred. A few dove directly for the sinking pellets and ignored the floating flakes completely, while the rest shot straight to the surface and splashed around like a frenzy of man-eating piranhas.

I didn't check the chemical balance in the water as Mrs. Harwick had directed me to do occasionally. I felt a little twinge of guilt about that, but I figured I'd performed my duties and then some for the Harwick family already, and frankly I was physically and emotionally spent. I wanted to get out of that house as soon as possible.

Plus, the sun was setting, and I had one more item on my to-do list before I could throw my exhausted bones into bed and put this whole day out of its misery.

15

When my grandparents moved here, the Key was a completely different world. First of all, there weren't nearly as many houses as there are now, not to mention condos and high-rise apartment buildings and restaurants and shops and chic hotels. It was just a quiet fishing village, and what few houses there were certainly never made it onto the cover of *Fancy-Pants Mansion* magazine. Secondly, there was no such thing as a "private" beach. Even when Michael and I were kids, we would roam for hours on end exploring every inch of the island, and not once did we ever encounter a NO TRESPASSING sign. Back then most of the island was covered in sea grape and sugarberry trees and live oaks that towered over jungles of saw palmetto, wild olive, and creeping moonflower vines. It felt like our own personal jungle for two.

These days people like to joke that if you look away too long, the jungle starts to creep in and reclaim its stake. That definitely seems to be the case on Windy Way, where the houses peek out from behind a densely woven curtain of tree limbs and vines, and you have to carefully maneuver your car around the occasional island that's opened up in the middle of the one-lane road, where patches of saw grass have sprouted and overly ambitious cabbage palms are poking their way through.

I pulled into the driveway of a low-slung ranch house with pale gray siding and a lipstick red front door. A huge live oak huddled over the house like a regular at the neighborhood bar, resting its leafy elbows on the peak of the roof. Mrs. Langham was sitting in a beach chair in the open bay of the garage with her feet propped up on an old ice cooler. She was stick-thin with salt-and-pepper hair and bright pink lipstick. Perched on the bridge of her nose was a pair of bifocals attached to a string of white plastic beads around her neck, and she was busily pulling a needle and thread through an embroidery frame—probably an applique for a dress she was working on. As I walked up she laid the embroidery frame down in her lap and slid her glasses off.

"Well, well, look what the cat dragged in!"

I said, "I know, I know. I've been meaning to call you forever."

"Oh, don't you worry about it. I knew you'd come sniffing around one of these days when you got desperate enough. Come on back. It's in the sewing room."

The last time I saw Mrs. Langham was months ago when I had dropped by on a whim. She had been my grandmother's seamstress, so I'd known her since I was just a little girl. I remembered lying on the floor of the sewing room in this very house, playing with her black poodle while she and my grandmother talked about clothes and men and neighborhood gossip. It turned out she had made a few outfits for my mother, too. Seeing me had reminded her how stylish my mother was, and before I knew it she was measuring me for an evening dress and talking about "low cut" this and "plunging" that. I went along with it because I didn't want to hurt her feelings, but when she called to let me know the dress was finished, I chickened out.

When I was nine, and my mother ran away to start a new life or hide from her old one—I've never been quite sure which—she left nearly all her things behind, including most of her clothes. We still have a trunk of them in the attic. I used to sneak up every once in a while and go through them, remembering how pretty she was, what she smelled like, how she looked in a particular hat or dress— a dress more than likely made in this very sewing room. So when Mrs. Langham had called to tell me the dress was ready, it set off some strange emotional reaction in me, and I just didn't want to go back. Plus, the thought of wearing some sexy getup made me feel like I had a fur ball stuck in the back of my throat. I'm nothing like my mother. I'm a T-shirt and shorts kind of girl. Always have been, always will be.

Mrs Langham didn't give up easily, though. She called several times over the next couple of months, and each time I made up another excuse to postpone a fitting. Finally, after a couple of unreturned messages, she just stopped calling.

I followed Mrs. Langham through the house to the guest bedroom, which had been converted to a sewing room with worktables and sewing machines in the middle, a full-length mirror on one wall, and a pegboard with hundreds of spools of colored thread on the opposite wall. Mrs. Langham swung open the doors of a huge armoire in the corner and pulled out a dress with a dramatic flourish. It was about the most hideous shade of purple I'd ever laid eyes on.

I tried my best to sound happy. "Oh wow! It's purple!"

"No, no, no. It's rose. Now, I know what you're thinking. Just give it a chance. You have the same coloring as your mother. I promise you, this shade was perfect for her, and it's perfect for you. It will look stunning with that beautiful blond hair of yours."

I stood there speechless, racking my brain for some excuse to make a quick escape.

"Come on, Dixie," she said, holding the dress out. "Trust an old lady."

Reluctantly, I stepped out of my clothes and slid the dress down over my head. There was a dressmaker's form on a stand in the middle of the room. Mrs. Langham wheeled it aside, and I stepped in front of the mirror. When I looked up, I nearly gasped out loud.

She was right. It was a good color on me. In fact, it was beautiful. It wrapped over both shoulders, crossing in the front to form a plunging neckline, but not in a vulgar way, and then gathered in very close at the waist and dropped down just above the knee.

"Oh," I said. "I look good."

Mrs. Langham perched her glasses on the tip of her nose and looked me up and down like a rancher appraising a prize steer at market.

"No, my dear. You look *hot*."

16

The next morning, I woke at 4:00 A.M. to the sound of my radio alarm playing "Walk Like an Egyptian." My thoughts bopped along to the beat of it for a few short but blissful moments.

Slide your feet up the streets, bend your back.
Shift your arm then you pull it back.

Then everything that had happened the day before came rushing into my brain like a hangover headache. My right shoulder ached as if I'd competed in a one-armed weight-lifting competition, and I realized with a jolt that it was from pulling Mr. Harwick's heavy, water-sodden body up to the edge of the pool. I switched on the bedside lamp and sat up. If it weren't for the fact that there were half a dozen animals depending on me for breakfast, I would've pulled the plug on the alarm clock and slept the rest of the day with the blinds closed.

I dragged my legs off the bed and walked zombielike

into the bathroom and splashed myself with cold water. I looked at my bleary eyes and puffy morning face in the mirror as I brushed my teeth. From the back of my head I heard a tiny voice say sarcastically, *Oh, you're gonna look great for Ethan tonight!*

I pulled my hair into a ponytail, grabbed clean shorts, a bra, and a tee from the closet, and slid my bare feet into a pair of white Keds.

It was still pitch dark outside, but I could see glittering reflections of the moon off the waves rolling in on the beach. I leaned on the porch railing and let the cool salty air fill my lungs. Along the edge of the horizon was a sliver of coral pink light edging the night sky out of its way.

Like I always do in the morning, I checked out the situation in the carport. My Bronco was sitting there all by its lonesome except for a couple of pelicans dozing on the hood. Paco's Harley was parked in the corner, but his truck was gone, which meant he was still out somewhere on an undercover job, hunting down a drug kingpin or infiltrating a street gang. The Special Investigative Bureau isn't exactly a nine-to-five job, so no one ever knows what Paco's schedule is, and Michael and I both worry about him when he's not home.

I breathed a sigh of relief when I remembered that Michael's shift at the firehouse would be ending tonight. With everything that had happened in the last twenty-four hours, I'd be happy to have a big strong man around.

My brain felt like it was repeatedly shuffling a deck of cards, except instead of clubs and spades and diamonds and hearts, the cards were all images of everything that had happened in the last several days: Mrs. Harwick sprinkling fish food across the surface of the tank, Becca rolled up in a sobbing mess on the bathroom floor, Mr. Harwick's stupefied face staring up at me on the side of the pool. I was suddenly filled with the most profound feeling of dread, and then all the cards in my head scattered, leaving behind one lonely image: Ethan Crane.

Sweet Ethan Crane. He was a good man, and he cared for me, but I was stupid to have agreed to go on a date with him. It would never work. For one, I was still reeling from my parting with Guidry, and . . . and what? It just didn't feel right. If I was being honest with myself, it was impossible to know if what I was feeling for him was love, and not loneliness or lust or fatigue looking for a resting place.

Anyway, if a woman decides it is love she feels, how can she ever be sure the man she loves is the right one? Then I pictured myself in that ridiculous purple dress and laughed out loud. I must have been a fool to think I could pull that off.

Alright. Clearly I had fallen into a funk.

I knew it had mostly to do with Mr. Harwick, and I tried to give myself a break. Apparently, failing to save a man's life can put a real damper on your mood. I sighed and looked up at the starlit sky. Somehow without even trying I had yet again gotten myself mixed up in a whole mess of trouble, and yet again I had no idea why it kept happening. One day I'm minding my own business, brushing out cat hair and picking up dog poop, and the next I'm locking lips with a dead man on the side of a pool. I needed to try to keep my mind on my own problems and my own life. I'm a pet sitter, damn it, not a social worker, not a

marriage counselor, not an emergency medical techni-
cian, and *not* a homicide detective.

I told myself that Mrs. Harwick was no shrinking violet.
She was a smart, capable woman. She didn't need me to
help her with the death of her husband, and no matter
how much experience I had in that department and no
matter how strong the bond I had felt with her, there was
nothing I could do to make what she was about to go
through any easier.

Furthermore, Becca had a loving mother and a loving
brother. She could depend on them for any support she
might need, and it was completely egotistical and frankly
a little crazy for me to think that I could help her through
her stepfather's death or the mess she and Kenny had gotten themselves into. No matter how much I could relate to
what they were going through, there wasn't a single thing
I could do to make it easier on any of them. The only thing
that was going to help was the passage of time.

I didn't know what to think about Kenny, but I decided
he was none of my business either. I'd spent too much
time and energy defending him and trying to help him
out, and now I was beginning to see that Michael and
Paco had been smart to be suspicious of him. Perhaps Paco
was right and I had been swayed by Kenny's scruffy good
looks, or maybe somewhere hidden deep inside him was a
genuinely good person, but he was clearly making some
very bad choices.

And if he'd had anything to do with Mr. Harwick's
drowning, I knew it wouldn't take Detective McKenzie
very long to figure it out. She didn't need my help either.

I told myself that if there was anybody that needed me right now, it was Corina, and there was plenty I could do for her. She might have made some bad choices, too, but at least she was trying her best to do better and make a better life for herself and her baby, and she wasn't hurting anybody in the process or acting out of pure selfishness or greed. All she needed was a little push in the right direction and she'd be fine.

As for Ethan, I'd have to figure out a way to let him down easy. I needed to take things a little slower and with a little more thought.

I remembered how I hadn't been filled with so much angst and doubt when I first met Todd. I didn't believe in love at first sight, but Todd changed that. There was never even the slightest doubt that he was the right man for me. When I held him in my arms, it literally felt as if our hearts beat at the same exact rate. Sometimes I wonder if my heart will ever find that particular rhythm again.

I decided that I'd been through too much bullshit in my life to complicate things now, and losing Guidry to New Orleans was no bed of roses either. If Ethan didn't understand that, then he wasn't the right man for me in the first place.

Feeling emboldened, I clattered down the stairs and hopped into the Bronco. The two pelicans on the hood sullenly unfolded themselves and flapped off toward the water as I backed out of the carport. I rolled down the driveway and turned onto Midnight Pass Road, determined to have a nice, normal, boring day.

Rufus was as happy as usual to see me. As soon as I

opened the front door he came clicking across the hard-wood floor, hopping up and down on his back legs and pawing the air excitedly. Then he ran barking into the living room and grabbed his chew toy. He shook it with all his might and then came racing back and dropped it at my feet as a welcome gift.

Whenever I spend the night with any of my dogs, which I usually do if their humans are going to be out of town, I always take their collars off before bed. I figure they don't want to sleep in their day clothes any more than I do, and I think they actually sleep better that way. Now almost all of my clients do the same thing. Rufus scampered around my feet while I got his collar out of the drawer in the hall desk. He stood as still as he could, or at least as still as his eagerly wagging rump would allow, while I fastened his collar around his neck.

Rufus isn't a power-walking type of dog. Most schnauzers would rather sniff and hunt when they're outside, and Rufus is no exception. He's always on the lookout for lizards and squirrels and snakes. I don't think he'd have the slightest idea what to do with one if he ever caught it, but he thoroughly enjoys the chase. I brought along my handy thirty-foot retractable leash so Rufus could skitter here and there while we walked.

I hooked the end of the leash to his collar and snapped a couple of clip weights to the handle and headed out the door. While Rufus did his business and scampered about, I did some arm raises and bicep curls. I wanted to keep myself occupied. From now on I was going to start being a little more disciplined with myself, and that included getting a good workout every day. I must have looked like a deranged person flapping my arms up and down at the end of Rufus's leash, but I didn't care.

After a perfectly uneventful walk around the block and a good long brushing session, I gave Rufus a kiss on the nose and a little hug. The Graysons were taking him to visit their son in North Carolina later in the afternoon, so I knew I wasn't going to see him for a few days.

At the Kitty Haven, Marge was on the phone talking to a rescue center in Jacksonville about two older cats they had brought in but couldn't afford to keep. If Marge didn't take them, they'd have to be put down. She was arranging for Jaz to make the four-hour drive to pick up the cats and bring them back to the Haven. Marge waved and pointed me to the back, where I found Charlotte in one of the private cubicles.

She was her usual snarky self. With all the food and love she was getting from Marge and Jaz, I wasn't too worried about her, but I knew she'd probably be a lot happier once she was back in her own home. I didn't allow myself to think about what her life was going to be like without Mr. Harwick, or whether she knew that he was gone. It was too much to bear.

She hissed dismissively at me as I sat down on the floor next to her, but I knew she didn't really mean it. Stroking her from head to tail while she arched her back and pushed herself against my hand, I told her it wouldn't be much longer before she was back home, and I did my best to form a mental picture of her curled up among the pillows in the Harwicks' big canopy bed. I like to do that just in case cats can read minds. Of course it's crazy, but I do it anyway.

Tom Hale was out of town at a convention and had taken Billy Elliot with him, so I was pretty much done for the morning. I figured by now the news was probably out about Mr. Harwick, and since one of the reporters had seemed to recognize me, I didn't feel like making an appearance at the diner. I knew everyone would be full of questions, and I was trying my best to forget about yesterday's events. Also I imagined Judy would want to know all about my D-word with Ethan, and if she found out I was planning on canceling it she'd probably want to give me a good beating.

At the intersection of Beach Road and Midnight Pass, I turned left and followed Higel's dogleg over the north bridge. Another left and I followed Tamiami Trail around the bay, where tall-masted ships rode at anchor, their masts sparkling in the bright sunshine. A quick zag off course, a quick swing through Whole Foods for some soup and some other goodies and a bouquet of daisies, and then I was back on Tamiami Trail to the Bayfront Village, a posh retirement condo and one of the worst architectural disasters ever to blight Sarasota.

Bayfront is home to several hundred well-to-do seniors who either don't notice the folly of mixing Ionic, Gothic, Elizabethan, and Colonial architecture all in one building or are too busy having fun to care. The interior design is as bad as the exterior, with murals of foxhunting scenes keeping company with paintings of circus clowns, the Mahabharata, and bucolic fields of sunflowers and bluebonnets. But happy, energetic seniors bounce past the bizarre decor on their way to tennis or golf or theater, and not one of them seems to mind living in an interior decorator's living version of hell. These are what I call "don't-give-a-damn" seniors. They're more active than most people half their age, they're having more fun than most people half their age, and, well, basically they don't give a damn.

The concierge waved to me from her sleek French Provincial desk and gestured for me to go on up. As soon as I got in the elevator, the knot I had felt in my chest ever since I'd discovered Mr. Harwick's body loosened a bit. Just knowing that Cora Mathers was waiting for me on the sixth floor made everything feel a little lighter.

Cora is eighty-something years old, and I am lucky to know her, although the way we met is not the prettiest story in history. Her granddaughter, Marilee, had been a friend and a client, and to make a long story short, Marilee was murdered by a crazed neighbor. Marilee had already set her grandmother up in Bayfront Village with enough money to live comfortably for the rest of her life. The remainder of her estate, which was sizable to put it mildly, was willed to her cat, a blue Abysinnian named Ghost. She made me the executor of Ghost's estate.

Once I found a good home for Ghost, I put the estate in Tom Hale's hands and have pretty much avoided thinking about it ever since. After Marilee's funeral, I continued to stop in now and then to make sure that Ghost was being well cared for, and I also visited Cora at least once a week. At first I'd done it out of a feeling of misplaced guilt and responsibility, but that had changed, and Cora and I had become genuine friends. I don't think there's any topic that we haven't thoroughly discussed, some of which would be a surprise to most people. Women my age and women Cora's age aren't assumed to have much in common, especially when it comes to romance and sex and love, but that's a lot of hooey. The only difference between Cora and me is that she has more wrinkles and more experience. Otherwise, inside our skins we're both the same.

I smelled Cora's apartment as soon as the elevator doors opened. About once a week, she makes bread in an ancient bread-making machine. At some point in the kneading process, which Cora keeps a secret, she throws in a cup of frozen semisweet chocolate chips. The result is a chewy bread with a crunchy crust filled with little lakes of oozy chocolate. Cora insists that the bread be torn into hunks rather than sliced, and when those hunks are slathered with butter, I guarantee that strong women will swoon and muscled men will whimper with weak-kneed delight.

The concierge had alerted Cora that I was on the way up, so she was outside her door waiting for me when I stepped out of the elevator and went down the hall towards her apartment. Cora is the size of a malnourished sixth grader, with knobby little knees and freckled arms. Her hair is thin and fine as goose down and floats above her scalp in a cottony cloud. She whooped when she saw me, rising up and down on her toes in a semblance of jumping for joy.

I said, "Do I smell chocolate bread?"

"It's still cooling! What's that you've got?" As greedy as a child, she grabbed the Whole Foods bag and peered inside. "Oh, goody goody! I just love their soup!"

"There's some beautiful blood oranges, too, and a slice of apple pie."

"I'll have the pie for supper and the soup for dessert."

I followed her into the apartment, practically stepping

in place at times because she moved so slowly. Her condo was lovely, with glass doors opening to a long sun porch facing the Gulf. I knew that if Marilee were alive today, she'd be happy to see how Cora has turned her little apartment into such a lovely and comfortable place to live. It was all pink marble and turquoise linen and shafts of sunlight.

She stopped at a bar separating a minuscule kitchen from the rest of the room. While she lifted the sweating container of frozen soup from the bag, I went around her to the kitchen, where a fresh round loaf of chocolate bread was steaming on a wooden board on the counter. Cora always keeps her kettle warm, just in case company comes, so it only took a minute to put tea bags in a Brown Betty pot and pour hot water on them. While I got down cups and saucers, Cora took a chair at a skirted ice cream table by the windows.

She said, "Now, don't slice that bread. It's better if you tear off pieces."

She always says that.

I rummaged in the refrigerator for butter to add to the tea tray. "I know."

I always say that.

I put the daisies in a little pink vase by the sink and brought the bread and the tea tray out to the table.

Cora cleared her throat, carefully sliding her saucer and cup closer. "Was it you that found that drowned man?"

I sighed. "How did you know about that?"

In the sunlight from the glass doors, her face seemed to fracture into millions of tiny, fine lines. "Well, Dixie, the news said the man was found by his pet sitter, and it was on Siesta Key. Who else could it be?"

I sat down and poured the tea. "It was awful."

"I imagine so." She pushed the bread toward me with a smile. "This should help."

I broke off a small chunk and buttered it. It was so warm there were little curls of steam rising up and the butter melted right into it. I put it in my mouth and allowed myself a tiny moment of sheer bliss.

"Oh my God," I moaned. "I needed that."

Cora took a piece herself, and we sat in silence for a while, luxuriating in the simple joy of it. Occasionally Cora hummed a little tune to herself. I loved that we could sit in perfect silence and feel completely comfortable doing it. That's a sign of real friendship.

After a while she said, "So what do you hear from that fellow of yours?"

She meant Guidry. "He's not my fellow anymore, remember? He ran away to New Orleans."

She nodded. I could tell she was disappointed, but Cora wasn't one to cry over spilt milk, and I think she understood why I couldn't follow Guidry to New Orleans, even if she didn't completely approve of it.

I smiled coyly. "But I am having dinner with someone tonight."

Her eyes brightened. "Oh? Do tell!"

"Don't get too excited. It's not that big a deal."

"It's with that Ethan Crane fellow, I can tell by the look in your eyes."

"Oh, stop it, no you can't."

"Really? So who's your date with tonight?"

I laughed. "It's not a date."

She clapped her hands. "I knew it! You've had your eye

on him for a long time. I knew his grandfather, you know. He was a lovely man, too."

"Well, don't have a cow, it's just dinner. It's not like we're going to live happily ever after. In fact, I'm seriously thinking about canceling it completely. I'm not ready for anything serious, and it's not right to lead him on."

Cora's smile fell away, and she set her cup down with a little clinking sound against the saucer. "Dixie, you think those people chose to leave you?"

"Huh?"

She reached out and laid her hand on top of mine. "You think love can't last, is that what it is? That anybody that loves you will eventually leave?"

"Cora . . ." I couldn't finish. Tears instantly sprang to my eyes. I knew exactly what she was getting at.

"Dixie, sometimes our minds believe things our hearts know aren't true. You've had a rough go of it, so I can't blame you, but it's time to put all that behind you."

I dabbed at my eyes with my napkin and tried to compose myself while she tore off another piece of bread and smoothed some butter on it. She was right. I think there was a part of me that was beginning to wonder if I would ever be able to hang on to anything that I loved. First my father, then my mother, then my daughter and my husband, and then Guidry . . .

"You can't go on being mad at everyone that's ever hurt you. At some point you just have to forgive them."

I said, "I'm not mad at anyone."

"Oh, sweetheart, of course you are. For years I was mad at my own granddaughter for leaving me. And she was murdered! Certainly wasn't her fault. But that doesn't make any difference. It's just natural human feelings, but you can't live the rest of your life all swaddled up and protected. Sooner or later you have to forgive. You have to let that anger go or your heart will just dry right up."

I nodded silently. I knew she was right, but I wasn't sure how I could just let all of it go. We watched the boats out on the ocean sail by, and after a little while I said, "I think maybe I'm just a little scared, too."

"Well, let's talk about that. What are you scared of?"

"You know, you have to make such big sacrifices to be in love, and I like my life the way it is. I have all my friends and my family and my pets to take care of. But when you're with someone, you have to do all kinds of things to make it work. You have to compromise and share and change."

Cora fixed me with her clear blue eyes. "Dixie, those are all *good* things." She smiled mischievously. "And as I recall, that Ethan Crane fellow is about as delicious as . . ." She waved a piece of chocolate bread in the air and popped it in her mouth.

17

I t was exactly two minutes after eight. I was wearing my purple dress and standing next to Ethan, or to be exact, I was wearing my purple dress and teetering next to Ethan on my three-inch high-heel shoes.

We were watching the waiters set our table. It was next to the window, but with a perfect view of the entire candlelit dining room. There were sparkling wineglasses and silverware on all the tables, which were covered in crisp white linen. As we followed the hostess in, I noticed more than a few people watching us with knowing looks. I wasn't sure exactly what it was they were all knowing, but I felt happy and proud to be seen in public with a man as stunning as Ethan.

His fingertips were on the small of my back, and I suddenly had the strongest feeling of déjà vu I've ever had in my life.

When we sat down, a young man handed us menus, telling us his name was Paolo and that he would be our waiter for the evening. I ran my eyes up and down the menu a couple of times before I realized it was all in Spanish and I wasn't comprehending a single word of it. I peeked over my menu to see if Ethan was doing any better.

As usual, just looking at him made me a little short of breath. He was wearing a dark fitted jacket over a crisp white shirt and a narrow lavender tie. With his thick locks of curly black hair and high cheekbones, he looked like a silent-film star. There were tiny beads of sweat on his forehead, and I realized with a twinge in my heart that he was just as nervous as I was.

He looked up and caught me spying on him. "You look amazing, by the way."

I rolled my eyes and retreated back behind my menu. I felt like a complete and utter idiot, but in a good way.

A stocky man with a handlebar mustache and a white dinner jacket set two glasses of red wine on the table. Ethan immediately jumped out of his seat, and the two men bear-hugged and slapped each other's backs.

Ethan said, "This is my very good friend Alfred."

"You must be Dixie," he said, taking both of my hands in his. He spoke with a slight Spanish accent. "It is so very nice to meet you. Welcome to Yolanda. Ethan has told me all about you—I was beginning to think he had made you up, so I am very glad to finally meet you in the flesh."

Ethan blushed and nudged Alfred. "This is Alfred's restaurant. We were roommates at law school."

I said, "This place is beautiful. You must be very proud."

He nodded. "Thank you. My mama, she loved to cook. When I was a little boy, I used to sit for hours and watch her all day long. Those were the happiest times. Then one day I am a lawyer. I am at work, I have a pile of files on my desk and phone calls and pressure, and I hear my mama's voice in my head, 'What are you doing sitting there all day? Go out and play!' and that's when I knew I didn't want to sit behind a desk anymore. Now, here we are." He slid the wineglasses to the center of the table. "These are for you two lovebirds, and while you look at the menu I will bring you our special appetizer of the evening."

He winked at Ethan and rushed away.

Ethan raised his glass. "Cheers."

I raised an eyebrow. "Lovebirds?"

He blushed again. "Yeah, I have no idea where he's getting that, I swear."

Our glasses touched. Suddenly all my doubts about Ethan melted away. There was something about just being in his presence that made me feel completely comfortable and safe. Whether it was love or lust or loneliness or all three combined, I didn't care. It just felt right.

Alfred returned shortly with a small silver plate and set it on the table with a flourish. There were two golf-ball-sized mounds of what looked like bright, kelly green scoops of ice cream.

Ethan said, "What is it?"

Alfred whispered conspiratorially, as though he had prepared it especially for us, "It is sorbet, but not sweet. Spicy! It is my own creation, made of peppers from my own hometown of Padrón."

I had never in my life seen such a thing, but I had to admit it looked absolutely scrumptious.

Ethan said, "Green pepper sorbet? Really?"

"Trust me," Albert said, giving each of us a spoon. "It is delicious!"

Ethan looked at me, a little hesitant. "Well, I'm game if you are."

I dipped my spoon into one of the mounds and tried it. There was an immediate tangy sweetness, almost like a key lime, and then there was a good spicy kick. It literally put a smile on my face.

I nodded at Ethan as I scooped up another spoonful. "Oh my gosh, it's so good. Alfred, you're a genius."

Alfred smiled at me and folded his burly arms across his chest. "I am always telling him this, but he doesn't believe me. You Americans, you are always afraid to try new things."

I tried to impress him with my worldliness. "It's such a beautiful color of green, too—the same color as René the Frog."

Ethan looked puzzled. "René the Frog?"

I glanced up at Alfred for support, but he looked just as confused as Ethan. I said, "You know, like Kermit the Frog, but in Spain you call him René."

Alfred nodded. "Oh yes! Kermit the Frog! But in Spain, we do not call him René. We call him Gustavo."

I was just about to take another spoonful of sorbet. "Huh?"

"Gustavo the Frog."

"You don't call him René?"

"No, miss, I have never heard this before."

"Are you sure?"

"Yes, *la rana* Gustavo! My daughter, she loves this frog very much. Now, I want to tell you that everything on the menu is very good, if I do say so myself, but I especially recommend the red snapper, which is served on a bed of roasted fennel, and we also have some very fine stone crab dipped in garlic butter. Have a look at the menu, and I will send Paolo over to take your order. Dixie, it was a very great pleasure to meet you."

I nodded. "Thank you so much for the sorbet."

I watched him as he made his way through the dining room toward the kitchen, shaking hands and saying hello to other diners as he went.

Ethan said, "Dixie? You okay?"

I realized I was watching Alfred walk away with my mouth hanging open. "Well, I'm not sure. Remember when I asked you about my friend? The one that was helping that illegal immigrant?"

"Yes?"

"Well, that was actually me."

"You're an illegal immigrant?"

"No, dummy! I was the one helping her."

He grinned. "Yeah, I knew that."

"I figured. Thank you for playing along."

He reached out and put his hand on top of mine. "You're welcome."

I told him the whole story of how we found Corina in the woods with a newborn baby and took her to Joyce's house, and all about the exotic bird that had miraculously come back to life. He listened without interrupting me once. I love a man that knows how to listen.

"The problem is: Corina told me she was from Spain. She said in Spain, Kermit the Frog is known as René."

"So . . . she lied."

"Yep. I had a feeling at the time that she wasn't telling the truth."

Ethan shrugged. "Look, she probably snuck into the country from Cuba. She's just protecting herself."

"Well, there's something else. Joyce found ten thousand dollars in Corina's purse."

Ethan's eyes widened. "Ten thousand dollars—cash?"

"Yeah."

"Wow. Okay. That's a lot of cash to be carrying around, homeless or not."

"I know. And you know what I think? I think it was payment for whoever smuggled her here. I think somehow she snuck away without paying them and now they're looking for her, and that's why she didn't check into a hotel or go to the emergency room. She knew she wouldn't be safe."

Ethan nodded solemnly and looked down at his menu.

I said, "I'm sorry. I didn't mean to talk all night about all this."

"No, no, it's okay. I'm just . . . Look, it's none of my business, but if you're right about Corina, I'm a little worried, that's all." He leaned forward and lowered his voice. "I've worked on a couple of cases where smuggling operations were involved, and to be completely frank with you, some of the shit these guys are up to is pretty fucking scary."

I blinked a couple of times. I realized I'd never even heard Ethan say "darn" before, and I'm embarrassed to admit that at that very moment I felt my nipples perk up. In my book, a man that doesn't cuss is sexy, but when that man lets a couple of cuss words slip out in the heat of the moment, it's not just sexy. It's *damn* sexy.

Dinner was nothing short of exquisite. I had a filet of salmon, which had been seared to perfection on an open wood grill. When the waiter set it on the table, I gasped.

Really. It came with a side of thinly sliced red cabbage sprinkled with coarse black pepper, lime juice, and olive oil. Next to that was a little bird's nest of the thinnest, crispiest french fries I've ever had the pleasure of putting in my mouth. I actually felt like I was cheating on Tanisha as I ate them.

Ethan had the red snapper, which looked absolutely delicious, but I was so taken with my dinner that I refused to insult it by having even a tiny bite of Ethan's.

By the time we finished dessert, which was a beautiful yellow Spanish flan with a crispy flamed crust of caramelized sugar and a dollop of freshly whipped cream on top, it was well after eleven o'clock. Also, I'd had at least four glasses of wine. Big red-wine glasses, the size of cereal bowls. I'm not much of a drinker, and red wine especially goes straight to my head, so by the time we were ready to leave, I was as relaxed as a limp cat soaking up sunshine on a redbrick porch. I was as loose as a black snake drooping out of a tree. Floppy as a worn-out pair of flip-flops. In other words, I was hammered.

Luckily, I'd had the forethought to call my friend Pete Madeira to take my appointments the following morning. Pete sometimes fills in for me when my schedule gets a little too busy, and since I'd suspected I might be staying out pretty late, I figured it couldn't hurt to give myself a break and take part of the morning off. I didn't feel too guilty about it, especially since it would be Saturday, and my schedule is always slower on the weekends. Plus, Pete is retired and always looking for things to do, so he jumped at the chance. I knew my pets would be well taken care of in his hands.

There were only a few people left in the restaurant when we said goodnight to Alfred and thanked him for the lovely meal. He and Alfred shook hands and then hugged good-bye. Outside, the night air was warm; there was a slight breeze coming in from the Gulf and the palmettos were waving gently.

I think I must have been waving gently, too, because Ethan took me by the hand and led me down the sidewalk toward his car.

Pointing behind us, I said, "Wait, my car ish back there."

"Yes, I know that, but you're not driving it."

I said, "Oh, no way. I'm not going home with you tonight, so jusht forget it."

He laughed. "I know you're not going home with me. I'm driving you home, and we'll get your car tomorrow."

I was in no condition to argue. Plus, he looked so cute, I would have jumped through hoops for him if he wanted me to. Then I imagined myself actually jumping through hoops in my low-cut purple dress and my high heels, and that threw me into a giggling fit. Almost as soon as we got in Ethan's car, I leaned my head on his shoulder and instantly fell asleep.

I woke to the familiar sound of car wheels on my crushed-shell driveway. My head was still plopped over on Ethan's shoulder, and I shuddered at the thought that I might have drooled all down the front of his nice jacket, but luckily it looked fine and he didn't seem to be utterly disgusted with me. In fact, he smiled sweetly when I raised my head and looked around.

"You were sound asleep."

"Oh, no. How completely embarrassing."

"No, not at all. You only snored just a little bit."

I punched him in the arm and hoped to God he was kidding. As we pulled into the carport, I was relieved to see there were no other cars. I could just imagine the teasing I would have gotten from Michael and Paco if they'd been home to see me arrive completely snoggered and holding on to Ethan for dear life. I wasn't sure if Paco would be home later, but I knew Michael's shift at the firehouse would be ending at midnight, so by the time he got home I'd be in bed, all alone and fast asleep.

I was just about to turn to Ethan and thank him for a truly wonderful evening and apologize for downing so much red wine when I heard him saying my name.

"Dixie."

"Huh?"

"Dixie. You're home."

I opened my eyes and found Ethan looking down and grinning at me. We were on my balcony in front of my door. He was holding me in his arms. He had carried me all the way across the courtyard and up the stairs.

I shook my head and wailed, "You have got to be kidding me. You had to carry me to my door?"

He looked down at me, and his grin widened. I felt myself falling into his big brown eyes. He bent down to kiss me, and just before my lips touched his he said, "Front door service, ma'am."

18

I opened my eyes and tried to get my bearings. It was dark, and as I looked around the room trying to figure out where I was, I realized I was holding on to something. I looked down to find Ethan's hand in mine. We were both lying on top of the bedspread in my bedroom. Our heads were barely touching, and our bodies were laid out at almost a ninety-degree angle to each other.

Ethan was sound asleep with his legs dangling halfway off the side of the bed. He was still wearing his dinner jacket, his tie still wrapped loosely around his neck, and I, thankfully, was still wearing my purple evening dress. I raised my head up and looked down at my feet. No shoes.

Then I heard it—a very faint knock on the front door. I sat up so fast that Ethan nearly bounced right off the bed.

He said, "What! What happened!"

"Shhh. There's someone knocking at the door."

"Jesus, what time is it?"

I looked at the clock on my bedside table. "It's three in the morning."

All kinds of thoughts flew through my head. It might have been Michael getting home from his shift. He might have seen Ethan's car in the driveway and gotten worried, although it would have been unlike him to just come up the stairs and knock on the door. He was bound to know that would scare the living daylights out of me. He would have tried to call first. The other thought I had was: What if there actually were some bad-ass thugs out looking for Corina, and what if they'd talked to that doctor and gotten my name and tracked me down and were here to either collect Corina or their ten thousand dollars or both?

I reached over and opened the drawer under my bed. When I left the force, I turned in my department-issued gun, a 9 mm SIG SAUER, but every law enforcement officer keeps a backup, and I still had mine: a Smith & Wesson .38. I keep it inside a specially made case next to Todd's 9 mm Glock, which hasn't been touched since he died. I pulled the .38 out of its black velvet niche and slid the drawer closed.

Ethan's eyes widened. "Uh, is that really necessary?"

I whispered, "You're the one who said Corina could be mixed up with some bad-ass thugs. What if they're here looking for her? I'll see who it is. You stay here."

His jaw dropped open. "What? Fuck that! No way in hell am I staying here. I'm coming with you."

Suddenly my sweet man that never cussed was developing the mouth of a drunken sailor, but I decided to address that later. We tiptoed into the living room. Standing at the French doors was a dark shadow in the shape of a man, silhouetted by the light from the porch. As I crept forward, my gun raised at the ready, the man knocked again, very lightly. I felt a shiver go down the entire length of my body. Ethan had pulled out his phone and was about to call 911 when the man stepped back a bit to look down the stairs and the porch light illuminated his face. I recognized him immediately. It was Kenny Newman.

I made a motion to Ethan to wait before he called the police and crept closer to the door.

I said, "What do you want?"

"Dixie, it's me, Kenny."

"I know, Kenny. What do you want?"

"Please, I need to talk to you."

"What you need to do is turn yourself in to the police."

I looked over at Ethan. He still had the phone poised to dial and was staring at me wide-eyed. *This poor man*, I thought. *He has no idea what he's getting himself into hanging out with me.*

He whispered, "Who is Kenny?"

"It's okay. He works for me, but he's got himself in some trouble."

Ethan threw his palms open. "What kind of trouble?"

Kenny said, "Dixie, please. I'll go to the police. I'll do whatever you want me to do. I just need to talk to you first."

I said, "Okay, Kenny. I'm going to open the door, but I'm not alone, and I have a gun."

Ethan whispered, "Dixie! You sure about this?"

I turned to him and took a deep breath. "Thursday morning I found one of my clients drowned in a swimming pool. Kenny was his pool man, and the police have been looking for him ever since. I didn't tell you because I didn't want to talk about it for our whole date. I know Kenny didn't do it. At least I'm pretty sure he didn't. He had other reasons to run away, which I can explain later. Okay?"

Ethan's eyebrows were raised halfway up his forehead, and his arms were hanging limply at his sides. He nodded slowly and sighed. "Okay. I'll have to trust you on this one."

He switched on the lamp by the couch, and I reached out and unlocked the door, keeping my gun down but in plain view so Kenny would see it right away. I nodded at Ethan, as if to say "Ready?" and he smiled feebly and nodded back. I swung the door open.

Kenny stood in the doorway, his shoulders slumped forward, a complete and utter mess. He wore a wrinkled plaid work shirt and scuffed cargo pants that were rolled up at the ankles. His beachy good looks seemed to have been worried away, and he looked like he'd aged ten years. His eyes were bloodshot and swollen.

He glanced down at the gun hanging at my side. "You think I killed him, too."

As his eyes welled with tears, I said, "Kenny, I don't know what to think anymore, but I do know that you need to turn yourself in to the police."

"I know it. I just needed to talk to you first." He looked over my shoulder at Ethan. "I'm sorry."

Ethan nodded. "It's okay, man."

I said, "Come in and we'll talk, but then you're going straight to the police."

Ethan pulled a chair over for Kenny and sat down on the couch with me. Kenny slumped down in his chair.

I said, "First of all, is Becca okay?"

"I don't know. We had a fight, and I haven't talked to her in days. I was going to ask you how she was."

"Kenny, Becca's been missing since we found Mr. Harwick's body."

He looked away for a second, then put his face in his hands and shook his head silently. His ears turned beet red, and tears squeezed out between his fingers and ran down his forearms. I looked over at Ethan, who stood up and grabbed a box of tissues off the kitchen bar. He placed it on the coffee table in front of Kenny and then sat back down next to me.

I said, "Tell me what's going on."

With his face still buried in his hands, he said, "Oh, man, I don't even know where to start."

Ethan said, "Just start at the beginning."

Kenny nodded and sat up, trying to compose himself. He let out a half-laugh and wiped his face with the back of his arm. "Okay."

He pulled a scallop-edged black-and-white photo from his breast pocket and laid it on the coffee table in front of him. From my point of view it was upside down, but I could tell it was a portrait. A young man in a white V-neck T-shirt with a crew cut and a rugged, handsome face.

He said, "This is my father. When I was little, he used to get up every day really early with my mom, and they would make breakfast together. She'd make eggs, scrambled or fried or however he wanted them that day, and he would make the coffee and toast. Then he'd come in my room and wake me up. I'd have breakfast with my mom while he got ready for work. He was always dressed in the same thing when he left. Sandals. A V-neck T-shirt and dark blue surfing trunks. We lived in Oceanside, California. His work was two blocks from the ocean. So every morning on his way to work, he'd stop and swim a couple miles. Then he'd get changed into his suit in the car and head off to work. He did that every day for years. Then one day he didn't show up at work. His boss called my mom, and she called the police. They found his car at the beach, and they found his footprints going from his car down to the water, and they found his shirt and sandals in the sand. But there weren't any footprints coming in. They never found his body. Probably sharks got him. I was eight years old."

He paused and rubbed his forehead with the tips of his fingers, like he was trying to massage the memories away. I glanced over at Ethan. He gave me a little wink, which normally I would have thought was completely inappropriate, but it wasn't. It was reassuring.

I said, "Go on, Kenny."

He seemed to have gotten completely lost in his thoughts, and I knew what was happening. I wasn't sure if he'd had a hand in Mr. Harwick's drowning or not, or even if he knew who did, but one thing was certain: It must have tapped in to some locked-away reservoir of emotion deep inside him.

"My mom was devastated. He had bought a huge insurance policy a couple of months before, and he drowned the day it took effect. She got a big payout, enough to pay for me to go to school and for her to live comfortably for the rest of her life. And then the cops got suspicious. They said she must have talked him into getting the life insurance policy and killed him for the money. Eventually they dropped it because there was no proof, but my mom was never the same. One day she made a big pile in the back-yard of all his stuff and every photo of him and set it on fire. She stopped caring about anything, starting taking all kinds of medicine for depression. Ten years later, the first week I left for college, she killed herself. Took a bunch of pills. They found her at the beach where my father drowned. That was in July last year. A month later, I got this in the mail."

He flicked the photo with one finger and it slid across the table, turning right side up as it came to a stop in front of us. The man in the photo did look a little bit like an older version of Kenny. But what I didn't expect, what Kenny must have known I would recognize right away, was that the man in the photo looked remarkably familiar.

I looked up at Kenny with astonishment.

"Yeah," he said. "That's Roy Harwick."

I picked the photo up and studied it closely. It was true. The man in the photo was in fact Mr. Harwick, perhaps twenty or thirty years younger. He had a full head of hair and a virile, ruddy complexion—nothing like Mr. Har-wick now, but the expression in his eyes and the shape of his face were instantly recognizable.

I looked up at Kenny and then back at the photo, and then back at Kenny again. I'd never once considered that there was even the slightest similarity between them. Where Mr. Harwick was a pudgy, balding ball of anger, Kenny was handsome and sun-kissed and thoughtful. But now I could see it. If you clipped back Kenny's long hair and shaved away his scruffy beard, he looked almost exactly like a younger version of Mr. Harwick.

I was beginning to feel like I'd been hit in the head with a two-by-four. "Kenny . . . what are you telling us?"

He let out a long sigh. "I'm telling you that Roy Harwick was my father."

19

Kenny had laced his fingers behind his neck and was staring up at the ceiling. I had about a million questions for him, but if what he had just said was true, I couldn't even begin to imagine what kind of pain he must have been in. He had lost his father at a tender age, and then his mother to suicide, and now he had lost his father all over again. I knew what it was like to be young and lose a parent, but this was something completely out of my league.

Softly, I said, "Kenny, I'm sorry."

He nodded. "That picture was in the first letter I ever got from him. At first he said he was my uncle. He said he'd read about my mother and he just wanted to know if I was okay. So I wrote him back, even though I knew something wasn't right. Nobody had ever mentioned I had an uncle. Eventually I started to figure it out, and he finally admitted who he was. It turned out he had planned his escape for months. The day he disappeared, he drove to the beach in the morning like he always did. He made sure he got there bright and early so nobody would see him. He parked his car and went down to the water. He left his shirt and sandals in the sand, but this time he took a change of clothes, wrapped up in a plastic bag and covered with tape. Then he walked out into the water a couple feet deep and trekked three miles up the coast, staying in the water and off the beach the whole time. When he figured he'd gone far enough, he came up on the beach, put on dry clothes, and hitchhiked out of town. He traveled all over the country for a couple of years, doing odd jobs and fooling around with girls. Finally he wound up here in Sarasota, got married, and never left again."

Ethan said, "Wow. That's heavy."

Kenny laughed sadly and shook his head. "I know. It's crazy."

"So, why did he get in touch with you?"

He shrugged. "Guilt. He felt guilty, and he wanted to make it up to me somehow."

We sat there for a few moments in silence. I wanted to believe him, as far-fetched as his story was, but there was still one thing I didn't understand. I was almost afraid to ask, because I didn't think I was going to like the answer.

I said, "Kenny, why did you come to Siesta Key?"

He shook his head. "I wanted to see him. I wanted to know who he was. I . . . I wanted to know *why*. Why did he leave us? I wanted him to look me in the face and explain it, man to man. I mean, I get it—he wanted to run away. Everybody feels like that once in a while, right? But how could he just leave his family like that? I felt like I couldn't go on with my life until I had an answer. So one day I just packed up my truck and drove down here. I didn't tell anybody where I was going."

"But how did you find him?"

"It was easy. The return address on his letters was always the same—a post office box in Siesta Key. There's only one post office here. So I just hung out in the parking lot until I saw somebody that looked familiar, and then I followed him home."

He picked up the photo and slipped it back into his breast pocket. "At first he had written that he lived like a bum, slept on the beach, jumped from job to job, didn't have any friends. But eventually he admitted that was a lie, too. Turned out he was filthy rich and he wanted to make it up to me. He said his stepkids were worthless and I could have it all. It was too late to change what he had done, but at least he could set me up for life. He wanted to buy me a house and everything."

I frowned. "So that's why you're here."

He shook his head. "No. No way. I didn't come here to get rich."

"Then why did you pretend to be a pool cleaner and work your way into his home?"

"I didn't pretend. I was broke. I started cleaning pools because I didn't have enough money to get back to California. So I made up some flyers saying I cleaned pools and could do odd jobs and started leaving them around town. One day this dude calls me up and asks if I can clean his pool, somebody had referred me. When he gave me his address I knew right away. It was Roy Harwick."

I said, "And you never told him who you were?"

"No. I was going to. But things got a little complicated . . ."

"You mean Becca."

Kenny's face flushed red as he looked down at his hands.
"Yeah. Becca."

Ethan turned to me and whispered, "Who's Becca?"

"Mr. Harwick's daughter. She's pregnant."

He nodded. "Ah, of course."

I could tell Ethan was getting a little impatient with the
whole story, and to be honest so was I. Kenny must have
wanted something more from the Harwicks. Why else
would he come all this way and infiltrate himself into their
home, not to mention their daughter?

"So when was the last time you saw your father?"

He looked down at the floor, struggling to keep his
emotions under control. "It was at his house. The night
before you found him."

I shook my head. "No, Kenny. You're lying. Mr. and
Mrs. Harwick were in Tampa that night."

He let out a little laugh. "Really? Well, as soon as he heard
what I had to say, he came right back home, didn't he?"

For the first time I could feel his anger, not just at Mr.
Harwick but at the world. I think I would probably have
felt the same. If he was telling the truth, his father's selfishness had triggered a chain of events that led to his
mother's suicide. He had already grieved away his child-
hood over the drowning of his father, and now it looked
like he was going to have to do it all over again.

I said, "What did you say to him?"

"When he answered the phone I said, 'Mr. Harwick, my

name isn't Kenny. It's Daniel. Daniel Imperiori. I'm your son.'"

The human brain is such an amazing thing. It's constantly absorbing new things and adapting and changing. Scientists have even proven that a person's intelligence isn't some static constant, like an IQ number, but something that can be improved just by giving it the right combination of food, rest, and exercise. It's like a kitten—but kittens can be very predictable. I guarantee that if you wiggle the tip of a peacock feather in front of a kitten, some magical unseen force will immediately take over, and that kitten will pounce on that feather without a moment's thought.

It's kind of the same with the human brain. It can be pretty predictable, too. As a cop, I learned to recognize certain signals that people give off when they're being less than honest. For example, if you're making something up that's not true, nine times out of ten your eyes will wander to the right without your even knowing it. But if you're telling the truth, trying to remember something that actually happened, most of the time your eyes will wander to the left. As Kenny remembered his conversation with Mr. Harwick, I noticed his eyes. He wasn't lying.

"What was his reaction when you told him who you were?"

"Nothing at first. I started to think he was going to hang up on me. Then he said, 'What do you want?' I told him I wanted to talk and that it couldn't wait, so he said to meet him at his house that night. He was whispering, so I knew he didn't want Mrs. Harwick to know about it."

"What time did you meet him?"

"Late. When I left it was almost midnight."

His words hung in the air. I knew Ethan and I were both silently thinking the same thing: *And where exactly was Mr. Harwick when you left?*

He looked from me to Ethan and then back again. "Look. I didn't kill him. I know what you must think, but it's not like I planned it to happen this way. I admit—it was totally cool to be able to watch him, to be right there under his nose. But once I saw what kind of person he was, the way he treated people, the way he made his money, I didn't want anything to do with him. I was sorry I ever met him. Dixie, you have to believe me."

I said, "I understand, but you're going to have a tough time convincing the police of that. Mr. Harwick was a very wealthy man. You show up, his only living son, the abandoned heir to his fortune, and then all of a sudden he's found dead in the bottom of a swimming pool and you were the last person to see him. It's a little hard to believe you wouldn't want all that money."

"Yeah, that's what he said, too. But I'm not stupid. I know what Sonnebrook is, and I don't want anything to do with that crap. I told him he could take his money and rot in hell—" He stopped himself and took a deep breath.

I glanced over at Ethan, and he looked at me out of the corner of his eye.

Kenny regained himself and said, "So that's why I gave him everything."

"Gave him what?"

"A big envelope with all the letters he sent me. All the letters where he admitted he was my father, where he said he wanted to leave everything to me. All of it. There were even checks he sent me that I never cashed. The only thing I kept was this photo, just to remind me of what could have been. He said he didn't care. He could still leave his money to me and I couldn't stop him. I said, 'If there's anything I learned from you, it's how to disappear. So good luck with that.' Then I left."

I said, "Okay. Kenny, or Daniel . . . what am I supposed to call you?"

He shrugged. "Doesn't matter anymore. Just call me Kenny. I'm used to it now."

"You're going to leave here, and you're going straight to the police. I'll back your story up. If you tell them everything you've told us, they'll believe you."

Kenny nodded. "You have to promise me one thing, though. That message I left on your machine. When I said I was about to do something big, I was talking about leaving town. I was going to leave those letters, say good-bye to Becca, and disappear."

"It's okay. I figured that out."

"That's why I wanted to talk to you. If the police get ahold of that tape, they'll think it's a confession. They'll think I planned it all along. They can't ever hear it."

I wasn't sure what to say. I believed everything he had told us, or at least, I believed *he* believed everything he had told us. I believed his father had disappeared in the ocean when he was a child. I believed his mother had committed suicide on the beach where his father had disappeared a decade earlier. I think I even believed that his father was in fact Mr. Harwick. Still, there was a rage in Kenny, bubbling just beneath the surface, that I had never seen before. I couldn't be sure that even he was aware of the kind of power that rage might have over him—the kind of power that could make him capable of murder.

Ethan cleared his throat and leaned forward, resting his elbows on his knees. "Okay, this is where I come in. As an attorney, I can tell you without a doubt that you won't be doing yourself any favors if you try to hide anything from the police. I'm sure Dixie would love to make that promise to you right now, but you've got to face the facts: If the detectives don't already have a record of every phone call you made in the days leading up to the murder, they soon will. They'll see right through it. You'll just be digging yourself in a hole that you can't get out of."

Kenny looked at me, and I tried to reassure him with a smile and a nod, but inside I was thinking, *Yeah. What he said.*

By the time Ethan and I watched Kenny descend the stairs down to the driveway and disappear into the night, it was just after 4:00 A.M., my normal rise and shine. I looked up at the moon and said a little prayer of thanks to the powers that be for giving me the forethought to ask Pete Madeira to cover my pet visits for the morning. We stepped back inside and shut the French doors. I looked at Ethan and he looked at me, and we both let out a huge sigh of relief.

I said, "Well, there's not much point in you going home now. The sun will be up soon."

He collapsed onto the couch. "I have to be at work in a few hours, and we still have to get your car."

"But it's Saturday. You still have to go to work?"

"Yep. Unfortunately."

"Well, I can bike into town later and get my car, so don't worry about that." I sat down on the edge of the coffee table and crossed my arms over my chest. "I'm sorry."

"For what?"

"For getting you involved in all this."

He grinned. "Dixie, how long have we known each other?"

"I don't know. A long time."

He reached out and pulled me toward him. "Yeah. Long enough for me to know better."

20

I opened my front door a crack and squinted at the bright morning light slanting in through the trees. Michael and Paco were sitting out on the deck at the table my grandfather built when we were kids. They had laid out a breakfast fit for a king. There was hot coffee, freshly squeezed orange juice, a bowl of locally grown strawberries and blackberries, and a platter heaped with glistening slices of cantaloupe, mango, and kiwi. Holding court at the center of the table was a basket of Michael's freshly baked scones, still warm from the oven. I was only just a little bit disappointed not to see a platter of bacon, but since I was apparently going to be seeing more of Ethan from now on, I figured I could do without it. A moment on the lips, a lifetime on the hips, my grandmother always said.

It all looked so good I practically skipped down the stairs and across the deck to the table. I could tell by their empty plates that Michael and Paco had already eaten, but waiting at my seat was an absolutely yummy-looking slice of spinach and mushroom quiche, lying on a bed of bright green baby lettuce. I couldn't remember the last time I'd been able to stay in bed this late, and I was pretty confident Michael and Paco had both been fast asleep when Ethan left for work. Not that I was trying to hide anything. I can do what I want. I'm a grown, mature woman, sort of.

In fact, Michael and Paco had been encouraging me to go out with Ethan for months, so I knew they'd probably be pretty happy about it, but I just wasn't in the mood to be bombarded with a hundred and one questions.

Turns out I was out of luck. The moment I saw the looks on their faces, not to mention the stack of newspapers spread out in front of them, I knew I was in for a good ol' session of Q and A with M and P.

Of course they had read all about Mr. Harwick's death, and now there were a number of articles in the paper with my name in them, and a quote from the police department saying there was a search under way for the primary person of interest: Kenny Newman, the Harwicks' pool man. I told Michael and Paco the whole story of everything that had happened, excluding Kenny's revelation about his father. I did tell them that Becca had revealed to me that she was pregnant, and that both of them had been missing ever since Mr. Harwick's body was discovered.

Michael and Paco sat quietly and listened, except when I was describing the ordeal of pulling Mr. Harwick out of the pool and trying to revive him. I must have looked pretty shaken, because Michael got up and came around the table and put his hands on my shoulders.

When I was finished, we all sat for a while in silence. Finally Paco said, "So, Michael, I think we should all agree right now to not ever say 'I told you so' about Kenny Newman."

Michael squeezed my shoulders and said, "Yeah. I totally agree, we should definitely not ever say 'I told you so' about that guy."

I rolled my eyes and said, "Hilarious," but I knew their teasing was only meant to make me feel better about the whole thing. In fact, I was pleasantly surprised that Michael wasn't more upset—I hoped it meant that he was beginning to feel a little less responsible for looking out for me all the time. He had a few gray hairs mixed in with the blond, and I knew every one of them had my name on it.

Paco said, "So still no sign of him, huh?"

"Not exactly."

Michael said, "What do you mean, not exactly? You know where he is?"

I took a bite of quiche and reveled in its buttery, cheesy deliciousness for a couple of moments. "Not really, but he paid me a visit last night."

Michael's voice rose. "What? He was here? Goddammit, Dixie, what were you thinking?"

"Michael, I know this is going to be hard for you to understand, but I just don't think Kenny Newman is a dangerous person."

Michael started to interrupt, but I cut him off. "I know what you guys think about him, and I agree it doesn't look good that he disappeared after Mr. Harwick died, but he has an explanation for all of it, and I think I believe him."

Michael took a deep breath. "Okay, I'm sorry. So what did he want with you?"

"He wanted to talk to me about a message he left on my answering machine the night before I found Mr. Harwick. He was worried that if I turned it over to the police, they'd think it was a confession."

I could tell Michael was getting a little more agitated. He rolled his eyes and said, "Oh, great. I can't wait to hear this. What was the message?"

I sighed. "He said he was about to do something. Something big. And that he was sorry."

Michael sat back down and rubbed his temples with the tips of his fingers. "Dixie . . ."

"I know, I know, I know," I said. "But there's something else, something that explains why Kenny has led such a secretive life here."

Michael raised his eyebrows. "What is that?"

I said, "Mr. Harwick is Kenny's father."

Michael had just taken a sip of coffee and almost spit it out all over the table. "What? How is that even possible?"

I told them Kenny's entire story, and even Michael, who's about the most skeptical person I've ever known, had to admit it was almost too crazy to make up. He also brought up a point I hadn't thought of before: Even though Kenny worked for me, he didn't have anything to gain by explaining himself. If he had been planning on murdering Mr. Harwick, why would he have called me first to warn me about it? Any fool would know that would've aroused suspicion about him right away.

I felt a sense of relief that Michael saw some logic in the

whole thing. So much had happened in the last forty-eight hours I wasn't sure I still had the ability to see straight. I was grateful he didn't think I'd finally gone off the deep end.

Paco had grown more and more quiet the whole time we'd been talking. Now he was holding his newspaper out in front of him, taking an occasional sip from his coffee cup.

I said, "Paco, what do you think?"

He lowered the paper. "Hmm?"

We both saw it in his eyes immediately. Paco's not normally one to hold back his opinions, especially when it comes to matters of law and order. There was a reason he wasn't chiming in with his thoughts. He knew something.

I said, "What did you think of Kenny's story about Mr. Harwick?"

He nodded nonchalantly. "Yeah. Sounds about right to me," he said and went back to his paper.

Michael and I shared a look. As a member of the special crimes unit, Paco has a lot of experience with all kinds of investigations. One week he might be meeting with an informant to root out an illegal narcotics ring, and the next he might be working undercover as a temp in a law firm, gathering evidence for a corporate fraud investigation. If he was somehow involved in an investigation into the affairs of Sonnebrook or the Harwick family, that was about as much as we would get out of him.

Michael turned to me. "So please tell me Kenny isn't running out of town."

"No. By now he's turned himself over to the police. I made him promise he'd go straight there after we talked."

He sighed. "Good. So your work is done. Right?"
I bit into a juicy slice of mango. *"Right."*

Weekends are usually busy on the Key, especially on a nice day. I was riding my bike up Midnight Pass, and I thought to myself, *It's not just a nice day. It's a* glorious *day.* The sky was a deep periwinkle blue, there wasn't a cloud in sight, and the sun felt warm and healing on my body. The road was chock-full of cars and joggers and couples on bicycles. Every twenty feet or so I passed a family or a group of kids, all draped in towels and carrying chairs and coolers to the beach.

Right before I got to the village center I took a quick detour down a side lane so I could ride by a pair of ancient magnolia trees. They've been there for about as long as I can remember, and I always make a point of going by them when I'm on my bike. They were in full bloom, their white cuplike blossoms tilted toward the sun. Their heady, sweet perfume was so powerful I could taste it on my tongue.

I pedaled into town and found the Bronco right where I'd left it the night before, parked just a couple of doors down from Yolanda, which was in the midst of a bustling brunch crowd. There were six or seven tables on the sidewalk outside, and I saw Alfred bringing out a tray of drinks. I indulged myself in a tiny fantasy in which Ethan and I were sitting at one of the tables sharing a frozen margarita. Something about having a margarita in the middle of the day always seems so decadent and wrong. I resolved to make that happen with Ethan as soon as possible.

I threw my bike into the back of the Bronco and headed

over to Tom Hale's condo. I knew Pete had been by there earlier and let Billy Elliot out to do his business, but I had a feeling that Billy might not have gotten a good run in— Pete's knees aren't what they used to be. So I thought I'd stop by and take him for a short whirl around the parking lot. Plus, I had some other business I wanted to get Tom's help with.

The entire way over I couldn't get Ethan out of my head. Every time I blinked I saw his deep brown eyes looking into mine, and when I gripped the steering wheel and turned the Bronco into the parking lot at Tom's, I could feel the back of his neck in my hands. I looked at myself in the mirror as I rode up the elevator to Tom's apartment. For somebody who'd been drunk the night before and barely slept a wink, I didn't look too bad, if I do say so myself.

I tapped on the door and opened it a peek. "Tom?"

"I'm back here, Dixie."

I found Tom sitting in his wheelchair at the dining table with his laptop and a stack of papers laid out in front of him. Billy Elliot came racing to the door to greet me as I came in.

Tom took off his glasses. "Hey, we missed you this morning. You know Pete stopped by already, right?"

"I know. I'm sorry, Tom. I had a busy schedule today, so I had to ask Pete to fill in for me, but I thought I'd take Billy Elliot out for a jog if that's okay."

"Not a problem at all. We thought maybe you were sleeping in because you had a big date last night."

Before I could stop myself, I said, "What? Who said that?" at about the highest, shrillest level my voice is capable of.

Tom's eyes widened. "Whoa, I was kidding there, Dixie, but looks like maybe I hit on something."

I pulled a couple of wandering strands of hair away from my face and smoothed them over my ears. "No, not at all, I'm just surprised because . . . because . . ."

He was grinning, and I'm sure my eyes were wandering willy-nilly all over their sockets as I searched for some plausible reason to be yelling like a howler monkey.

"Okay, fine. I had a date last night. Big deal!"

He chuckled. "Hey, I'm pretty good, huh? Maybe I should be a private detective."

I said, "Huh. Funny you should mention that, because I actually have some detective work for you. I was talking to a friend of mine, and she told me that in Spain, Kermit the Frog is known as René, but last night I was at a Spanish restaurant, and the owner told me that in Spain they call him something different."

Tom put his glasses on and slid his laptop over. "Hmmm, let's see."

His fingers clicked away at the keyboard. I've always been resistant to computers, or anything electronic, for that matter. I think I was the last person I know to even get a cell phone. I held out for as long as I could, but eventually I realized the whole world was going to leave me in the dust if I didn't break down and get one. I was beginning to feel that way about computers.

Tom said, "Yep, he was right. They call him Gustavo in Spain."

"Huh."

He scrolled through a couple more screens. "That's funny. Why don't they just call him Kermit?"

I shrugged. "Beats me. I guess the name Kermit doesn't translate right in Spain for some reason."

Billy Elliot came trotting up and dropped his leash at my feet. I think he'd had enough talk about Kermit the Frog for now. I clipped his leash on his collar while he wagged his tail like a helicopter blade.

"Alright, Mr. Elliot, let's go out for a spin, okay?"

He wiggled his whole body with excitement, and we started for the door.

Tom was still looking at his computer screen. "Yeah, here it is. This says Kermit the Frog is called René in Guatemala."

I slid to a stop, and Billy Elliot looked back at me.

"Huh?"

He squinted at the screen. "Yep. Guatemala. Your friend just had it mixed up. They call him René in Guatemala."

As Billy Elliot raced around the circular driveway pulling me behind him, my thoughts raced around what Tom had just told me. Instead of feeling I knew more about Corina now, I actually felt like I knew less. I had one pretty good reason why she might lie about where she was from, but I didn't want to admit it to myself. At least not yet. So I racked my brain trying to come up with an explanation.

Why would she lie? Spain sounds glamorous, but then so does Guatemala. Hell, I've never been outside Florida, so Peoria, Illinois, sounds pretty glamorous to me. Was it possible that perhaps she'd just misunderstood what we were talking about? Maybe she was just struggling with the language?

No. I knew I was only fooling myself, and the sooner I owned up to it the better.

The question to ask was: What next? I wasn't completely sure, but I knew I needed to get over to Joyce's and talk to her as soon as possible.

As usual, Billy Elliot and I rode up in the elevator panting like two rabid hyenas. I gave him a pat on the rump and told him he was a good boy, then hung his leash up in the hallway and called out to Tom.

"Thanks for the research, Tom! See you later."

He said, "Hey, hold on a minute. You never told me about your hot date last night."

As I closed the door I called out, "I know!"

I raced over to Joyce's house, trying to figure out what my game plan was. I figured she'd be upset when I told her what I thought. She and Henry the VIII had a nice life they'd set up for themselves, but I knew having Corina and the baby in the house had given their little family a much-needed jolt of excitement. Plus, I think she enjoyed having the feeling that there were people at home who needed her.

I slowed down again as I approached the place in the park where we first saw Corina. Just as I passed, a homeless man in a filthy yellow tank top and dirty white shorts stepped out of the bushes. His skin was tanned dark brown, but his face and neck had the shiny red flush of an alcoholic. He had a red bandanna tied around his head to hold his scraggly, sun-bleached hair back, and he was carrying several overstuffed garbage bags and a milk carton. He waved as I went by, and I sheepishly waved back.

As I pulled into the driveway, Joyce was unloading groceries out of the backseat of her station wagon.

She waved as I got out of the Bronco and walked over. "Whew! Perfect timing! You can help me carry all this stuff in."

Her backseat was filled with packs of bottled water and groceries, and there was a big fat watermelon strapped into the baby chair.

I said, "Joyce. Before we go in, there's something we need to talk about. Is Corina here?"

"Sure. She's taking a nap with Dixie Joyce. What's the matter?"

"Good. I need to tell you something about her, and I don't think you're going to like it."

She frowned and set the bag of groceries she was holding down on the hood of the car. "Hmm, that doesn't sound good."

"Well, I could be wrong—but it's something we have to consider."

She leaned against the car and folded her arms. "I think I know what you're going to say."

"You do?"

She nodded. "Is it about the bird?"

"Yeah."

"You think Corina was going to sell it."

I nodded. "Joyce, I think she lied when she said she was

from Spain, and she may be poor, but I don't think she's homeless. You said that bird was from Guatemala, right?"

She nodded sadly.

"Well, my friend Tom looked it up—Kermit the Frog isn't called René in Spain, he's called Gustavo."

Joyce looked down and shook her head. "Oh Lord."

"I know. And guess what he's called in Guatemala."

She nodded. "I think I knew all along and I just didn't want to think about it. She was on pins and needles the whole time that bird was at the vet's, and if you'd seen how quickly he took to her . . . it was like he'd known her all his life. "

"I think maybe he has known her all his life. Poachers steal eggs from nests in the wild and then sell them for a profit to people like Corina, who hatch the eggs and raise them by hand. The more exotic and rare the bird, the more it's worth. So Corina smuggles some birds out of Guatemala, sells them to a dealer here in Florida, and that dealer turns around and sells them to collectors and exotic pet stores for a handsome profit. Pound for pound, a bird like René is probably worth more than cocaine, gold, or even diamonds. On the black market, he could easily go for thirty or forty thousand dollars, possibly more."

"So that explains the cash in her purse."

"Yeah. She had probably already sold one bird, and I think she was on her way to deliver René to another dealer that morning we found her, but then there was a little snag in her plans. Remember the doctor said she was at least a month premature?"

Joyce shook her head again. "She probably thought

she'd be back home in Guatemala by the time she had the baby."

"Yeah, and with enough money stashed away to raise her right."

She smiled wanly. "I think maybe we just figured out why they call it a nest egg."

21

Joyce and I were perched shoulder to shoulder on the hood of her car, trying to figure out what we should do about Corina and the resplendent quetzal. I have to admit, I was at a complete and utter loss. I kept waiting for Joyce's inner marine to take over and start handing out orders, but I think she must have been having as much difficulty as I was figuring out what in the world our next step should be.

In spite of everything, I didn't want to make things harder for Corina than they already were, and I knew Joyce was feeling the same way. I kept thinking about what Corina's life must have been like in Guatemala, how terrible the conditions must have been—terrible enough to compel her to take on such a dangerous, high-risk job. And what if she was caught? Smuggling an endangered species from one country to another is an international crime. I shuddered to think what would happen if Corina was arrested. She'd end up in prison, and then where would her baby be? How in the world could she have been so reckless?

But I knew the answer. I would have done the same thing for my daughter if it meant the difference between feeding her or letting her go hungry.

Still, I couldn't ignore the fact that what Corina was doing was not only illegal, it was unethical. It went against everything I believe in. I couldn't just stand by and do nothing while an innocent, endangered animal was passed from person to person for money with little or no regard for its well-being.

Finally we decided the best thing would be to try to convince Corina that what she was doing was wrong, and that if she agreed to stop, we would do everything in our power to help her and her baby, even if that meant letting her stay at Joyce's rent free until she was able to get herself back on her feet.

As for whether or not it was wrong that we weren't immediately reporting Corina to the police, we decided to leave unanswered for now.

Joyce stood up. "Alright, let's get this show on the road. My ice cream is melting."

We unloaded the rest of the groceries and brought them up the walk to the front porch. Joyce pushed the door open with her foot, and Henry the VIII came prancing in from the living room. He raced around our legs barking a mile a minute while we carried everything into the kitchen. I think he must have been trying to tell us what we'd missed while Joyce had been shopping.

I put the last of the bags on the counter, and Joyce fished out a pint of ice cream and put it in the freezer. "The rest of this can wait. I'll go wake her up."

She disappeared down the hall while I sat down on the

couch and braced myself. Henry the VIII jumped into my lap and pawed at my hand, trying to get me to pet him.

From down the hallway, Joyce let out a little laugh and then I heard, *"Ay dios mío."*

As I rubbed Henry the VIII behind the ears, I wondered how angry or afraid Corina would be when she heard what we had to say. I didn't think she was capable of violence, but I also knew that anybody, animal or human, can be pretty unpredictable when backed into a corner. I hoped she would understand that we were only looking out for her best interest, but I wasn't sure how easy it was going to be to get her to see that.

Joyce said, "Hey, Dixie, why don't you come back here?"

Henry the VIII jumped off my lap and went scampering down the hall ahead of me. Joyce was leaning in the doorway of Corina's bedroom with a sad smile on her face.

"She's gone."

The room had been meticulously cleaned. The bedspread was completely smooth, its corners neatly tucked in, and the pillows were leaned up against the headboard with their edges perfectly parallel to one another. Lined up on the edge of the bed and organized in neat piles were all of the things I had bought for the baby. The clothes, the diapers, the creams, the bottles, the blankets. Everything.

On the dresser in front of the mirror was Joyce's antique birdcage. It was as clean as if René had never existed, and inside, leaning against one of the little wooden perches, was a plain white envelope. Joyce opened the cage door and pulled it out. Written in a childish hand on its face were the words I'M SORRY.

We both slumped down on the bed and sat numbly for a minute or so.

Finally Joyce said, "Well, I guess I better open it."

She slid her fingers across the flap of the envelope and took a deep breath.

There was no letter inside.

Just two slightly wrinkled thousand-dollar bills.

I have a theory about cats. It's based on my own ranking system, which I call the Kitty Craziness Factor, or KCF. It measures the level of feline loopiness in a household—like how much racing up and down the stairs there is, or climbing on furniture and pouncing on imaginary mice. The higher the Kitty Craziness Factor, the more loopiness. So in a household where the KCF is high, there might be, for example, spelunking down the living room curtains or skydiving off the refrigerator.

The process of determining the Kitty Craziness Factor is pretty simple. You just count the number of cats. A household with only one cat has a KCF of one. A household with two cats has a KCF of two. A household with three cats has a KCF of seven. I don't know why a household with three cats has more than three times the loopiness of a household with only two cats, but it's a scientific fact.

Betty and Grace Piker were two retired sisters who had a long-standing agreement with each other. If one found a cat and wanted to bring it home, the other would stop her—using physical force if necessary. They had seven cats, all rescues. It wasn't even possible to measure the KCF in their household; it was completely off the charts.

The Piker sisters had gone to Orlando to visit their niece, who had just given birth. They were only staying for the day, so all I needed to do was check on the cats and feed them. The sisters were planning on being back home that evening.

All the cats were napping when I arrived, so things were relatively subdued. I washed out the food bowls and lined them up in a row on the kitchen counter. In each bowl I mixed a cup of dry cat kibble with just a little warm water from the tap. Then I opened the cabinet and pulled out a can of sardines.

Suddenly all seven cats stampeded into the kitchen, circling at my feet and bleating excitedly. I hadn't even opened the can yet. I could swear they knew the sound it made when it clinked down on the countertop.

As I distributed the bowls around the kitchen to give everybody a little elbow room to dine in private, I felt like Dame Wiggins of Lee, a character from one of the books my grandmother used to read to me when I was a little girl. The book had been a gift to me from my brother on my very first birthday. Dame Wiggins had seven wonderful cats that could all cook and sew. When they weren't outside ice-skating on the pond or flying kites, they were inside helping Dame Wiggins of Lee with all her daily chores.

I said, "Anybody want to come home and help me with the laundry?"

There were no takers. They were all too busy concentrating on their yummy sardines to pay me any mind.

While they ate, I did a quick run through the house, righting overturned trash baskets and checking for any other accidents. In the guest bathroom, somebody had made confetti of the toilet paper roll, and there was a scattering of kitty litter that had been pawed out of one of the three litter boxes in the laundry room. They might not have been as neat and tidy as Dame Wiggins of Lee's cats, but they were just as wonderful.

By the time I had cleaned the litter boxes and put everything back in order, everyone was done with dinner and the Kitty Craziness Factor was through the roof. Usually I worry about leaving my pets all alone in their houses— even if I've spent a good chunk of time playing with them— but these guys provided each other with so much attention and exercise that I didn't feel guilty leaving them. In fact, I think if they'd been able to open a can of sardines by themselves, they wouldn't have needed me at all.

I was headed out to the car when my cell phone rang. It was Detective McKenzie. I imagined Kenny had told her his story by now, and she was probably calling to find out what he'd told me and if our stories matched.

Before I answered, I took a deep breath. I wanted to be ready for whatever tricks she had up her sleeve.

"Dixie, I wanted to let you know our crime units are pulling out of the Harwick house now."

I said, "Oh, okay. I guess I can bring the cat back?"

"That's why I'm calling. Mrs. Harwick isn't coming home yet. She's afraid to sleep in the house until the killer has been caught. She's asked if you could continue to feed her fish for a little while longer."

I could tell by the tone in McKenzie's voice that Mrs. Harwick was probably still in a state of shock. If it were me, I don't think I'd ever want to go home again.

The last time we had talked, McKenzie mentioned that a doctor had been called in for Mrs. Harwick, probably to prescribe some sort of sedative to help her sleep. I wanted to know if that had helped at all, but I knew it wasn't my place to ask.

McKenzie said, "Still no word from Kenny Newman?"

I closed my eyes and silently shook my head. "Oh, no."

"What? I'm assuming you've not heard from him?"

I sighed. "Detective McKenzie, he showed up at my apartment late last night. I'm sorry I didn't call you. He promised he was turning himself in as soon as he left. I just assumed he was telling the truth."

There was a slight pause on the line, and then she said, "We need to talk. Where's convenient for you?"

We agreed to meet near the pavilion at Siesta Key Beach. We were alone except for a group of teenagers in swimming trunks and bikinis, huddled around their soft drinks and eating hot dogs at one of the picnic tables. They were tearing little pieces of their hot dog buns and tossing them to the sparrows that were pecking around under the tables.

Detective McKenzie was waiting for me at one of the benches that face the beach. In her plain tan skirt and navy blue blazer, she stood out like a sore thumb. I got the feeling she didn't spend a lot of time on the beach, and she had probably never worn a bikini in her life. She was wearing a pair of big-framed sunglasses, and her frizzy sorrel hair was pulled under a wide-brimmed straw hat, which provided some protection for her pale, freckled skin from the hot afternoon sun.

When I walked up, she stood and shook my hand firmly.

"Thanks for meeting me, Dixie. It's much easier to talk in person than on the phone."

I muttered something vague like "Sure is," but the truth was I didn't want to talk to her at all. For some insane reason I still felt a lingering loyalty to Kenny, some inexplicable desire to protect him, even though he'd given me his word that he would turn himself in to the police as soon as he left my apartment. Apparently he'd had other plans.

As I sat down she said, "First of all, does he have Becca?"

I shook my head sadly. "No. He says he has no idea where she is."

"Alright. And I don't suppose he told you where he's staying."

I shook my head again. "No."

She smiled uncomfortably. "Well, now that we've got that over with. Tell me everything that happened last night."

I told her the entire story, including how Kenny had asked me not to let the police hear the message he'd left on my answering machine. She pulled her clipboard out of her bag and made a few notes as I talked, but she didn't say a word until I got to the part where Kenny said he was Mr. Harwick's son.

She held up one hand to stop me. "Wait a minute. He's been working in the Harwick house for months."

"I know. He was going to tell them who he was, but I think he was scared."

"So he never told them?"

"He did. He called Mr. Harwick."

"When?"

"The night before I found him in the pool."

"Does Mrs. Harwick know about this?"

I said, "I don't think so. Mr. Harwick was whispering on the phone, so Kenny got the impression he was trying to hide it from her. They agreed to meet at the house, and Mr. Harwick drove back from Tampa that night. They met alone. He told Kenny he was sorry, and he wanted to make it up to him. He said he would buy Kenny a house and give him money and put him in his will, but Kenny didn't want anything to do with it. He told Mr. Harwick that he wasn't there for money. He just wanted his father to tell him to his face why he had run away."

She took off her sunglasses and looked me squarely in the eye. "Dixie, let me get this straight. It's the middle of the night. This man who's been missing since Mr. Harwick drowned shows up at your door out of nowhere. You know the police are looking for him. You're all alone. Why in the world would you let him in your house?"

I wasn't sure how to respond, but I suddenly felt my cheeks turning red. "Well . . . I wasn't alone, actually."

She waved her hand like a teacher erasing a chalkboard. "Okay, forget that. Why would you let him in your house *at all*?"

I thought for a moment, but I couldn't come up with a good answer. "It was stupid. I shouldn't have let him in. I guess I trusted him."

She put her sunglasses back on. "Yes, I'm beginning to see that. So how did their meeting end?"

"Kenny told Mr. Harwick he didn't want anything from him, including his money. And to prove it, he gave him an envelope with all the letters that Mr. Harwick had ever sent him, including checks that he never cashed."

I paused for a moment. I knew that what I was about to say was not going to sound good, but I also knew I didn't have a choice. "He also said that he told his father he could take his money and rot in hell. Then he left."

Detective McKenzie frowned. "This packet of letters, did he say where it was?"

"No. He said he gave it to Mr. Harwick before he left."

She nodded. "That's interesting. There was no packet of letters in that house when we searched it."

The teenagers had gone down to the beach and were running in and out of the waves and laughing in that carefree way kids do. A small brown sparrow perched on the table next to ours and pitched a couple of bossy chirps at us. I think he was checking to see if we had any hot dog buns for him.

It was hard to tell what Detective McKenzie was thinking. She had laid her clipboard down in her lap and was resting her hands on it.

"Dixie, tell me what you know about Becca."

"I've only met her a couple of times, but she seems like a sweet girl, just a little in over her head."

"Mrs. Harwick tells me that Becca can be emotional. Does that sound right to you?"

"Yeah, I would say she definitely has a flare for the dramatic."

"And that day you found her crying on the floor in her parents' bathroom, did you wonder why she was there, instead of her own room?"

"No. It's a pretty nice bathroom, and the aquarium is kind of soothing, so I got the impression she spent a lot of time in there."

"Did anything seem strange about her?"

I said, "Other than that she was totally freaking out?"

"I understand she was upset, but the way you described it made me wonder if there wasn't something else going on, something that might have been influencing her behavior."

"You mean . . . like drugs?"

She nodded.

"It's possible. Like I said, I didn't know her before all this, so I couldn't say if the way she was acting was normal for her or not. But she did say her brother had been involved with drugs. That's why he got a job at the golf club, because the Harwicks cut him off when they found out."

She nodded. "Mrs. Harwick mentioned that. She also told me she overheard an argument between Becca and August. Apparently something was missing from August's room, but Becca denied having anything to do with it. Do you know what that might have been about?"

"No. She didn't say anything about that to me."

"Alright, one last thing. I keep going back to your porcupine fish. You didn't notice if it was alarmed that morning you talked to Becca?"

"No, definitely not, I would have remembered that for sure."

"Do you think a loud noise could have caused it to puff up like it did?"

"Definitely. Especially if the noise was nearby."

Detective McKenzie pursed her lips together. I could tell she was making an effort to choose her words carefully.

"Like a scream, for example. Could a scream have set off that kind of reaction?"

I nodded slowly. "I think any loud noise could have set it off."

"Okay. That's helpful."

I looked down at my hands. "Detective McKenzie, do you think Becca is still alive?"

She looked at the water for a long time. Eventually I figured out that she wasn't going to answer me, which was fine. Her silence was answer enough. No matter what had happened the night Kenny met with Mr. Harwick, the fact that Becca had been missing ever since was not a good sign. If she had witnessed what had happened, it was possible that she had been discovered hiding in the bathroom. Becca was tough, but she was still just a teenager and probably not more than a hundred pounds. I don't think she would have been able to defend herself. Whoever killed Mr. Harwick that night might have taken her. Or worse.

Detective McKenzie turned to me and said, "When my husband died, I felt like I was instantly a member of a secret club, where only people who've lost a husband or a wife before their time can understand me. Do you ever feel that way?"

I waited a couple of moments before I answered. "Yeah. I know exactly what you mean. It's like a club you wish you weren't in, but you're glad it's there all the same."

"Yes. That's exactly it. I don't know what it's like to lose a child, Dixie, but I imagine it must be that same feeling, multiplied a million times over."

I nodded. That felt about right.

We sat for a while longer, not talking, just watching the

kids play on the beach. I think we were both thinking the same thing: For every hour that Becca was missing, the odds that she was alive got smaller and smaller.

It was bad enough that Mrs. Harwick was now a card-carrying member of Detective McKenzie's secret club. I hoped with all my heart that she wasn't about to be a member of mine.

I wouldn't wish that on my worst enemy.

22

After Detective McKenzie left, I stayed a while longer and watched the waves crashing in on the beach. Our meeting had left me reeling, and I just needed to sit and rest for a while. There was something about that woman that always made me feel like I'd just lived through a hurricane or run a ten-mile marathon. She was drab and plain on the outside, but on the inside her mind was spinning at about a hundred miles an hour.

I bought a hot dog from the food stand at the beach pavilion and slathered it with hot mustard and relish. By the time I got halfway to the car I'd already downed it, so I went right back and bought another one.

Sitting in the Bronco in the parking lot, I chewed on my second hot dog and tried to sort everything out in my head. McKenzie had hinted that August wasn't the only one in the Harwick family with a drug problem. If Becca had been high on something, I wasn't sure I would have recognized it. I never did drugs when I was a kid, and neither did Michael. Not that I was a goody-two-shoes or anything; it's just that living by the ocean was a good enough high for me. Plus, I'm sure my grandmother would have taken a belt to my backside if she'd ever caught wind of drugs under her roof. My grandmother was a pretty strict guardian, but she never spanked me with a belt, and I wanted to keep it that way.

There was something else bothering me, though. When I mentioned the packet of letters that Kenny had given his father before he left, Detective McKenzie seemed genuinely puzzled, and I didn't think it was some kind of trick she was trying out on me. She had probably known right away what was just now trickling into my brain: Either Mr. Harwick had hidden that packet somewhere in the house before he was killed, or someone had taken it.

Of course, there was one more possibility: that Kenny had made the whole thing up and was playing me. He knew I would report everything he said to the police.

My second hot dog wasn't nearly as satisfying as the first, but I ate it all anyway. Sometimes my stomach doesn't listen to my brain. At Beach Road, I turned left and took the long route around the Key toward the Harwick house. To be honest, I wasn't looking forward to being in that house alone. Up until now it had been filled with crime-scene technicians and police every time I'd gone over, but now it would be empty.

On the way, I called the Kitty Haven. Now that the investigation at the Harwick house was over, I wondered if Charlotte might be happier at home, even if it meant staying there alone. Being in a strange place with so many other cats can be stressful, especially for a cat as grumpy as Charlotte, and sometimes grumps like to be left alone. Believe me, I know that from firsthand experience.

Marge said, "No, she's doing just fine. Not nearly as jittery as she was when you first brought her in. Jaz has been spending lots of time with her, and cats always pick up on the energy of the people around them. You know Jaz, she's always happy."

That was welcome news, not just for Charlotte but for Jaz as well. When I'd first met her, there were a lot of things you might have called Jaz, but happy was not one of them. It seemed working with Marge at the Kitty Haven was doing her a world of good.

I thanked Marge and told her I didn't think it would be much longer before Charlotte could go back home, even though I really didn't know if that was true or not. Detective McKenzie had made me wonder if Mrs. Harwick would ever go back home again. I figured August might be moving back in at some point, but it was entirely possible that he'd be staying with his mother until she was back on her feet.

When I pulled up to the Harwick house, the first thing I noticed was that all the yellow police tape was gone. Luckily for me, the gang of reporters that had been hanging out on the street had finally picked up shop and moved on, too. Until the coroner's report on Mr. Harwick was made public, there wouldn't be anything new to report. They were probably all camped out at Mrs. Harwick's hotel, hoping to get a shot of the fabulously wealthy grieving widow.

When I opened the front door, my heart did a little skip.

The alarm didn't make its familiar beeping sound, which meant someone had turned it off. I immediately had that same creepy feeling I'd had the morning I found Mr. Harwick—that someone was in the house.

I rolled my eyes and said out loud, "Oh, get over it!"

I dropped my ring of keys into its pocket on my backpack and went over to the marble staircase and called up. "August?"

There was nothing but silence.

Then I realized, of course the alarm wasn't on. The crime-scene units had only finished their work today. I doubted they even knew the code to set the alarm.

I let out a big sigh of relief and told myself I needed to stop being so dramatic. But just to be on the safe side, I went back over and locked the front door. That's when I smelled it. Cigarette. Something moved in the corner of my eye. I walked through the main entry where the two Roman statues were standing guard and saw the back of someone's head.

Mrs. Harwick was sitting on the couch in the living room, staring out at the pool. A plume of white smoke was trailing up from a cigarette perched on the edge of the coffee table.

I stepped lightly up to her side. "Mrs. Harwick?"

She turned her head in my direction but didn't look directly at me. "Oh, Dixie. I didn't hear you come in."

"I'm so sorry to interrupt you. I didn't realize anyone was home. I just stopped by to check on the fish."

"Oh, good." She stared blankly ahead, her eyes fixed on the pool area. "The police left a little while ago. I came by to get a few of my things. I was going to send the driver in to get them for me, but at the last minute I changed my mind. I told him to leave me here and come back in an hour."

Her voice was small and distant, as if it were locked away inside a safe.

"Mrs. Harwick, I'm so sorry."

"Oh, thank you, Dixie. I'm sorry, too. That must have been a terrible ordeal for you."

She tilted her head to the side and closed her eyes.

I suddenly realized that I'd completely intruded on her quiet, and more than likely she just wanted to be left alone.

I said, "Well, I'll just check on the fish and then I'll be out of your way."

As I turned to leave, she stopped me.

"It's so odd, isn't it? You think you know people. I've never been very close to my son, August. He's always been a little distant, even when he was a baby. People say that's just the way boys are. Maybe it's true. It's always been Becca that was there when I needed her. But not this time. Not now. Becca's gone. To be honest with you, I think she's gotten herself mixed up with drugs, and now it's August taking care of me. All the paperwork, the police, everything. I don't know what I would do without him."

My first instinct was to tell her I was sure that if Becca could be here she would, which of course was about the dumbest thing I could possibly have ever said. Sometimes my mouth starts running before my brain has any idea what's going on. As my grandmother liked to say, "The wheel is spinning but the gerbil ain't home."

Luckily this time I caught myself. Mrs. Harwick was in a state of deep shock. She knew Becca was missing, but she'd somehow managed to avoid considering what everybody else feared: that Becca might have witnessed something that night, and right now could be in very grave danger.

I said, "I know Becca's been going through a lot of things in her life. When you're a teenager, sometimes you think the world revolves around you. You shouldn't take it personally."

She was sitting perfectly still, her back ramrod straight, staring numbly out at the swimming pool.

She said, "Becca and I were riding bikes one morning. She couldn't have been more than five or six, because I remember her bike still had training wheels. We were coming around a curve, and I rolled over a stick that had fallen in the path. It popped up and got stuck in the bicycle chain. The next thing I knew I was flying over the handlebars. I landed flat on my face. It nearly knocked me out. Becca saw me fall, but she just kept on riding. I remember her little legs just pumping away on the pedals."

She looked down and spread her palms open.

"I broke the fall with my hands. I'm convinced that's where my arthritis came from. Dixie, do you have someone?"

That caught me off guard. I said, "What do you mean, someone?"

"Someone special in your life."

"Umm. I do. Sort of. I mean it's complicated."

She stared at me, unblinking, with a desperate look in her eyes. I knew she wanted an honest answer.

I said, "I've been alone for a while, so it's hard. I mean, it's such a compromise . . ."

"A compromise?"

"Well, I mean I like my life the way it is. It's just hard to compromise no matter how much in love you think you are."

She thought for a moment and then looked out at the pool. "I think you should stay away from Kenny Newman. I'm afraid of him."

"Mrs. Harwick, I'm not involved with Kenny Newman, and I never have been. I really only know him through work."

She nodded slowly. "I'm sorry. I don't know why I jumped to that conclusion. To be honest, I think I was a little jealous. I'm ashamed to admit that I've always had a little crush on Kenny, which I'm sure you can understand." She smiled sadly. "Well, I'm glad you have someone you can share your life with."

She looked down at the cigarette, still lying with its lit end over the edge of the coffee table, only now there was a half-inch-long tail of ashes. She flicked the ashes into the palm of her hand and dumped them along with the cigarette into a bowl on the table next to the couch. She shook her head. "Disgusting habit. I haven't smoked in twenty years."

The doorbell rang.

"That's the driver."

She stood up slowly, and we walked to the front door.

"Dixie, I hope you don't mind feeding the fish a while longer. I realize it's not at all what we planned, but until they find out who did this, I can't stay in this house."

"It's not a problem at all. I can feed them as long as you

want, and I've already talked to the Kitty Haven. Charlotte can stay there as long as necessary."

Her eyes glassed over, and she nodded mutely. I watched from the porch as the driver helped her into the backseat of the car. She had been so vital and strong that first day we met. Now, just a few days later, she seemed old and frail.

The driver closed the door, and as he walked around the front of the car and got in the driver's seat, Mrs. Harwick sat perfectly still, her eyes wide open and gazing forward. I was waiting to give her a smile or a wave, but as the car moved forward she didn't look back.

I trudged up the stairs with heavy legs. Mrs. Harwick seemed to have lost not only her husband, but her soul mate. I had been wrong about them. They had been together so long their bickering had become just another mode of communication. What I had thought was bitterness and sarcasm was really just harmless play, like two old dogs rolling around in the grass and chewing on each other's ears.

In the master bathroom, I slid open one of the pocket doors on the side of the aquarium and opened the cabinet where all the food and chemicals were kept. I pulled out a water-testing strip and dipped it into the aquarium for a few seconds, then watched the little squares on the strip change color. I compared them with the examples printed on the side of the bottle. Everything matched perfectly, which was a relief. I didn't have to add any chemicals to the tank. I remembered Mrs. Harwick saying that just the slightest imbalance in the chemistry could be fatal to the fish.

After I sprinkled some food in, I slid the lid of the tank closed, flicked off the light, and closed the pocket door behind me. The bathroom was the same, except the towel that had been lying on the counter was gone, along with all the little yellow evidence markers, and the harp-toting angels flying around on the ceiling looked a little more heavenly and glowing in the late-afternoon light.

I thought to myself, *If I were Becca, I would probably have spent a lot of time in here, too.* I went over to the little alcove opposite the aquarium and sat down on the velvet bench. I closed my eyes and the image of Mrs. Harwick's face came into view. There was so much sorrow in her vacant stare that I could barely take it. She must have been so terrified when she woke up that morning in Tampa and realized that her husband wasn't lying in bed next to her. I hoped someone had been with her when she was told what had happened. The thought of her sitting alone in a hotel room to hear that news was just too terrible to think about. And now it was beginning to look like Detective McKenzie might have been right about Becca, that she was on drugs.

That's when it finally dawned on me.

Becca had said that Mr. and Mrs. Harwick had basically disowned August for getting mixed up with drugs, and that he'd been forced to get a job at the golf club. That was one of the main reasons she'd been afraid to talk to her parents: She was worried they'd cut her off, too. And who could blame her? If I'd had that kind of money growing up, I don't think I'd be too happy about losing it either.

Now, though, I remembered something August said the first day I met him. He had just searched through the house and found Charlotte out on the lanai. We were walking up the driveway together, and when we passed his car he said, "How do you like my new wheels?" If he'd been cut off financially from his parents, forced to get some menial job at a golf course, how in the world could he have afforded to buy a brand-new, expensive-looking sports car? Where would he have gotten the money for something like that?

It was simple. I don't know why I hadn't seen it before.

August wasn't "mixed up" in drugs. He was dealing them, and Becca knew it. Detective McKenzie had mentioned Becca had taken something from her brother's room. Was it possible Becca had found his stash of money and drugs and stolen it?

Then there was the question of that packet of letters that Kenny supposedly gave Mr. Harwick. Where was it? And if it wasn't hidden in the house, who had taken it?

My brain was starting to hurt. I rubbed my hands over my eyes and took a deep breath. Somehow I'd done it again. I'd gotten all mixed up in something that was none of my business. I had told myself that it was none of my business a hundred times, but somehow that didn't matter. I just kept getting sucked in.

I looked up at the fish tank. The mermaid was sitting inside her simple, peaceful little world with that same insipid look in her eyes and stupid smirk painted on her face. As I was about to mutter something disparaging about her ridiculously exaggerated boobs, I stopped myself. *Wait a minute,* I thought. *This mermaid is trying to tell you something.*

She was gazing serenely out one of the bathroom windows, as though she was mesmerized by how the sun was glittering through it and sending little prisms of color reflecting around the room, as though she was being transported to some magical, far-off land.

I thought, *You're exactly right. I need to do that. I need to gaze off into the distance with an empty head. I need to wear a bikini. I need to drink some margaritas in the middle of the day. I need a damn break. I need to* get away.

And I knew exactly who I wanted to get away with.

23

I looked at my watch. It said exactly 4:38, which meant it was exactly a minute past 4:30. I like to be on time, so I trick myself. I set all my clocks seven minutes fast. That way if I'm running late or hit traffic, I always have a few minutes to spare. I knew Ethan usually left his office around 4:30 every afternoon and walked over to the café for a cup of coffee. I decided I'd drive by and see if I could catch him. It was silly, but I knew it would cheer me up. My conversation with Mrs. Harwick had put me in a lousy mood.

The coffee shop is right on the corner at the light. As I pulled up to the curb, Ethan was just coming out the door with a coffee and a bagel. I honked the horn and rolled down the passenger window. He was deep in thought, probably mulling over the details of a case he was working on, but when he saw me his face lit up and he came bounding over and stuck his head in the window. If he'd had a tail he would have wagged it.

"Hey! Fancy meeting you here!"

"Well, not really. I'm sort of stalking you. I know you usually get coffee around now, so—"

"Hold on. You drove over here just so you'd run into me?"

I shrugged. "Well, I was sort of in the neighborhood, but basically yes."

"Wow. That is the best thing that's happened to me all day."

I could literally feel my heart racing. "Me, too."

"So, when am I seeing you again? I am seeing you again, right?"

I said, "Yes. In fact I have a fantasy that we're sharing a margarita on some faraway island in the middle of the day."

"I have some fantasies, too, but we can go over those later."

Huh.

He looked at his watch. "I wish I'd known you were going to be stalking me. I would have made some excuse not to go back to the office."

"No, it's okay. I need to get home anyway."

"Maybe I could stop by later?"

"Definitely."

He smiled. "Good. I'll call you. I had a great time last night. I even enjoyed all the crazy drama."

"There won't be any more craziness, I promise."

His eyebrows went up, and I braced myself for whatever sarcastic yet witty remark he was about to make. Instead he said, "Damn, look at this beautiful automobile."

He tipped his chin at a car that had just rolled up next to us and was waiting for the light to turn green, but I didn't look over. I had no interest in some silly car. I was more interested in how excited Ethan was. He was beaming like a dog in a butcher shop.

"That's a Fiero Miyata. They only make about a hundred of them a year, and you need major connections just to get on the waiting list. That little baby probably costs a cool hundred thousand at least."

I'll never understand what it is with boys and their cars. Don't get me wrong, I appreciate a nice car as much as the next person, but as far as I'm concerned, cars are just like shoes—they help you get from one place to another. I wouldn't waste a hundred thousand dollars on a fancy designer car any more than I'd waste it on a pair of fancy designer shoes. Except that I have been known to have a weakness for shoes. So I might fantasize about buying a hundred-thousand-dollar pair of shoes, if they even make such a thing, but I'd never actually do it. I mean, they'd have to be pretty nice shoes.

Ethan saw the grin on my face as I was watching him. "What?"

I said, "I'm just wondering if I'll ever see that gleam in your eye when you're looking at me."

He laughed. "Oh, you're way hotter than that car. But still . . . you have to admit. That is one nice car."

With a cheesy wink, he headed off down the sidewalk. I watched him go and thought to myself, *and that is one cute butt.*

As the light changed to green, I turned to look and my smile instantly vanished. I couldn't see who was driving, but I recognized the car immediately. It was the same black sports car that August was driving the first time I met him outside his parents' house. In and of itself, that was no big deal. We live on a tiny island, so people's paths are bound to cross every once in a while, and I run into people I know all the time. What made my jaw drop open and my eyebrows jump was that I thought I recognized the person that was sitting in the passenger seat.

The windows were rolled up and slightly tinted, so I couldn't see the face clearly. I waited until the car had gone through the light, and then I pulled out onto the road a few cars back. I followed it all the way up Higel Avenue and through Bay Island to the bridge that crosses over Roberts Bay onto the mainland. At Tamiami Trail, the car turned north and headed out of town. I kept a safe distance just in case they saw me and got suspicious. We drove on for about five miles, and then finally made a right onto University.

I realized we were headed for the Sarasota International Airport, but then the car passed by the main entrance without even slowing. About a mile farther, it made a quick turn down a long gravel road that led into what looked like an old, abandoned factory. There were several hulking cinder-block structures with vaulted roofs clad in corrugated iron, clustered around a sprawling expanse of white-hot concrete baking in the late-afternoon sun. At the far end was a row of small, single-engine airplanes. I realized the buildings must have been airplane hangars. Adjacent to the concrete yard was an open field choked with tall grasses and weeds. I couldn't see it from the street, but I knew there would be a long single-lane runway cut through its center.

There was no way I could have followed the car in without drawing attention to myself, so I sped on to the next light and made a U-turn. Before I got to the lane where they had turned, I pulled in behind a long, low warehouse with rusted corrugated roofing and slid to a stop, sending a cloud of dust into the air. I caught a glimpse of myself in the window as I shut the door. I knew what I was doing was completely foolish, but I needed to know if I was right about who was sitting in the passenger seat of that car.

I hustled across the graveled surface to the far end of the warehouse and carefully peeked around the corner. A field of grassy weeds lay between me and the cluster of airplane hangars. I could see the black sports car parked in the center of the concrete courtyard, and there were a couple of men in black shorts and dark blue polo shirts making their way toward the car. The driver's door opened, and a tall, shaggy-haired man wearing a black suit stood up, but it was too far to make out his face through the waves of heat coming up from the concrete. I needed to get closer.

There was a chain-link fence smothered in vines alongside the warehouse, creating a narrow strip of dried-out brush about two feet wide.

I whispered to myself, "You are one hundred percent out of your mind."

I squeezed through the gap between the chain-link fence and the warehouse and inched my way closer, ducking behind the weeds and dodging broken bottles and rotting trash banked up against the side of the building. At the end of the fence, I came to what looked like an old electrical generator, surrounded by a low concrete wall. I ducked down behind the wall and peered over the edge.

The man standing by the car was indeed August. He was talking to one of the traffic control men while one of the planes positioned itself at the head of the runway. It must have been a private charter plane. Another car had arrived now, a gray Mercedes sedan, and a conservatively dressed middle-aged couple was waiting with small rolling suitcases. They were probably wealthy travelers off to a private island resort somewhere.

As one of the men opened the door on the plane's side and lowered the folding stairs, another man wearing a pilot's cap came sauntering out of one of the hangars. The man talking to August shook his hand and then signaled for the couple to bring their bags over. August walked around to the passenger side of his car and opened the door. A woman stepped out, holding a small package in one arm and an overnight bag in the other.

It was Corina—and the small package she was holding was Dixie Joyce, wrapped in the fleecy pink blanket I'd bought her at Walmart.

I held my breath as August reached into the front seat of the car and brought out Corina's handbag. There was a gentleness in the way he handed it to her, and the thought flashed across my mind that they were a couple. She draped the handbag over her shoulder, and they walked together to the plane. August handed her overnight bag up to one of the men inside and then watched as Corina made her way up the steps with Dixie Joyce in her arms. When she got to the top, she looked back nervously at August. He waved at her, and then she disappeared inside.

The two ground crewmen folded the steps up and latched the door, and then one of them whistled and gave a thumbs-up to the pilot. He and August waved to each other as the plane started rolling forward.

Just as the plane lifted off the ground, I felt two things. First was an extraordinarily confusing mix of thoughts and emotions—I knew it would be a while before I'd sorted through this one. Second was a firm tapping on my left shoulder. It was so unexpected that a high-pitched scream spontaneously flew out of my throat as I spun around, my hands raised in front of me like two karate sticks. Standing before me was an elderly man in a dark blue security uniform with trembling hands and a look of terror in his face equal only to mine.

"Young lady, this is private property you're on."

"I know, I'm so sorry—I'm leaving now."

"Well, now hold on, missy. I have to report you for trespassing, so I'm gonna need to see your driver's license first."

I had to think fast. If he worked for the people that operated the private charter planes, the last thing I needed was a trespassing report with my name on it. They seemed pretty chummy with August, and I didn't want him to find out that I had been snooping around watching him.

Of course, I could have made a run for it. The poor old security guy was so befuddled it was almost comical. He had pulled out a yellowed report pad that had obviously never been used and was shaking a ballpoint pen in the air, trying to get the ink to flow. I noticed a silver loop-chain ID bracelet on his wrist. My grandfather had worn the exact same bracelet.

Summoning up my inner busty blonde, I pointed to August's car and said, "Oh, please don't report me. Do you see that man? He's my boyfriend. He just put his mistress on a private plane. I thought he was cheating on me, and now I know it for sure."

"Little lady, that's none of my business. I still gotta fill out a report."

I started rummaging through my pockets, pretending to look for my wallet. "Great. My boyfriend finds out I got heart trouble and right away he runs out and gets another girl, and now I'm gonna get busted for it."

He looked up. "You got heart trouble?"

I shifted my weight and glared at him. "Yeah, and I gotta take Plavix every day and I got a twenty-four-hour head-ache from it, too, but what do you care?"

He held out his wrinkled hand and showed me his ID bracelet. It had a white symbol printed on it, like a six-sided snowflake.

I said, "So what is that supposed to be?"

"It's my medical ID bracelet. It says I take a blood thin-ner every day to prevent another heart attack."

I said, "Huh. Am I supposed to wear one of those?"

He'd suddenly taken on a fatherly tone. "Well, you should. If you ever got knocked out and taken to the hos-pital, they'd need to know. And if you're having headaches every day, you gotta report that to your doctor. That's not a good sign at all, young lady."

I pushed my hands down in my pockets, slightly squeez-ing my breasts together with my arms. "Seriously?"

My friend Judy at the diner always says, "If you've got tit, flaunt tit." I'm not particularly proud of myself in these moments, but it works. He led me back down the side of the warehouse, kicking the occasional piece of trash out of the way, and helped me into the Bronco.

I said, "Thank you so much for letting me go this time. I really appreciate it."

He shook his head angrily, and I felt a little guilty for riling him up.

"What kind of asshole runs out on his girlfriend just cuz he finds out she's got heart problems? I hope you're gonna dump his ass right away."

I nodded as I put the Bronco in gear. "Oh, yes, sir. That man has no idea what I got in store for him."

24

I drove home in a daze. Paco's truck was under the carport, and so was his Harley, but Michael's car was gone, which meant they'd probably gone out fishing for dinner. I stripped off my clothes and took a good long shower, letting the hot water soothe my aching brain and body. I padded naked into the combination closet-office and sat down at my desk, looking at all the unopened bills I'd let pile up. The last thing on earth I felt like doing now was going through bills, so I pulled on a pair of sweatpants and an old faded T-shirt and tied my hair back in a ponytail.

I stripped the sheets off my bed and threw them in the washer with some dish towels and a couple of pairs of work shorts. Normally I would have checked the pockets to make sure I'd emptied everything out first, but I didn't this time—either I was too tired or too lazy or both. You'd think by now I'd know better, considering I once washed my cell phone on the delicate cycle. Turns out it's not so delicate.

While the washer hummed along doing its mindless

job, I did the same in the kitchen with a brush and a bottle of bleach spray. I started with the countertops, which are made of some unlikely amalgamation of white marble and plastic that was popular when my apartment was put in, and then I moved on to the metal-faced cabinets on the wall. I scrubbed the stovetop to within an inch of its life, and by the time I had finished with the kitchen sink, it glittered like a cat's eye in the mirror.

I took a deep breath and let the lingering chlorine vapors fill my lungs and hoped they were disinfecting me on the inside. I collapsed on the bare mattress in my bedroom and stared up at the ceiling. The sun was sinking low in the sky, and the only light was a melon orange glow coming through the long narrow window near the ceiling.

I knew now that it wasn't drugs that August was dealing. It was birds. Sarasota may have a lot of birds, but we've got nothing on Guatemala. There are at least seven hundred species there, and more than twenty of those are rare and endangered, meaning they're more likely to fetch a pretty penny on the black market. Guatemala was the ideal place for August to get all the fine-feathered merchandise he needed to keep his "shop" fully stocked.

Also, I finally knew for certain why Corina had so much cash in her purse. August had hired her to smuggle the birds into the country for him. He had probably paid for her transportation, tacked on a few thousand dollars per bird for her trouble, and then passed the merchandise on to rare-bird collectors, pet shops, and dealers. With just one or two resplendent quetzals a month, he could make enough money to buy a new Fiero Miyata and have plenty of cash left over to party.

I knew all about the average bird enthusiast, like Joyce, who gets great pleasure and joy from her "collection" of rare-bird sightings, but it was hard to imagine the type of collector who wants more, who isn't satisfied with mere sightings but will pay thousands and thousands of dollars to hold that rare bird, alive, in his hands—even if it means taking that bird away from its home and stuffing it in a metal cage for the rest of its life. Not to mention risking the total extinction of the species as a whole.

That's a kind of pure selfishness that I just cannot comprehend.

I could, on some level, come up with a way to forgive Corina. In her case it was a means of survival, of providing for her newborn baby. She was just a cog in the wheel of a much larger, more sinister machine—an important part of that machine, for sure—but I doubted even she knew exactly what kind of damage she was partly responsible for.

August, on the other hand, I couldn't explain away so easily. He'd had every advantage in life that a person could ever hope for. Wealthy, white, male, educated, with parents to take care of him and put a roof over his head. There was no excuse. With the death of his stepfather, I knew he'd be going through a rough time, and with his mother so distraught, things were certainly not going to get easier for him anytime soon. But I also knew I didn't have a choice—I would have to report what I knew about him.

I heard a car coming up the driveway to the house, and I recognized it right away. Michael's car makes a particular kind of sound as it rolls over the crushed shells. I don't know if it's the weight of the car or the width of the tires or what, but I've heard it so many times I could probably recognize it in my sleep. Then I heard the sound of car doors shutting and their footsteps crunching across the courtyard to the deck.

"Hey, Dixie!"

I hopped off the bed and ran through the apartment to the French doors. Michael and Paco were posed under the balcony, holding up a line of freshly caught fish and grinning up at me, all shirtless and muscled. They looked like one of those racy postcards all the souvenir shops sell that show perfectly tanned, hunky men with bulging muscles, and have cheesy captions like NICE CATCH!

I said, "Hey, nice catch!"

Michael grinned. "We're firing up the grill. Dinner in twenty minutes."

I threw my fists in the air and cried, "Yippee!"

It looked as if the day might end on a high note after all. I raced over and turned on my CD player, and while Michael Jackson's "Smooth Criminal" pumped through the apartment, I shuffled into the closet, shucked off my sweatpants and T-shirt, and starting pawing through my sad collection of clothing. I wanted to look nice for dinner, not just because I was excited to have my men back and a nice home-cooked dinner, but because I remembered Ethan had said he might be stopping by for a little bit.

I pulled on a clean pair of faded jeans and a gauzy white dress shirt and finished it off with a cute pair of wedge sandals. Then I bopped my way into the bathroom and pulled out my little makeup kit. I was half surprised it wasn't covered in cobwebs. I put on a love smudge of eyeshadow and some nearly translucent pink lip gloss. My hair was still a little damp, so I pulled out my hair dryer from under the counter and blew it out.

Just as I was about to sprint out the door, my office phone rang. I ran over and shut the music off so I could hear who it was, but no way in hell was I answering it, unless of course it had something to do with one of my pets.

I jumped a bit when I heard Detective McKenzie's familiar voice. "Dixie, we just got the report from the medical examiner on Mr. Harwick. I have a couple of questions for you. Can you call me right away?"

As if it had a mind of its own, my hand reached out to grab the receiver, but I stopped it. Detective McKenzie could at least wait until after dinner. There couldn't possibly have been anything in that report that required some urgent piece of information from me. I waited for the machine to click off and then skipped down the stairs two at a time.

Michael and Paco had laid out a picnic on the outdoor table. On their way home, they'd stopped by Morton's Market and picked up some of my all-time favorites: a creamy potato salad with fresh dill, crusty sourdough baguettes, and pear and blackberry tartlets. The fish was whole snapper that Michael had marinated in white wine and olive oil while the grill heated up. It was cooked to perfection, crispy on the outside, light and flaky on the inside, sprinkled with coarse sea salt and freshly ground pepper and topped with a few aromatic sprigs of fresh rosemary.

It was heavenly.

Paco set a bucket packed full of ice and frosty bottles of beer on the ground next to the table. "Hey, did you hear they found the Harwick girl?"

I stopped with a forkful of snapper poised at my lips. "What?"

"Yep. She was in Miami."

"Miami? Where did you hear that?"

"It was on the news. They said she went to visit a friend who's in college there."

Michael narrowed his eyes and looked at me. "Did you know about that?"

I saw him notice my hair and makeup, but if he thought anything about it he didn't say. "No, I swear she didn't say a word about that to me."

Paco said, "She says she didn't know anything about her stepfather until she saw it on TV, but nobody's buying it because her whole family didn't know where she was. I guess the cops still think she's a suspect."

I said, "Oh, no. I think I might be partly responsible for that. I told Becca she'd have to tell her parents she was pregnant sooner or later, but she was terrified. I wonder if she decided it would be easier to just run away."

Michael muttered, "Seems to be a lot of that going on lately."

"So where is she now?"

"She's back. They said she's in a hotel with her mother and brother."

I said, "Yeah, the investigators are done with the house, but Mrs. Harwick isn't ready to go back yet. I still have their cat at the Kitty Haven."

Paco nodded. I could tell he felt sorry for Charlotte, but he was also holding something back. Whatever he knew about the Harwick case, he wasn't saying.

Michael said, "Okay, can I interject here for a second?

We have this amazing fish and all this fantastic food in front of us, and all you guys can talk about is pregnant teenage runaways and dead bodies. Can we please talk about something else?"

My cell phone rang. I fished it out of my pocket, ignoring Michael as he shot a disapproving look in my direction. It was Detective McKenzie again. I muted the ringer and laid it back down on the table.

Paco smiled mischeviously. "Okay, let's change the subject. Why don't we tell Dixie what you said to that woman at the market today."

Michael said, "Oh, let's not."

"What happened?"

Paco said, "This woman saw all the cartons of potato salad and prepared foods that Michael was putting in the basket. She winked at Michael and said, 'Looks like somebody needs a woman to cook him up a nice homemade meal.' So Michael said, 'Yeah, except I think my partner wouldn't be too happy about that.' Well, apparently she thought he meant his *business* partner, because she said, 'What kind of business are you in that he has a say in it?'"

I laughed. "Oh, no. What did you say to her?"

Michael deadpanned, "I said, 'Monkey business.'"

I nearly fell out of my chair laughing.

Paco put his arm out to keep my chair from falling over backward. "She said, 'Oh, that's interesting!' and just kept on shopping, like it was the most normal thing in the world."

Michael grinned. "I think she must have thought I was a monkey trainer for the circus."

It felt good to just sit and laugh, to forget about everything that was happening outside of our little world. We finished our beers and watched as the sun sank deeper behind the ocean, leaving behind a slow-motion trail of undulating ribbons of pink and orange light in the darkening sky.

My cell phone rang again. This time I jumped for it. It was Ethan.

Michael started to shoot me another of his signature disapproving looks, but I rolled my eyes and said, "Oh please, you don't scare me. I have to answer this one."

I walked away from the table and flipped open my phone.

"Hey."

"Hey there. What are you doing?"

Even the sound of Ethan's voice made my heart speed up a little bit. "I'm sitting here with my favorite men in the world having dinner."

"Your favorite men? Shouldn't I be there?"

"Yes, you should. Come over. We've got fresh fish on the grill and ice-cold beer."

"Nice! I'm on my way."

I hung up and walked back to the table.

Michael said, "Who was that?"

"Ethan," I said demurely.

Michael raised one eybrow. "Really?"

He and Paco shared a look.

Paco said, "How's he doing, anyway?"

I sat down and scooped another serving of potato salad onto my plate.

"You can ask him yourself. He's coming over."

.   .   .

When Ethan arrived, he and Michael and Paco all stood around on the deck with their hands in their pockets, swaying back and forth and talking in that deep-toned, monosyllabic way that men do when they're a little uncomfortable. Then suddenly Michael and Paco disappeared inside, and Ethan and I were left alone.

We walked down to the beach and sat down on the sand and watched the waves crashing in. The birds and crickets were still in the throes of their evening performance, and at times it was all so loud we had to speak up a little just to be heard over them.

Finally I said, "I'm scared."

He tilted his head. "Of what?"

I waved my hand back and forth between us. "You know. *This.*"

"Yeah, I know. So what else is new?"

"Very funny."

"I wasn't joking."

I looked up at him. I could tell by the look in his eyes that it was true. He wasn't joking. He was dead serious.

"I'm sorry, it's just sometimes I feel like we're at a carnival, and we keep getting on the same carousel over and over again because you're afraid to get on the big-kid rides."

I said, "Ethan, do you have any idea how many people die every year on roller coasters?"

He rolled his eyes.

I said, "Okay. I know, I know. Believe me, I know. All my friends are saying I need to just move on with my life and stop being so . . ." I searched for the right word. "Safe."

Ethan said, "Wait a minute, you talked to your friends about me?"

"Well, no, not you in particular, just about relationships."

"Ah."

He looked a little disappointed. Then I thought of Cora popping that piece of chocolate bread in her mouth and the twinkle in her eye as she reminded me how delicious Ethan was.

I smiled. "Okay, maybe I did mention you a couple of times."

He grinned and looked out at the water. "That's good, I guess."

"I'm sorry I'm so neurotic. I'm really trying to change. Believe me, I don't want to spend every moment of my life feeling like I'm hiding from something."

He turned to me. "Well, maybe it's time to change that. Maybe it's time to start living every moment as if you're finding something. What if every moment is a discovery?"

I laid my hand on top of his and looked up into his big brown eyes. I said, "That is the corniest fucking thing you have ever said in your entire life."

He burst out laughing. "I know, right? High five!"

I clapped my hand into his and he pulled me closer. I did my best impersonation of a self-help hippie guru: "What if every moment is a beautiful blooming lotus blossom of discovery?"

He chuckled, and we both sat there a while longer and listened to the waves and the dying chorus of birds and crickets.

Finally he said, "But you have to admit, it's not bad advice."

. . .

As we were walking up to the house, I saw Michael and Paco out on the deck clearing away the dinner dishes, but when they saw us coming they scattered back inside like mice.

I walked Ethan over to the carport. Before we even got to his car he pulled me into his arms.

"Tell Paco and your brother I said thanks for the beer, and call me if you need me."

I felt his strong arms slide around the small of my back and a wave of goose bumps flowed across my entire body.

"I will. Thanks for coming by. You totally made my day."

I could feel his chest rise and fall against mine with every breath he took. He cocked his head to one side and said, "Your hair looks good."

"I know. I dried it with a hair dryer."

"Totally works."

I laid my hand on the back of his neck and gently drew his lips to mine.

25

I walked behind Ethan's car a little ways down the lane until his taillights disappeared around the curve. Then I came back up with my arms wrapped around my shoulders like I was giving myself a good hug. I was halfway up the steps to my apartment when Michael poked his head out of the house.

"Hey, where's your gentleman caller going?"

I put one hand on my hip. "He's going home, Michael. Where do you think he's going?"

He smirked. "I figured he'd be going right up those stairs with you, like he did last night."

I suddenly felt like a fifteen-year-old girl caught making out with a boy on the front porch by her father. My cheeks turned red hot, and I started back up the stairs.

He pumped his fist. "Yes! Busted."

I stopped and turned. "You know what, Michael? Grow up!"

Paco appeared in the doorway and started pulling

Michael back inside, but he wasn't giving up that easily. "Hey, if the carport's a-rockin', don't come a-knockin'!"

I said, "Hilarious," and slammed the door behind me.

I heard Paco say something, and then Michael shouted, "Oh, come on, Dixie! I'm just teasing!"

No matter how old we get, no matter how mature or well adjusted we are, we all have our own inner child hidden somewhere deep inside us. I think there's also an angst-ridden teenager in there, too. In my case, sometimes she gets out and tears things up a bit, especially since there's nothing better than having an older sibling around to get that inner teenager riled up. Every once in a while I turn into the haughty, emotional fifteen-year-old brat I once was, and Michael turns into my sadistic, teasing older brother.

I stretched out on the mattress, wishing I'd put the clean sheets back on earlier, and pulled the comforter over me. I fumed for a little bit, but I knew by the morning it would all be fine. I wasn't even sure what I was so steamed about. Either I was embarrassed that Michael and Paco knew Ethan had spent the night, or I was embarrassed that I had tried to hide it from them, or I was just embarrassed that I was embarrassed.

Whatever it was, I felt like an idiot. I'd have to apologize to Michael for reacting like a pubescent diva. I knew he was thrilled that I was getting closer to Ethan, and I knew there was nothing he wanted more than for me to be happy.

. . .

That night, I dreamed that I lived on a deserted island in a grass hut, with a bed made out of bamboo sticks and palm fronds, and a little shelf over the bed made out of abalone shells. Eventually I realized it wasn't just any island I was on. It was Gilligan's Island, and it wasn't a TV show, it was real. There were other grass huts all around mine where all the other castaways lived, everyone except Ginger, who lived at the other end of the island in a huge glass-and-steel football stadium with a domed roof and a huge expanse of green Astroturf carpeting.

I was standing next to Ginger in the center of the stadium. It was completely dark except for a few shafts of light cutting through the blackness and making pools of green light on the floor. There was someone climbing up one of the walls, dangerously high—he must have been almost ten stories off the ground. I turned to Ginger and said, *Who is that?* Her wavy red hair was cascading over her shoulders and glistening in the light. She said, *Dixie, that's Todd.*

He was climbing across some kind of scaffolding that extended all the way to the top of the dome, and as he climbed higher and higher, he was poking little holes in the ceiling with the tip of a pool cue. Occasionally we would see dust and little pieces of the dome come floating down in the shafts of light.

I was just about to ask Ginger if her red hair was natural when Todd lost his footing. I watched in horror as he fell all the way down to the ground. He landed in a pool of light about thirty yards away from us. I ran as fast as I could to his side, but when I got to the place where he'd fallen, his body was gone. Lying on the bright green Astroturf was a small embroidery frame. It was oval shaped, with little pegs to hold in place a piece of fabric stretched across it. But instead of fabric in the frame, there was a paper-thin piece of balsa wood. I laid the tip of my finger on the center of the wood and felt a steady heartbeat.

I took the frame home to my hut and placed it on the abalone shelf over my bed. Throughout the night, I would wake up, reach out, and touch the thin membrane of wood to feel the heartbeat. It never stopped. At some point before morning came, Ginger snuck in and was gently nudging my shoulder. I looked up at her, and she said, *Dixie, I found it!*

I shot straight up in bed and said out loud, "I know where those letters are."

When I backed out of the carport, I was still reeling a little bit from the dream, which was about the strangest, most surreal dream I'd ever had. I rolled down the lane with the headlights off. Michael and Paco are pretty heavy sleepers, but I didn't want to take any chances, so I drove as slowly as I could until I got to the end. I didn't switch on the headlights until I was heading north on Midnight Pass. It was the middle of night, and there was nobody on the road but me.

I drove through the deserted village in the center of town and past the park where Joyce and I found Corina. At Jungle Plum Road, I made a left and drove at a snail's pace along the trees lining the street where the Harwicks' house was. As I pulled through the gates and up the long driveway, I breathed a sigh of relief. There were no cars in the parking area.

I pulled my ring of keys out of my backpack and unlocked the door. The alarm system beeped when I went in, and with a trembling hand I punched in the security code to disarm it and then closed and locked the door behind me. It was pitch dark inside, but I was a little reluctant to turn on any lights. I told myself that technically I wasn't really doing anything wrong. Nobody had told me I couldn't come and check on the aquarium in the middle of the night, but still I didn't want to arouse the suspicions of any of the neighbors.

I fished out the little flashlight I keep in my backpack and made my way across the foyer and up the marble stairs to Mr. and Mrs. Harwick's bedroom. Even though I knew the house was totally empty, I was terrified. It seemed like every time I thought I was alone in this house, I was dead wrong.

I passed through the bedroom suite and made my way slowly down the short hall toward the master bathroom. Very gently, I pushed the door open and waited just in case there was someone hiding inside, which of course there wasn't. Still, I could literally feel my heart pumping in my chest. I tiptoed across the marble floor directly to the little alcove with the peach-colored velvet bench and sat down.

I took a deep breath and slowly raised the flashlight. I followed the pool of light as it slid across the floor to the tank, to the edge of the mermaid's tail fanned out across the aquarium floor, then up her glittering turquoise body. As her face came into view, her pouting red lips, her pale porcelain skin, and her deep violet eyes, I knew I was right.

She had been moved.

On that morning I had searched the house looking for Charlotte, the same morning I found Mr. Harwick at the bottom of the pool, I had sat in this exact same place. I distinctly remembered looking up and seeing two pairs of eyes staring directly at me: the porcupine fish's and the mermaid's. But earlier today, after Mrs. Harwick left, I sat here and imagined the mermaid was looking out the window and fantasizing about some faraway land. At the time I didn't think anything of it, but now I knew I was right. She had definitely been moved, and recently. She wasn't looking at me at all. She was gazing off at least three feet to the right, directly at one of the stained-glass windows.

My eyes floated down to the black-and-gold treasure chest she was sitting on. I wasn't one bit happy about what I was about to do, but at the same time, I felt like I didn't have a choice.

I needed to see what was inside that chest.

I slid one of the large pocket doors open and stepped through the hidden pathway and around to the back of the aquarium. The nets and poles with hooks on one end were hanging in a row on the wall behind the tank, and the fish were all drifting about aimlessly in the darkened water. When I switched on the overhead light, they all darted around a bit, and I whispered an apology for waking them up and intruding into their silent world. I rolled up my sleeves and slid my arms down into the tank. I was worried the mermaid would be too heavy to move by myself, but she must have been hollow, because it was surprisingly easy.

As all the fish retreated to the far corners of the tank,

I put both my hands on the back of the mermaid's head and tilted her forward. I felt a momentary jab of pity when I saw the lid of the treasure chest lift up with her. I thought, *No wonder she just sits in here all day. I'd do the same thing if I had the lid of a treasure chest fused to my butt.*

I brought her up a little farther so that she was balanced on her own against the front wall of the aquarium, and then I pointed my flashlight down into the open treasure chest.

Inside was a black rectangular package, wrapped in what I thought at first was twine but then realized were rubber bands. I reached behind me and brought one of the wooden poles off the wall and lowered it down into the tank. As carefully as possible, I looped its hook under one of the rubber bands and then gently drew the package up out of the water.

The whole thing had taken less than a minute. I spread a towel on the floor and laid the dripping package down on top of it. It was light, about half a pound. The rubber bands were wrapped around what looked like a black plastic garbage bag, and I thought of Kenny and how he had described his father wrapping a change of clothes in a plastic bag and carrying it into the ocean.

Carefully, I took the rubber bands off one by one and laid them in a neat pile on the floor next to the towel. Before I looked inside the bag, I glanced up at the tank. The porcupine fish was floating aimlessly in the middle of the tank, puffed up like a beach ball and covered in sharp white quills.

I whispered, "Sorry about that."

Slowly, I opened up the package and pulled out two clear

plastic bags. They were the gallon-sized type with water-tight zippers across the top.

Inside one of the bags was a collection of envelopes, exactly as Kenny had described them. They all had a post office box here in Siesta Key for the return address, and they had all been sent to the same person: Daniel Imperiori—Kenny's real name. There were probably about ten enve-lopes total. The other bag had only two things in it. One was a piece of paper, like a receipt, and the other was a small, amber-colored plastic bottle with a white label.

I brought the plastic bag up closer and squinted at the tiny print on the bottle. It read BUTORPHANOL, 40 ML.

I should have known.

I never aced a chemistry test in high school, and I don't have a medical degree, but I have spent a lot of time around animal clinics, so I know a thing or two about animal medications. Vets use butorphanol every day. It's powerful and relatively tasteless. It's mostly used for sedating ani-mals before surgery, but I had a feeling it might come in handy in other situations as well. For example, if you needed an animal to be quiet for a few hours. Like, during a plane ride.

It all started falling into place. Those drugs Mr. and Mrs. Harwick had found in August's room—he wasn't us-ing them on himself, and he wasn't dealing them, either. He was using them to sedate the birds he was smuggling into the country, to keep them quiet so they wouldn't be discovered. That was why the bird Joyce and I found in the park had been knocked out. It hadn't flown into a window. Corina had drugged it.

I knew it didn't take long for a narcotic like butorphanol to take effect. Corina had probably squeezed it into the bird's mouth with an eyedropper in the taxi or the bus on her way to the airport in Guatemala. By the time she boarded the plane, the bird would have been out like a light, sleeping away in a drug-induced stupor inside her handbag.

I turned the bag around and read the faint blue machine-printed text on the receipt inside: ALLIED TAXI, $79. At the bottom of the receipt was a Tampa address, written with a purple felt-tip pen in round, childish handwriting, followed by a short sequence of numbers and letters, "230A1P."

Calmly, I folded everything back together with the rubber bands and slid the package down into my backpack. I switched off the light in the hidden closet and pulled the sliding door closed. My mind was racing at about a thousand miles per hour. I was so distracted that it wasn't until I'd gotten back in my Bronco and was rolling down the cobblestone driveway that I realized I'd forgotten to put the mermaid back down on her treasure chest, and I had left the wet towel lying on the floor in the access closet behind it.

But it didn't matter. I had more important things to do.

First, I dialed Detective McKenzie. She answered as if it was the most normal thing in the world to get a phone call in the middle of the night.

"Dixie, thanks for returning my call. I have a question about when you tried to revive Mr. Harwick."

I interrupted. "You want to know if a large amount of water came out of his lungs when I pressed on his chest."

"Uh, yes. How did you know that?"

I said, "Because if he drowned, there would have been water in his lungs, but there wasn't. That means he was already dead or had stopped breathing before he went into the pool. And they found a massive amount of narcotics in his body, right?"

"Yes, they did."

"I know. It was butorphanol, wasn't it?"

"Dixie, what the hell is going on?"

"Detective McKenzie, I think I know who killed Mr. Harwick. I don't have hard proof of it, but I think I know how we can get it. I'm on my way to Kenny's boat at the dock behind Hoppie's Restaurant right now. Can you meet me there in ten minutes? I can explain everything then."

There was a long pause on the other end, and for a second I thought the call had dropped.

I said, "Hello?"

McKenzie said, "Okay. Listen to me. I don't know what you're up to, and I'm not sure I like it, either. But I'm going to meet you at Hoppie's in ten minutes, and I don't want you to do a goddamn thing or talk to anyone else until you've explained everything to me first. Understand?"

I gulped. "Yes."

She sounded relieved. "Thank you. I'm on my way now."

Before she hung up, I thought about the gun that August carried in his glove compartment and said, "Oh, Detective McKenzie?"

"Yes?"

"Bring backup."

26

After meeting with Detective McKenzie, I waited in the sleeping cabin below the main deck on Kenny's houseboat. I had situated myself in a musty old armchair next to Kenny's bed. The cabin was completely dark except for the glow from the fire I'd built in a small wood-burning stove in the corner and a faint patch of light spilling in under the cabin door from a lantern on the dock. There was a small kitchenette next to the stove, and lined up along the countertop was a row of canned tuna and several bags of dried pasta.

Hung about the walls were various coils of rope, fishing rods, maps, hooks, and bags of shells. There was a battery-operated radio hanging by a string tied around its broken antenna, and there was a huge, yellowing map of the Gulf. Tacked in the middle of it was an old photo of a young couple, a man and a woman, sitting in a swinging porch chair. The caption read, "On the patio with Danny holding Tiger." There was a little boy sitting on the man's lap, and he was beaming at the camera. Cradled in his arms like a baby was an orange tabby kitten.

I took a deep breath and reached into my backpack. Pulling out the business card that August had given me the day I met him at the Harwick house, I thought about how cocky and sure of himself he had been. I'm sure he fantasized that if he ever got a call from me, it would be a booty call. Never in his wildest dreams would he have imagined the call I was about to make.

I punched his number into my cell phone. When he answered, his voice croaked and his words were a little slurred. He was either half asleep or drunk or both.

I said, "August, it's Dixie Hemingway. I'm sorry to call so late, but I thought your mother would want to know. I think I've figured out who's responsible for your step-father's death."

That woke him up. He said, "Excuse me?"

"I know, I'm sure it's a shock. I found a package of letters that your stepfather wrote. They were stashed away in your mother's fish tank. I've hidden them on Kenny Newman's boat at Hoppie's Restaurant. It's the last place he'd ever think to look for them. In the morning, I'll turn them over to the police."

There was a moment of silence. I could hear the wheels spinning in his head.

He said, "That's interesting. So, you read the letters?"

I said, "Yeah. I did."

"And what did they say?"

I said, "August, I really can't tell you. I don't think it would be right. Once the police have the letters, I'm sure they'll be very happy to explain everything to you."

There was a long silence. "Okay. Well, I'll be sure and tell my mother right away."

I said, "You do that. I think she'd definitely want to be woken up for this."

"That's not a problem. She doesn't really sleep anymore."

I nodded. I could tell by the sound of his voice that he wasn't making that part up. "Well, now you can tell her she'll be able to rest soon."

He said, "I will," and the line went dead.

The bay was calm when I had first arrived, but now the wind had picked up a bit and the houseboat was rolling gently back and forth. I could hear the water lapping up against the sides of the boat, and occasionally a deep, creaking moan rose up from the hull as it nudged up against the edge of the pier. A couple of iron pots hanging from hooks over the wood-burning stove were tapping into one another with sullen, metallic clunks like a retarded cuckoo clock.

The fire had died down, so I got up quickly and threw in a few more pieces of driftwood and crumpled-up newspaper from a pile that Kenny kept next to the cabin door. I wanted to keep it burning.

As I sat back down in the chair, a slow rain began. I could hear it tapping on the metal roof. It started with just a few drops here and there but gradually grew to a steady hiss, like quiet static on a radio. There were two small round windows on both the port and starboard walls, and a flash of headlights moved from one to the other, lighting up the inside of the cabin briefly. I couldn't hear anything but the rain, so I wasn't sure if a car had gone by on the road or if someone had just pulled into the parking lot alongside the dock.

My stomach tightened into a knot, and thoughts were bouncing around inside my head like balls in a pinball machine, but I told myself to keep calm. I took a deep breath and allowed my eyes to close for a moment. I tried to imagine my gentle, babbling brook with all its polished pebbles and butterflies flitting about. I tried to see the steps leading down to the water and the flowers gently swaying in the breeze, but then the unmistakable sound of footsteps coming down the dock broke through the soft hum of the rain, and my eyes shot open.

When the boat tilted slowly to the starboard side there was no doubt. Someone had stepped on board.

My heart started to pound so hard that for a moment I thought I might have a heart attack. I heard footsteps moving slowly across the upper deck as I glanced over at the port side window, but all I could see were tiny reflections of light in the falling rain.

The footsteps stopped for a moment but then crossed directly over my head. There was another pause, and then I knew someone was slowly descending the steps. A shadow appeared in the narrow strip of light under the cabin door directly in front of me.

I moved my hand to the side and slid it down between the cushions of the armchair. It came to rest on the barrel of my Smith & Wesson .38 pistol. I could feel its cold, hard steel on the tips of my fingers.

Closing my eyes again, I took a deep breath. This wasn't exactly the craziest thing I had ever done, but it was definitely right up there in the top ten. For some reason, though, I felt okay. I thought to myself, *No matter what happens, I've done the right thing.*

I heard the cabin door swing open, and I raised my eyes.

Standing in the doorway, silhouetted by the light shining down from the dock, was Mrs. Harwick.

She didn't see me at first. She fumbled around in the outer pocket of her shoulder bag and then pulled out a small yellow flashlight. When she flicked it on, the light pointed directly at my face. She jumped back, and her hand flew up to her mouth, stifling a scream.

I said, "Mrs. Harwick, it's Dixie."

"Oh God! Dixie, you scared me to death. What are you doing here?"

I said, "I brought the letters here to hide them. Didn't August tell you?"

She put her hand over her heart and tried to regain her breath. "He did. That's why I'm here."

"But I told August I would give them to the police in the morning."

She said, "I know, Dixie, but I came to get them. When the police read those letters, they'll know why Kenny Newman killed my husband. He wanted revenge, and he wanted money. But I'm worried about you. They already think you and Kenny are lovers. They'll think you were involved somehow, and I don't want that. I should hand them over myself."

I said, "You think it was Kenny?"

She nodded. "I do. I'm sure of it."

I leaned over and pulled the package out of my back-pack and handed it to her.

She held it to her chest. "I'm going to take this to the police right now. The sooner they have it, the better. In the meantime, you should go home. You look like you could use a drink, and it's late. I don't think we're safe here."

As she turned I said, "Mrs. Harwick. Do you want me to bring Charlotte back home now?"

"Oh, Dixie, I'm really not much of a cat person. Maybe your cat kennel could find a good home for her?"

I nodded mutely. I had more or less expected her to say that, but it still made me a little sad to hear it out loud. Charlotte had really been Mr. Harwick's cat.

She turned toward the steps, but I stopped her again. "And you knew your husband was Kenny's father?"

She sighed and looked back at me. "I did. He never told me, but I figured it out long ago."

I could feel my heart pounding out of my chest, and for a second I worried she would actually hear it. I said, "I remember something you told me the first time we ever met. We had walked out to my car, and you were telling me about checking the water in the fish tank. Do you remember? You said fish seem like such strong creatures, but given just the slightest chemical imbalance, they can wind up dead at the bottom of the tank."

She had an exasperated look on her face. "Why are you telling me this?"

"Because when I found that little plastic bottle of butorphanol, which I'm sure has your fingerprints on it, I wondered if you hadn't planned on killing your husband for a long time."

Her eyes turned to narrow slits. "How dare you. How dare you accuse me of such a thing. I have no idea what you're talking about."

"You found your son's supply of butorphanol, and you took some of it. That's what he meant when he accused Becca of stealing something from his room."

Mrs. Harwick leaned against the doorway of the cabin, and I was reminded of that first day I met her, when she stood with her arm on the back of her neck in the doorway of the living room and looked so beautiful and elegant.

"Oh, my," she said. "You're such a smart girl, aren't you? And then what happened?"

I could feel myself trembling, but I held on to the arms of the chair. I didn't want her to see how terrified I was. "I think Mr. Harwick did tell you he was Kenny's father. In fact, I think he even told you he was going home to meet with Kenny the night he died, and I think you went home with him. You must have hid upstairs and listened. You heard their entire conversation. You heard your husband say he wanted to give his fortune to Kenny. You heard him say his stepchildren were useless. Then, after Kenny left, you came downstairs and had a drink with your husband. I imagine you might have been arguing about Kenny. At some point, when he wasn't looking, you poured that vial of butorphanol into his glass."

Mrs. Harwick laughed incredulously. "This is ridiculous. What are you even saying?"

"Butorphanol is a narcotic. It acts very quickly. You must have led your husband out to the lanai. Once the drug took effect, either he fell into the pool or you rolled him in."

"And why in the world would I do that?"

"Because you didn't want to share his money. Because you were looking out for your own children."

She shook her head. "You stupid woman. I was in Tampa that night."

I said, "That's what I thought, too, until I saw that receipt, the one in the bag with the butorphanol. The receipt was for seventy-nine dollars, which is probably about what a taxi would cost from Sarasota to Tampa."

She shook her head. "You're crazy. You have no idea what happened."

I kept my voice level. "Mrs. Harwick, the taxi driver wrote an address on that receipt. I recognized it from the files your husband gave me with your contact information. It was the address of the hotel you stayed at with your husband in Tampa. 1146 Del Rio Way."

A smile played across her lips. "You certainly have it all figured out, don't you?"

I said, "No, not everything. There's some kind of code written at the bottom of the receipt. It says '230A1P.' I didn't know what that meant at first, but I knew it wouldn't be too hard for the police to talk to the taxi company and get their records, especially since it's all computerized these days. If I was a taxi driver, I think I'd definitely remember driving a beautiful older woman from Sarasota to Tampa in the middle of the night. Say around 2:30 A.M., and I think '1P' stands for 'one passenger.'"

She put her hand on the clasp of her shoulder bag, and I immediately had the feeling that August wasn't the only one in the family that carried a gun.

She said, "Dixie, I'm afraid you're going to be very sorry you ever met me."

I said, "Mrs. Harwick, you should know that when I heard your car drive up just now, I called the police. They'll be here any minute."

She was still holding the packet to her chest. She glanced around the room. I wondered if she wasn't thinking about running, but then she casually reached over and dropped the packet into the wood-burning stove. The flames leaped up around it, and the cabin filled with the smell of burning plastic.

She turned to me calmly and said, "When the police arrive, I'm going to tell them that you and your lover, Kenny Newman, called me here tonight to blackmail me. I'm going to tell them that you first tried to blackmail my husband. You threatened to expose his true identity. When he wouldn't cooperate, you drugged him and pushed him into the pool. I'll tell them you told me to take a taxi back to Tampa or you'd kill me, too, and that if I ever breathed a word of what happened that night, you'd kill both my children."

She drew a metal poker out of the wood bin and stirred the ashen remains of the packet around in the red-hot embers. "Roy was good at making money, but he wasn't a very smart man. If anyone ever found out that he had faked his own death, he would have gone to jail for insurance fraud and tax evasion. He would have lost his position at Sonnebrook, not to mention his stock, and my family would have been left with nothing. But apart from all that, Roy wasn't a very good person. I think you figured that out pretty quickly. So yes, you're right."

She laid the poker down on top of the stove and turned to me. Her eyes were sparkling like two black marbles, and her lips curled into a smile. "I killed him. Of course, without this packet, it's just your word against mine. And I do wonder who the police will believe. Me, the grieving widow of one of the wealthiest, most powerful men in the country? Or you, a small-town litter-box cleaner, who got kicked off the police force for mental instability."

I said, "Mrs. Harwick, I don't need that packet."

She leaned forward slightly. "And why is that, sweetheart?"

"Because I took everything out of it before you got here. That one was just stuffed with old newspapers."

Her face went white.

Shadows rose up behind her, and as she turned, Detective McKenzie and two deputies moved swiftly down the steps with their guns drawn and pointed directly at her.

McKenzie said, "Mrs. Harwick, that's good enough. Please drop your bag and raise your hands over your head."

Deputy Morgan moved into the room with his gun still fixed on Mrs. Harwick as she lowered her purse down to the ground. He glanced at me. "You okay?"

I felt dizzy, like someone had just hit me in the head with a frying pan. "Yeah—but I think she has a gun in that purse."

Detective McKenzie said, "Mrs. Harwick, you're under arrest for the murder of Roy Harwick."

. . .

By the time I came up out of the boat, Mrs. Harwick had already been read her Miranda rights and taken away. The whole area around Hoppie's was surrounded with police cars, and the parking lot looked like it had been turned into a disco of flashing red and blue lights. Except instead of dance music, there was only the sound of crickets, which had woken up when the rain stopped, and the chatter from the police radio in Detective McKenzie's unmarked sedan.

I was sitting in the driver's seat of the Bronco, waiting for the adrenaline that had been coursing through my bloodstream for the last hour to subside. It had left me feeling like a bowl of mush, and I wondered if that wasn't what a porcupine fish feels like after it's spent a couple of hours all blown up and spiny. All I wanted to do was go home, have that drink Mrs. Harwick suggested, and crawl into my bed.

Detective McKenzie came up to the window and said, "I'll need you to make a statement about everything, but I think it can wait until tomorrow. Will you be okay?"

I said, "I'll be fine, but I am worried about one thing. I'm afraid of what August will do when he finds out what's happened to his mother."

She nodded. "Dixie, I should probably tell you—the special investigative team conducted a sting operation at August's hotel tonight. They picked him up for smuggling endangered species into the country and selling them illegally. One of his couriers has agreed to testify against him, so I don't think you'll need to worry about that young man for a long time."

I nodded. No wonder Paco had been so quiet whenever

the Harwicks came up. He'd been in the middle of an investigation into August's smuggling operation.

Meekly, I said, "Do you by any chance know the name of that courier?"

She smiled. "Dixie. You know I can't tell you that."

I did, but I also didn't need her to tell me. I had a pretty good idea who it was.

She stuck her hand in the window and shook mine firmly. "Thank you for what you did tonight. Do you need someone to follow you home?"

"No, I don't have that far to go. My place is just up the road."

She nodded curtly and started to turn away, then stopped herself. "You know, people talk about you down at the station. They wonder why you keep getting involved in things like this, why you would put yourself through this kind of danger. They say it's crazy. But I think I know why."

I blinked dumbly at her. I hoped she would share it with me, because I had no earthly idea.

She said, "It's not fair how you lost your family. Believe me, I have an idea of what that feels like. So, I get it. I just wanted to tell you that."

She turned and walked away. I sat there for a few moments. I wasn't completely sure what the heck she was talking about, but it did dawn on me that seeing someone punished for wrongfully ending someone else's life felt good.

Really good.

I picked up my phone and punched in Ethan's number.

He answered on the second ring. "Umm, isn't it a little late?"

I said, "Remember tonight when you said to call if I needed you?"

"Yeah?"

I said, "I need you."

27

A light fog had risen up after the rain had stopped, but as I drove home I barely noticed it since my brain was already in a fog of its own. To be honest, I think I was in a state of shock. I couldn't help thinking about Mrs. Harwick. When she had pulled that poker out and stirred the burning embers in the stove, there had been a look of real fear in her eyes, but more than that, there was a look of certainty. She seemed driven, as though there was no doubt in her mind that what she was doing was right and that there were no other choices.

Had things gotten so twisted in her head that she really believed she needed to murder her husband in order to protect her children's security? Or perhaps it was never Mr. Harwick that she loved, but his money, and she wanted to keep it all for herself. I remembered with a shudder that she'd mentioned that Mr. Harwick was her second husband and that her first husband had died unexpectedly. I wondered if somebody shouldn't look into that.

I pulled into the curving lane that leads down to my

house and slowed to a crawl. I didn't want to wake anyone up. Ethan's car was parked under the carport next to Michael's, but of course Paco's was gone.

The Special Investigative Bureau was probably still booking August, and I had a feeling they had a lot of questions for him. I thought of Corina and how nervous she'd looked getting on that private plane. I knew why now. There had been a sleeping bird in that purse she was carrying. That's why August had handed it to her so gently. If she was the courier that was cooperating with the police, I wondered if she'd been caught in the sting as well or if she'd turned herself in voluntarily. I hoped it was the latter.

I'd get Paco to tell me. Or at least I'd try. He can be a tough nut to crack sometimes.

As I pulled into the carport I saw Ethan waiting at the bottom of my steps. He came over and opened the door of the Bronco, and when I stood up he hugged me. We just stood there for a long time, not talking, but then it all came pouring out of me and I told him everything. How I'd found the package of letters that Kenny had told us about. How when I saw that bottle of Butorphanol and the taxi receipt, I'd realized that Mrs. Harwick was probably not as grief-stricken as she was pretending to be. How she had drugged her husband and rolled him into the pool and had planned on framing me. He listened to the entire story and didn't interrupt once, not even when I got to the part about waiting in Kenny's boat with my gun hidden in the cushions next to me and the police hiding out nearby. He didn't say a word. He just listened.

Have I mentioned that I like that in a man?

When I was finished with the whole story, I fully

expected to hear a lecture about never putting myself in that kind of situation again, or how I should have let the police handle it, or what would have happened if, blah blah blah. Instead, he merely nodded with an impressed expression on his face, as if he'd just watched me hit a baseball out of the park.

"Nice job, Dixie."

He walked me over to the steps with his arm around my shoulder. I was thoroughly exhausted, but luckily this time he didn't need to carry me up.

When we got to the top, Ethan said, "Looks like somebody left you a present."

Sitting on my doorstep was a small paper gift bag, tied shut at the top with a scallop-edged pink ribbon.

I put my hands on my hips. "Did you put that there?"

"No. I wish I could take credit for it, but I didn't. Any other guys I should be worried about?"

I rolled my eyes at him. "Come on."

"No, seriously, I got here right before you did."

"Really?"

I knelt down and picked up the bag. Then it hit me.

I said, "Oh, no. I bet it's from Michael. He was teasing me earlier, and I got mad." I handed it to him and pulled my keys out. "He's so sweet. I was going to apologize to him in the morning, but he beat me to it. Open it up. Knowing Michael, I'm sure it's something good to eat."

I dropped my backpack just inside the door and collapsed on the couch. Ethan walked over to the kitchen counter and pulled the pink ribbon off and rustled through the tissue paper inside.

He said, "Cynar. Nice."

He pulled out a wine bottle with a red cap and a picture of a green artichoke against a red background on the label.

I said, "What the heck is Cynar?"

"It's really good. It's made out of artichokes."

"Ick! Artichoke wine?"

"No, it's liqueur. It's kind of bitter, but sweet, too. Tasty!"

It figured Michael would have gone out and bought me some strange, fancy liqueur. He knew damn well I'd be just as happy with some homemade brownies or a six-pack of beer, but he's always trying to get me to develop a taste for more sophisticated things. I felt like I recognized the label on the bottle, but I was pretty sure I'd remember drinking something made out of artichokes.

Ethan tossed a card on my lap. "Here."

I said, "He's really trying to make up with me, isn't he?"

"Let's have some. After what you've been through to-day, you deserve it."

"Okay. There are some glasses in the cabinet over the sink."

He opened up the cabinet and rummaged through my sad, ragtag collection of mugs, plastic cups, and wineglasses.

"Don't you have any liqueur glasses?"

I shot him a disdainful look.

He laughed and pulled down two mismatched wine-glasses. "Gotcha!"

I slid the card out of its envelope. It was the color of light butterscotch, with a black border around its edge. There was no signature, just a short note. It said, "Dear Dixie, love doesn't always have to be a sacrifice."

It was written in the tiniest, most precise handwriting I've ever seen.

Actually, that's not true. I had seen that handwriting before: when Mrs. Harwick handed me her feeding instructions for the fish.

I stood up and brought the bottle into the kitchen, studying the cap. I couldn't really tell if it had been tampered with, but I had a pretty good idea. I have to admit, I was definitely in the mood for taking chances, but drinking artichoke liqueur laced with a narcotic, or worse, was definitely not one of them. I twisted the cap off and tipped the bottle into the sink.

Ethan jumped. "Wait! What are you doing?"

"I'm pouring it out."

"What is this? Prohibition month? I promise you that is perfectly delicious stuff."

I clucked my tongue at him. "Don't be ridiculous. You have no idea where this came from. You can't just go around drinking whatever you find laying on your doorstep."

He grabbed my hand and tipped the bottle back up. "Dixie, seriously, just try a little. I promise you it's not that bad."

I sighed and looked him in the eye. "Ethan. It's not from Michael. It's from Mrs. Harwick."

He withdrew his hand and hopped back a little. "Oh."

"Exactly. She must have stopped by here on her way to Kenny's houseboat. Obviously, she didn't intend for her evening to end the way it did."

I tipped the bottle back over, and we both watched the amber liquid as it gurgled out and disappeared down the drain. As the last drop fell, we sighed in unison. I rinsed the bottle out several times with hot water and threw it into the recycling bin.

Ethan watched in silence. Poor sweet man. I'd promised him there wouldn't be any more drama, but it turned out the drama had only just begun. He pulled me close to him and wrapped his arms around me. I put my hands on the back of his neck.

He said, "I wish I'd brought a bottle of wine for you."

"I don't care. I didn't really need a drink. What I need is right here."

He said, "Talk about corny," and lowered his lips to mine. Again I felt that wave of goose bumps move with lightning speed across my entire body. When I opened my eyes, he was looking down at me and smiling.

He said, "Don't you even want to know if she put something in it?"

I thought for a second.

Did I want to know if Mrs. Harwick had planned on killing me so I wouldn't tell the police about what was inside that package? Did I want to know if I had just narrowly escaped being poisoned to death? Did I want to know if fate had dealt one card, but I'd picked up another?

I heard a voice inside my head say, *Hell no.*

28

It took a couple of days for Kenny to come out of hiding. He eventually turned himself over to the police, but of course he waited until the news got out that Mrs. Harwick had been arrested. I couldn't blame him. It would have been pretty hard for a jury to ignore the fact that Kenny had a lot to gain from Mr. Harwick's death, both emotionally and financially, and if there hadn't been any evidence against Mrs. Harwick, it's entirely possible that Kenny might have ended up in jail for a very long time. But Detective McKenzie had questioned him and let him go, and the last time I'd heard, he was planning on going back to California to try to pick up his life where he left off. As for Becca, I wondered if I would ever see her again.

I woke up early and made my regular morning rounds. At Tom Hale's place, Billy Elliot spotted a wild rabbit in the azalea bushes alongside the parking lot, so he'd gotten an extra good workout. In his glory days, Billy could probably have worked up enough speed to catch up with that rabbit, but now that he's retired, it's all just for fun. I think the rabbit was probably just toying with him, too, because after zipping back and forth in the parking lot a couple of times, it disappeared down a hole as fast as lightning. Billy came trotting back all happy and panting nevertheless. I could tell he was grateful to have somebody who could run at a respectable pace for a change.

After Billy Elliot I stopped at Timmy Anthem's apartment. Timmy is a former pro hockey player who coaches for the local high school team. They'd just won the regional playoffs, so as a reward he had taken the whole team to Sunrise, Florida, to watch the Panthers play. His pit bull, Zoë, was recovering from surgery to repair a torn ligament in her leg, so we couldn't play fetch in the courtyard like we usually did. Instead I made up for it with some peanut butter treats and lots of tummy rubs, which I think she was just as happy with. Pit bulls get a bad rap. She's one of the sweetest dogs I've ever known.

As I was leaving Timmy's place, my cell phone rang. It was Kenny Newman.

"Dixie, you know . . . I just wanted to say, like, I'm really sorry about everything, and I want to say thank you. I mean, no one's ever really stood up for me like you did."

I said, "I knew you couldn't have done something like that. I'm just sorry it turned out like it did."

"Yeah. Except maybe it's all for the best. It turns out Roy Harwick is the name of some dude that lives in Phoenix, Arizona. My father basically stole his identity. The police told me the feds were about to arrest him for insurance fraud and identity theft, but he drowned before they got to him. I don't think he would have been too happy in prison. I mean, he probably would have killed himself first."

I said, "Well, your father was pretty messed up, but he certainly was an interesting person."

He laughed. "Yeah. He was pretty smart, too. After he faked his death, he made up this bogus oil manufacturing company and then pretended he was looking to hire a consultant. He did a whole nationwide search and collected tons of résumés. Then he just picked out the one that was the closest to his own, with the same age, education, expertise, and everything. He hired the guy over the phone, got his Social Security number, and then disappeared into thin air. After that, he just started applying for jobs pretending to be that guy, Roy Harwick, and that's how he got hired by Sonnebrook. Everybody loved him. He was smart, funny, handsome. Eventually he worked himself right up to the top of the company."

I said, "Impressive."

"Yeah, except he was filing taxes the whole time. So the real Roy Harwick, he started getting notices saying he'd paid his taxes twice, but he just ignored them. He figured it was just some computer glitch or something. It took them almost twenty years to finally track it down to my dad."

I said, "Becca must be devastated."

"Umm, yeah. She's actually here with me now."

That was a shock. I couldn't think of anything to say except "Oh, good."

"She's having a pretty rough time, but she's gonna be okay."

I breathed a sigh of relief. He might not have realized it himself, but Kenny had planned on doing the same thing to his baby that his father had done to him. It's amazing how strong those patterns can be from generation to generation. When it came to being a father, Kenny only knew how to do one thing: run. I was glad to see he might be breaking that cycle.

I said, "If you think she's ready for it, I know a very good obstetrician."

There was a pause, and then he lowered his voice. "Yeah, well, about that. She may not be pregnant after all."

"Huh?"

I could tell he was struggling for the right words.

"It turns out, her monthly cycle is late, and, you know, she can be kind of dramatic."

I said, "Mmm-hmm."

"So . . . we don't really know for sure."

I hesitated. "But . . . you're staying?"

"I thought when she found out who I was, she'd never forgive me. But she lost her father when she was young, too, so she kind of understands why I did what I did. So, you know, we're gonna try to work it out."

I was smiling ear to ear. "That's great, Kenny. I'm really glad to hear that."

After we hung up I thought to myself that maybe all those things I'd bought for Corina and her baby wouldn't go to waste after all. I still didn't know if it was Corina who had agreed to testify against August Harwick or not. Paco wouldn't confirm it, but then again, he wouldn't deny it either. When I told Joyce what I suspected, she acted like she didn't much care, but I knew deep down inside she felt the same way I did. We both hoped that it was Corina, and we both hoped that one day we might see her again.

And Dixie Joyce, too.

29

I was wandering up and down the aisles at Walmart. Ethan was coming over later, and for once I was planning on cooking dinner with my own two hands in my own apartment with my own pans. I had stopped by to pick up a few basic things. Like a cookbook. And some pans.

I filled the cart up with all kinds of goodies. Some long tapered beeswax candles, a box of wineglasses, some cornflower blue place mats with matching napkins, a couple of nice kitchen knives, and some wooden salad bowls. In the clothing section, I threw in a bag of white ankle socks and a couple of pairs of fresh white Keds. My supply was getting a little low.

I wondered if I might run into the young girl that had helped me pick out all the baby things that day I'd found Corina. I kind of hoped not. I had liked her right away, but I knew she'd ask me how it had worked out with the pediatrician she recommended and how the baby was doing. I imagined myself saying, *Oh, I don't really know. I think that baby's in Guatemala now, but I'm not really sure.* I think she already thought I was a complete kook, and I didn't want to make things worse.

In the pharmacy, I grabbed some toothpaste, a bottle of lavender-scented hand cream, and a couple of tubes of lip balm. There was an older couple standing at the end of what they call the "family planning" aisle, and they were staring at the vast collection of condoms in every shape, size, and color of the rainbow with bewildered looks on their faces. As I rolled up to them, the woman stepped to the side.

She said, "Harry, move over."

The man jumped a little when he saw me and then shuffled over next to her.

I said, "Pardon me, just rolling through."

They both smiled pleasantly as I went by, and just as I turned the corner I reached out and grabbed a little purple and white box with bold black lettering. It read EARLY PREGNANCY TEST. As if it was the most normal thing in the world to buy, I tossed it into the basket with a flick of the wrist and headed for the registers.

On my way home, I pulled into the pavilion at Siesta Key Beach and walked across the gravelly parking lot to one of the weathered plank boardwalks that hover over the dunes. As usual, next to the steps at the end of the walkway were about two dozen pairs of sneakers, flip-flops, and sandals that people had slipped off before they went down to the beach. It's kind of a tradition.

Whenever anyone asks me why I live here, I talk about

the beautiful weather, all the birds, the pure white sand, the wonderful people. In my head, though, I think of all these shoes lined up in rows in the dunes, some of the shoes sitting next to the shoes of their friends and family—whoever they came to the beach with—and some of them just sitting next to perfect strangers' shoes, just hanging out. People have been leaving their shoes like this for as long as I can remember. I always think, *I live here because nobody wants to steal your shoes.* I wouldn't want to be anywhere else in the world.

There was a group of people playing an impromptu game of beach volleyball. I kicked off my Keds and placed them in the sand next to all the other shoes and walked down to the water to watch for a while. A flock of sandpipers was zipping up and down with the waves, picking through the foamy sand for fish eggs and bits of seaweed. I sat down and tilted my face toward the warm sun.

I thought to myself, *This is what it's all about, just to be able to breathe in the fresh ocean air and dig my toes in the cool sand.* All we have in this world is time, and we should be grateful for every single bit of it.

Life is good.